BURNING SKIES

THE LAST SANCTUARY: BOOK THREE

KYLA STONE

Printed in the United States of America

Cover design by Deranged Doctor Designs

Book formatting by Vellum

First Printed in 2018

ISBN 978-1-945410-14-7

Paper Moon Press

Atlanta, Georgia

www.PaperMoonPress.com

❀ Created with Vellum

To Jeremy, for your patience, understanding, and always believing in my work.

1

AMELIA

The night was a cold, black thing crouched just outside the ring of firelight. Eighteen-year-old Amelia Black shivered and wrapped her auto-warm blanket tighter around herself. According to the SmartFlex she kept in the side pocket of her cargo pants, it was a frigid forty-one degrees. It felt colder.

For the last week, they'd been inching closer to downtown, maneuvering their two trucks around the husks of thousands of abandoned vehicles clogging Interstate 75 leading into the heart of Atlanta.

"I still think a fire is too dangerous," her brother Silas grumbled. His lawn chair was pulled as close to the flames as possible, his shoulders hunched, his hands held palms up for warmth. The glow of the firelight revealed his features sharpened from the hard living over the last three months. His face was lean and wolfish. His gray eyes sparked. "Anyone could see us."

"It was start a fire or freeze," Micah said from beside her.

They'd had to build a fire every night—the risk of freezing to death was worse. Where they couldn't find firewood, they hacked up chairs and tables as kindling. Once, when they couldn't find a fireplace, they opened the windows and laid on the floor to escape the choking smoke, just thankful to be warm.

They slept with their weapons beside them, two people always on watch. They'd seen a few furtive movements from a distance, but they hadn't come into close contact with anyone since they'd left Harmony and Sweet Creek Farm after the Headhunters' attack, her mother's capture, and Nadira's death.

Though Harmony had betrayed them, she'd also warned them of the dangerous killers known as Pyros. This was a brave new world. Danger lay in wait everywhere. But they couldn't back down now. They were headed into Atlanta to ambush the Headhunters to rescue her mother before they reached the Sanctuary.

Amelia missed her mother like a physical ache in her chest. She'd spent far too long resenting and misjudging her, barely getting her back before she was taken by the Headhunters.

But her mother was still alive. She had to believe that. The Headhunters were violent but pragmatic. Her mother was worth more alive than dead.

After they rescued her mother, they'd find the Sanctuary. Hopefully, the scientists there could find a cure for the Hydra virus with Amelia's blood. There were answers waiting for them at the Sanctuary. It would be their salvation or their destruction; Amelia still wasn't sure which.

Willow slurped the last bite of her kidney beans and tossed the empty can at the fire. "That was filling. Not."

On Willow's other side, eight-year-old Benjie sat next to Finn, teaching him a new card trick from the tattered *Magic Tips for the Advanced Beginner* paperback that Micah had found.

Across from Willow, Celeste huddled on a stump, shivering in her lavender sweater, her mass of tightly coiled, cranberry-red curls bound in a ponytail. She was model-tall and svelte, but her cheekbones were sharp, the hollows beneath her eyes deep and shadowed. Her rich, earth-tone skin had a dull tinge to it.

She'd been uncharacteristically quiet since Nadira's death a week ago. They all had. Even Tyler Horne, the cocky former CEO, was more subdued. He obeyed Jericho without too much trouble, and took his watch shifts without complaining.

He and Jericho were guarding the outskirts of the camp they'd set up for the night. Once they'd gotten as warm as they could, they'd head inside the abandoned house and take shelter until morning. They were in a nice neighborhood of stately homes, wrought-iron fences, and massive, overgrown lawns. But the only thing that mattered now was whether the place was safe and clear of decomposing, disease-infested bodies.

Amelia tugged at the mask around her neck. She was immune, but she wore it anyway. They all wore them during the day, but pulled them off once they'd found a place to hunker down. They wore gloves, too—always careful, always mindful of the agonizing death that awaited from a single, tiny mistake.

Across the fire, Gabriel Ramos Rivera met her gaze. His full mouth curled into a lazy, sensuous smile.

Her heart gave that same treacherous jolt it always did when she caught him watching her. His broad shoulders and tall, muscular body cut an impressive form against the firelight. With his curly black hair, scruffy goatee, and bronze Puerto Rican skin, he was as roguishly handsome as ever.

No matter how much she wanted to, she couldn't forget his lips on hers, his dark eyes smoldering with desire and need and pain. Their desperate hours trapped in the belly of the hijacked *Grand Voyager* had linked them, connecting them forever whether Amelia liked it or not. She'd revealed her soul to him, and he'd turned around and betrayed her.

She wanted to break her gaze from his, but she refused. He was the one in the wrong. He was the one who should be filled with shame. As if reading her thoughts, his face contorted, a shadow passing over his features. He looked away first.

She shifted her gaze to the fire. She wasn't the same girl he'd handed over to the terrorists. She'd survived too much, come too far.

"You okay?" Micah asked quietly. He was a warm, comforting presence next to her. His face had grown leaner in the last several months, but it was still round and boyish, his wavy dark hair falling haphazardly across his forehead. His eyes behind his glasses were a soft, gentle brown. "How are you feeling?"

He meant her epilepsy. Anxiety roiled in her stomach. She'd gone without her medication for a week. Her mother had used the last emergency auto-injector on her when the fever from the Hydra virus had triggered a seizure.

Out here, without medical intervention, another seizure could disable or kill her. She sucked in her breath, forcing herself to focus. Worrying about it wouldn't change anything. "I'm fine, for now. Thank you."

"Are you sure?" He knew she was worried about what awaited them once they reached the Sanctuary, but he didn't know exactly why. She hadn't told him everything, not yet.

Her old life of secrets, lies, and distrust died hard. Her mother had cautioned her repeatedly about how dangerous it would be for Amelia and Silas if anyone found out the truth. *Trust no one,* she'd warned.

But Amelia was tired of fear. She'd lived in fear most of her life. A week ago, the night the falling stars streaked across the night sky, she'd promised herself she would open herself to hope. And to do that, she needed to trust. "Can I tell you something?"

"Of course." Micah placed the dog-eared copy of *Call of the Wild* on his lap.

Everyone else was busy chatting, fitfully dozing, or staring at the fire, lost in their own thoughts. This was as much privacy as they'd had all week.

She glanced across the fire at Gabriel. This wouldn't be easy. She wasn't used to trust, to vulnerability. Not after a childhood raised on fear and secrets. But she couldn't let them have any more power over her—not Gabriel, not Kane, not Simeon, and not her father. They'd all tried to break her in their own way. They'd all failed.

"I hope you'll forgive me for not telling you before," she said haltingly. There was no way to cushion her words, so she simply blurted them out. "The New Patriots weren't behind the Hydra Virus."

Micah stiffened beside her. Like everyone else, he'd believed that the radicalized group to which his brother belonged had not only hijacked the *Grand Voyager*, they'd also released the Hydra bioweapon, the genetically engineered virus that had killed ninety-five percent of the world's population in a matter of weeks. "What? How do you know?"

"Because—" She sucked in a breath, reaching instinctively for the charm bracelet bound to the leather cord circling her neck and tucked beneath her shirt. "Because it was my father who did it."

The chill seemed to deepen around her. Would Micah reject her? Hate her? Blame her?

"Tell me," he said gently. There was no recrimination in his voice. No bitterness or judgment.

She told him everything—how her father had designed the bioweapon and released it through the universal flu vaccine his company, BioGen, had distributed to the American public, carefully selecting one hundred thousand victims from the poorest communities to receive a fatal dose. "It was supposed to terrify the people into passing the Safe and Secure Act. The Unity Coalition had plans to monitor every citizen with the VitaliChip implant. Just one more step in cementing their power and control."

Micah glanced at Tyler Horne. "Was Horne in on it?"

He stood guard at the edge of the firelight, facing toward the street, his semi-automatic cradled in his arms. Both handsome and incredibly vain, he had symmetrical features, a square jaw, and floppy blonde hair that he still managed to style—even in the apocalypse.

Amelia shook her head. "I don't think so. Tyler Horne's company, VitaliChip Industries, was a subsidiary of BioGen. They stood to make billions when the microchips became mandatory. But my father and his associates wouldn't have trusted someone like Horne with the truth."

"Why would he want to kill his own citizens?"

"Because they planned to blame it on the New Patriots all along. A massive-scale terrorist attack would let them pass just about any law they wished, which they did. People will trade their rights for safety. The Unity Coalition had been consolidating their power for years. They wanted to take over the U.S. government, to wrest the last remnants of power. And they were willing to do it by any means necessary."

"But they killed billions."

"That wasn't their plan." Amelia remembered all the terrible things her father had said on the bridge of the *Grand Voyager*, his face bloodied, a gun to his temple, surrounded by terrorists who wanted nothing more than to kill them both, his eyes hateful and defiant until the end. "The virus they engineered interacted with the bat-flu virus that was already an epidemic. The new, mutated virus was highly contagious and deadlier than either of them put together."

"And my brother . . ."

"He still hijacked the *Grand Voyager*. But Gabriel told you the truth. The New Patriots were trying to stop the Unity Coalition and the microchip implant law. Once they found out about the bioweapon, they tried to force my father to give them the cure. But he refused. Gabriel had nothing to do with the Hydra Virus."

Micah let out a long, shuddering sigh. "Okay," he said slowly. "Okay."

Amelia clasped her hands on her lap. She stared at the flames until her vision blurred. "My father wasn't the mastermind. He was working with others. We don't know who. Vice-President Sloane— well, President Sloane, now—was a member of the Unity Coalition. So were several other senators and high-ranking government officials."

"You think they might be in this Sanctuary place," he said, reading her thoughts.

"Silas, my mother, Gabriel, and myself know the New Patriots were used as patsies. If any surviving members of the Unity Coalition were to find out what we know ..."

"They'd want to eradicate any threat to their power. Whatever's left of it, anyway."

Amelia nodded heavily, suddenly feeling her exhaustion. Her muscles ached. Her eyes burned. "Even in the apocalypse, some things never change."

Micah was quiet for a long moment. The wind picked up. The thin line of trees at the edge of the yard swayed. Bare branches sawed against each other, making strangely haunting sounds.

Almost like a violin. She touched the permanent indents on the pads of her fingers. "I've wanted to tell you for months. But I was afraid. And with everything going on, struggling to find our next meal and not get killed, it was easy to simply not tell you. But I hated that you believed that Gabriel was guilty of such a thing. I mean, he's guilty of plenty, but..."

7

"He's not guilty of destroying the world as we know it," Micah said wryly.

"You deserve to know the truth. Gabriel—" she swallowed around the sudden lump in her throat, "—he knew and didn't tell anyone, even though it made everyone believe he was a monster." Gabriel was an enigma. He'd both betrayed her and protected her, lied to her and kept her secrets. She couldn't wrap her head around it.

Micah touched his shoulder to hers. "I won't tell anyone either."

"It makes me sick," she whispered, "to know it was my own father who did this." It sickened and terrified her. Thoughts of her father always brought a knot of fear and anger and shame, of grief and loathing—and beneath it all, a tangled, bitter love.

"It was him, not you. We aren't responsible for the sins of others. Don't ever forget that."

Relieved, she gave him a shaky smile. Micah didn't resent or despise her, not even for withholding the truth about his brother for so long. He was the same old Micah—loyal, solid, always there to lean on. Her truest friend. "Thank you."

A twig snapped behind them. Amelia whipped around, twisting in her camp chair.

"What was that?" Benjie asked, his brown eyes wide. His black hair stuck up all over his head. He pulled his ratty Star Wars backpack onto his lap and clasped it to his chest, shivering.

"Just a squirrel," Celeste mumbled.

"Nothing set off the trip wire," Willow said, but she stood up anyway, her hand drifting to her holster.

The hairs on the back of Amelia's neck prickled. She peered past the circle of firelight into the darkness surrounding them. The fire made the shadows shift and sway. Anything could be out there in the dark.

Hunting them.

Something moved.

Fear spiked up her spine. It could be a violent gang. An armed, dangerous loner. A pack of infected dogs. Or something larger, a tiger or bear that had escaped from the local zoo.

The shadows deepened beneath the trees. They seemed to solidify, taking the shapes of monsters and demons, then melted back into nothingness.

She rose to her feet, the blanket slipping off her shoulders.

Silas screamed.

2

GABRIEL

Twenty-one-year-old Gabriel leapt to his feet, yanking helplessly against the handcuffs binding his wrists. His heart jackhammered into his throat.

A massive shadow plunged into the center of the clearing. It bounded past Silas, smashing into his chair and knocking him on his ass.

Silas let out another sound that sounded an awful lot like a scream. Jericho came running.

Willow was already on her feet, gun pointed at the massive black shape whirling in front of the fire, sparks flying all around it. "Oh, hell."

"It's that scary-ass dog," Silas growled from his position on the ground.

Gabriel might have laughed, if he wasn't slightly terrified himself. His senses cleared as Silas's words sank in. He let out his breath. "It's the wolf."

"Nothing gets past you, Sherlock," Willow quipped, lowering her gun.

The huge black wolf stood in front of the fire, mere feet from Gabriel, his massive head taller than Gabriel's waist. He stared at them with unblinking yellow eyes, his hackles raised, ears pricked, tongue lolling through sharp white fangs.

Before anyone could get their bearings or say another word, a figure sailed into the middle of the circle, dismounted a hoverboard, and dumped three dead rabbits and a bundle of sticks on the ground next to the fire. The figure pushed back the hood of a rain slicker, revealing a head of black hair and a pair of shining black eyes.

Everyone stared at her, their mouths open.

"You didn't trip the alarm," Jericho said, both alarmed and perplexed. Slowly, he lowered his rifle.

The girl's expression didn't change. "I watched you make it."

"How did you follow us?" Silas asked suspiciously.

"You're slow. And you bumble around like stampeding cattle."

Willow let out a sharp laugh. She slumped back into her camp chair and shoved her unruly bangs out of her eyes. "You about gave us a heart attack, Raven."

Raven was short, though not as short as Willow, who barely reached Gabriel's shoulder. Her Asian heritage showed on her delicate-featured face, though there was nothing delicate in her fierce, unyielding expression.

Silas stood up shakily and pointed an indignant finger at the wolf. "Just keep that...that *thing* away from me."

"Shadow goes where he wants. You try telling him what to do. See how it works out for you." Raven pointed at the animal carcasses at her feet. "We caught dinner."

Celeste looked appalled.

"I refuse to eat a *rabbit*," Horne said, aghast, his pompous nose turned up at the very idea.

"Then don't." Raven dropped her backpack with the hoverboard sticking out of it to the ground and pulled a hunting knife from a sheath at her waist. She crouched on the ground, picked up one of the rabbits, and made a small cut along its back.

Horne stared at her. "I will not be turned into a greedy, mindless animal."

"Greedy, mindless animals eat supper." Raven paused and looked up, meeting Gabriel's gaze. There was no fear or indecision in her dark eyes. "Do you know how to field dress a rabbit?"

He shook his head, suddenly embarrassed. Simeon had taught him to hack the government, how to fight, and how to kill people, not animals. He was a city boy. He didn't know how to hunt or how to cook what he'd hunted.

Raven tsked in disgust. "Slow *and* stupid." She grabbed the rabbit's fur on either side of the cut she'd made and tugged, pulling the rabbit's hide away from its body. She quickly chopped off the animal's head and feet. Her hands moved deftly as she carefully sliced the rabbit's belly skin from tail to chest. Its entrails slid out in a steaming pile.

"That poor rabbit," Finn said. "I think I'm going to be sick."

"Screw it," Celeste said, though her mouth was pursed. "I'm starving. Food is food."

Horne made a gagging noise. Amelia looked away, her milk-white skin growing paler. Only Willow sat forward, fascinated.

"How did you learn to do that?" Gabriel was fascinated himself. If they could learn to hunt the local wildlife, they wouldn't be so dependent on scavenging in dangerous towns and cities.

"Practice." Raven moved to the second rabbit, repeating the steps. She worked like she'd done this a hundred times—some skilled hunter and trapper transported from the pioneer days.

Within a few minutes, she'd skinned and dressed all three rabbits and set up a spit with the bundles of sticks she'd brought. She rocked back on her heels. "Now they cook."

Gabriel leaned forward, his cuffed hands in his lap. "How long have you been alone?"

"I'm not alone."

"Then what group are you with?"

She didn't bother to answer, just pushed one of the forked sticks deeper into the ground and turned the spit.

"She means the wolf, you bonehead," Silas said sullenly from his camp chair, where he hadn't taken his eyes off Shadow for a moment.

"How's he so big?" Benjie asked.

"He's a hybrid."

"That's impossible," Gabriel said. "The scientists said mods couldn't be bred with normal animals."

"The scientists were mistaken."

Willow snorted. "Seems to be a lot of that going around these days."

He wasn't sure if he believed Raven, yet Shadow was the largest wolf he'd ever seen. Mods were often larger than their original counterparts, but genetically engineered to be meek and docile. The wealthiest of the elites commissioned mods as pets. Since so many wild animals were extinct now, the remaining zoos, circuses, and aquatic parks were mostly filled with mods.

Or at least, they had been. Since the Hydra virus unleashed its wrath on the world, the animals had either been released by activists or starved to death in their cages.

The wolf stood next to Raven, refusing to lay down or relax, wary and vigilant. His ears were pricked, hackles slightly raised, his sharp eyes constantly shifting.

"How did you tame a wolf?" Benjie asked, awestruck.

Raven's expression was impassive. "Who says he's tame?"

Shadow yawned then, showing off a dramatic set of teeth. Benjie's eyes widened even further.

"Where did you find him?" Gabriel asked.

She didn't answer for a long moment, as if weighing how much to tell them. She looked like someone used to fending for herself. Someone used to being alone. "I saved him," she said finally. "Then he saved me."

She wasn't afraid, but she also didn't seem comfortable. Her eyes kept darting back to the shadows past the campfire. She gripped her knife in her right hand. And she kept her back to the fire, keeping as many of them as possible in her sight.

When the rabbits were ready, Benjie scavenged the abandoned house for plates and forks. He even brought out napkins. Raven chopped the meat into strips and passed it around, offering Benjie the first plate. As she moved, Gabriel noticed she heavily favored her left foot. At Sweet Creek Farm, she'd barely stepped off her hoverboard.

The fire crackled and popped. Everyone ate in silence, enjoying the hot, juicy meat and licking their fingers. Even Horne and Finn appeared to have overcome their misgivings. Celeste dug in, forgoing her cultivated manners to tear into the meat with her teeth. "This is amazing."

Gabriel ate hungrily, ravenously. He'd never tasted anything so delicious. It was stringy, but also rich and gamey—nothing like the faux foods and cloned meats he was used to. It had been a long time since he'd enjoyed a truly filling meal. Maybe not since the *Grand Voyager*.

At the naval base in Jacksonville, he'd been treated like a terrorist, beaten and starved. He pushed those memories out of his head. They served no purpose but pain. He had plenty of that already.

The wolf rose to his feet and nudged Raven's shoulder with his snout. She tossed him a chunk of meat. He gulped it down in one bite, teeth flashing. He turned his great head and regarded Gabriel with those keen amber eyes.

Gabriel remembered those eyes from the night Nadira died, when he'd dug her grave in grief-stricken silence. The wolf had come, standing still as a statue at the edge of the woods, simply watching him as he plunged the shovel into the earth again and again, blisters forming on his hands and pain rupturing his soul. The wolf had kept vigil, a witness to it all.

And when Gabriel had longed for death, challenging the wolf to come for him, to end him, end his guilt and shame and misery, the wolf had refused.

Gabriel moved his cuffed hands together and carefully shoved one hand into his pocket, fingering the folded cloth. He'd torn a small section from Nadira's eggshell-blue headscarf to keep with him, to remind him of the sacrifice she'd made.

Nadira, who was sweet and tender and one of those rare people who was genuinely good-hearted. In the midst of everyone's hatred and suspicion, even his own brother's, she alone had treated him with gentleness and respect. As though her god, Allah, could forgive the likes of him, as though he hadn't fallen so far that he couldn't climb back up again.

She'd believed he could earn redemption for his sins. She'd offered her life for his, ensuring that he wouldn't throw his own away.

He gritted his teeth. She haunted him now, both in his waking hours and his dreams, joining the dead of the *Grand Voyager*— joining the little girl in the yellow bathrobe, shot to death on the storm-tossed deck, her black hair fanning around her tiny face like a halo. He was responsible for their deaths.

The life he lived now must be worth something. He would spend it seeking redemption. Maybe someday, if he was lucky, he would find it.

Raven ripped off a piece of meat with her teeth and chewed noisily. "You shouldn't go to the city. There's a settlement. Northwest of here, a seven days' hike. My mother lived there before the break. She's not there anymore, but there are more people now. Good people. They'll take you in."

Gabriel wasn't sure if they would survive another community. Sweet Creek Farm had seemed welcoming enough, but in desperate times, people saved their own. They wouldn't stick their necks out for strangers. Why would they? He wouldn't. "If it's so great, why aren't you there?"

Raven tossed a rabbit bone into the fire. "Too dangerous for Shadow. He can't be fenced in. Neither can I."

"Thank you for the suggestion, but we can't." Amelia's voice was soft, but there was iron running through it. "We need to beat the Headhunters to the Sanctuary to rescue my mother, Elise."

Raven stood up quickly and shouldered her pack. "Have it your way."

"Are you leaving already?" Willow looked disappointed. So did Benjie. "Why don't you come with us?"

"No."

"Yet you came all this way," Gabriel said, studying her. "Surely it wasn't just to feed us dinner."

Her mouth tightened. Her eyes were shards of obsidian reflecting the firelight. "We'll meet you on the other side of the city. If you make it." She walked over to Benjie, limping with her left leg. Was it a wound that predated the end of the world, or a more recent injury? He doubted Raven would tell him if he asked. She was taciturn, a loner who kept her cards close to her chest.

She shoved her hand inside the pocket of her pants and thrust an object at Benjie. Benjie turned it over in his hands, his face lit with awe. Gabriel caught a glimpse of a wooden shape—carved wings, an elegant head, and curved beak. A bird. Likely, a raven. A ghost of a smile passed across her face. "Keep it safe for me."

Benjie nodded solemnly and protectively tucked the carved figurine inside his own pocket.

She turned to Jericho. "You'll follow I-575 once you're through Atlanta. There's a small town, Ball Ground. Exit 27. We'll wait for you there."

Raven yanked her hoverboard out of her pack, activated it, and set it on the ground. It hovered six inches above the grass, beating down the dry, brown blades with tiny, whirring rotors. "Be careful of the rats. They're scared of fire. Be more careful of the Pyros. They make the fire."

Unease twisted his gut. Harmony had warned them of the same gang. "What do you mean? What do you know about the Pyros?"

But she didn't answer. Raven stepped onto her hoverboard and whisked out of the clearing, passing between Silas and Horne, who both stared after her like she was some sort of ghostly apparition.

"You forgot your dog," Silas said, his expression petulant.

"He'll come when he comes," she said over her shoulder. She weaved expertly between the shadowy hulks of cars and houses and trees. The wolf heaved himself to his feet and bounded silently after her. Just like that, they were gone.

"Good riddance." Silas glowered at the fire.

Willow just laughed.

Micah stood up abruptly and crossed the clearing, stepping around the fire and coming to a stop in front of him.

Gabriel looked up in surprise. They'd barely spoken in the week since they'd left Sweet Creek Farm. Though Micah hadn't seemed quite so angry, there was still a deep tension between them, a yawning chasm Gabriel wasn't sure how to cross.

He had lied to his brother and betrayed him—the brother he'd sworn to protect all those years ago when their mother had died of cancer and their father had wasted away from grief and Silk. Back when it was only them against the world.

Every night before he slept, Gabriel repeated to himself the words he longed to say and hear in return: *Just us. Always.* He wasn't naive enough to believe he'd ever hear his brother say those words again. But he held them close to his heart anyway.

"What is it?" he asked now.

"Can I trust you?" Micah said evenly, his face tense, his expression unreadable.

"Yes," Gabriel said without hesitation. He couldn't hope for anything. He wouldn't allow himself to hope, to believe…but he sat up straighter, his heart beating fast.

Micah turned to Jericho, who stood half in darkness, turned toward the house but still listening. "I think we should uncuff him."

Everyone else fell silent, watching. Gabriel didn't move, didn't speak. Some part of him was afraid to break this spell, whatever it was. What was Micah doing? What was he thinking? His face was still inscrutable, the firelight reflecting in the lenses of his glasses.

Jericho rubbed his square, stubbled jaw and stared at Micah for a long minute. He was broad-chested and muscular, his brown skin gleaming darkly in the firelight. Jericho was tough and no-nonsense, a stickler for the rules, and the reason Gabriel was still a captive locked in cuffs. "You believe he can be trusted?"

Micah cleared his throat. "I believe he has proven so with his actions. He had plenty of chances to run, but he didn't. He had plenty of chances to turn on any one of us, but he didn't. He fought with us."

"To protect his own life," Horne spat.

Gabriel didn't speak. It wasn't his place. This decision was out of his hands. He gritted his teeth and waited, though every bone in his body thrummed with dark energy.

"And others," Micah insisted. "He almost died saving Amelia."

Gabriel's heart constricted. He hadn't died like he was supposed to. Nadira had died instead.

"Maybe we could give him a chance," Finn said amiably. He stuffed a hunk of rabbit in his mouth, then tore another chunk off the bone he was holding, which looked like a toothpick in his large hands.

"He's a New Patriot." Willow shot him a look, daggers in her gaze. "A *terrorist*. Don't forget what he did."

"I'm not forgetting," Micah said quietly but firmly. "But we're going into a dangerous city and we don't know what we're up against. We need every fighter. And Gabriel is good at keeping people alive."

"When he wants to," Willow muttered under her breath.

Gabriel ignored her. He knew why she hated him. His people had killed her sister and her mother on the *Grand Voyager*. But her hatred was harmless. He already loathed himself more than she ever could.

"I trust your judgment, Micah." Jericho gestured for Gabriel to hold out his cuffed hands. Jericho swiped in the code. The cuffs released and fell to the ground. As simple and easy as that.

Gabriel flexed and unflexed his fingers and rubbed his chafed wrists. He knew better than to believe this meant more than it did. He was strong. He knew how to fight. He was an asset to the group, but not in handcuffs.

They trusted him not to kill them in their sleep. That was still a far cry from earning their respect. Or their forgiveness. "Thank you."

Micah returned the cuffs to Jericho. He gave Gabriel a grim smile. There was something in his eyes. Not absolution, but something else. His gaze didn't hold as much bitterness or recrimination as before.

The realization hit him. Amelia must have told Micah the truth about the Hydra virus. He'd hated that Micah believed him capable of such an atrocity. He was guilty of great evil, but not that. He already had a lifetime of sins to make up for.

Gabriel glanced sharply at Amelia. She stared back at him, unflinching. Her beautiful face was carved in alabaster, her white-blonde hair cut into a ragged, wispy fringe, her ice-blue eyes steady.

He nodded in thanks. And then, amazingly, she nodded back.

He tried to ignore the tightness in his chest, the tingling that spread through his whole body when she looked at him. He wanted to push her hair behind her ear, to tilt her chin toward him, to feel her breath on his skin and her lips on his. He longed to hold her and never let her go.

But that was an impossible dream, futile and useless. The sooner he stopped wanting it, the better. The truth was, some things couldn't be fixed once you'd broken them—no matter how much you regretted it, no matter how deeply you wished things were different.

He knew this. Yet it was so easy to forget.

Jericho rose to his feet with a sigh. "Get some sleep, people. We need to rest as much as possible."

"I'll take the first watch," Gabriel said.

He took a shovelful of dirt and threw it on the fire. Sparks danced in the air like a hundred pairs of red eyes watching them in the night.

3
___

WILLOW

I t wasn't the way Willow would have chosen to spend her eighteenth birthday, but beggars couldn't be choosers. Not these days.

Amelia and Jericho's waning SmartFlexes still recorded the time and date, though they did little else. The morning of December eighth dawned cold and brittle.

Willow had made Benjie wear three layers of long-sleeved shirts they'd scavenged from someone's garage several miles back. He wore a turquoise knit hat low over his eyes. The bright color bobbing through the world of gray and brown made her heart ache. Turquoise had been her sister Zia's favorite color.

The sky was overcast, thick with a dreary, drizzling rain, and clotted with pillars of smoke. What leaves remained on the trees were shriveled and brown, clinging to their barren branches in defiance of coming winter. A white haze of frost filmed the overgrown grass and weeds choking the edges of the asphalt.

Two days ago, they'd abandoned the trucks just past Hartsfield-Jackson airport to the west. The road was too clogged with vehicles.

They continued on foot, trudging past signs for communities with names like Lakewood Heights, High Point, and Summerhill. As they headed into South Atlanta, townhouses and tenement tracts gave way to restaurants and shops, infotainment stores and grocery delivery warehouses. Above them, gleaming corporate towers, dazzling luxury apartments, and soaring skyscrapers cast long shadows.

"No talking above a whisper," Jericho had instructed. "Communicate through gestures when you can. This is hostile territory. The sooner we make it through, the better. Look alive, people."

"You hear that?" She squeezed her brother's hand.

Benjie nodded and tugged on her arm, pointing at something above them. Thirty feet over their heads, the AirRail track arced gracefully, winding between skyscrapers and hovering on slim columns over the congested streets. Constructed a decade ago, it was a sleek white hyper-speed maglev train that levitated over magnetized tracks.

The holoscreens attached to every building stared silent and empty, like giant blind eyes somehow still watching their every move. The scanners wouldn't read any SmartFlexes now. They wouldn't instantly glean a lifetime of purchasing history or social media data or tailor ads specifically to your unique preferences, no annoying advertisements directed at you every time you traveled down the street.

Her stomach lurched. She never thought she'd actually miss a holo ad.

The further they walked into the city, the heavier and thicker the smoke grew. The stench burned their nostrils and stung their watering eyes. Ahead of them, smoke poured from an Italian deli. On their left, only a burned-out husk remained of the Metropolitan Historican Artifacts Museum. Windows and doors were broken or boarded up. Spray-painted graffiti marked the walls.

There were bodies crumpled on the sidewalks. Bodies lying half-inside doorways. Bodies slumped inside cars. All of them in various states of decomposition. For most of them, the tell-tale blood stains rimming the eyes, nose, and mouth told the same story—the ravages of the Hydra virus.

Acid burned the back of Willow's throat. She tried not to gag. The N95 masks they wore did nothing to filter out the stench of rotting flesh mingled with burnt metal and wood and charred plastic.

Hawks and other carrion birds squawked over the bodies. A coyote with red on its muzzle growled at them, but scurried down an alley when Silas hurled a rock at it.

Crashed drones littered the streets, sidewalks, and roofs of shorter shops and cafes. Most were food and product-delivery drones, but there were plenty of surveillance and patrol drones. Many of them looked like they'd been blown out of the air, their metal bodies torn and mangled.

When she'd first learned of the billions of dead, her brain couldn't imagine it, couldn't comprehend the astronomical numbers, the sheer staggering mathematical figures. She still couldn't. But here in a massive city constructed of steel and glass and concrete, everything designed by people, for people, the silence was deafening.

They trudged past a dozen bodies slumped over each other next to a stoplight. The Hydra virus hadn't taken them. Bullet holes were drilled into the back of their heads.

She turned Benjie's face away. He didn't need to see that.

"What happened here?" Finn asked grimly.

"What didn't happen? Maybe that's the better question." She took a closer look at the buildings. Bullet holes punctured the brick facade of a posh college prep academy, the tuition probably more than Willow's mother had made in two years on the *Grand Voyager*.

A massive infotainment center sported craters a car could drive through.

Evidently, something had happened, some sort of uprising or gang turf war fought right in downtown Atlanta. The question was: when?

"This place gives me the creeps," she said softly.

"Tell me about it." Finn gazed up at the skyline, the crowns of skyscrapers a thousand feet above them disappearing into the smoky haze. "Makes me more nervous than a cat in a roomful of rocking chairs."

"It's eerily quiet…where are all the people?"

Jericho paused, holding up his hand. "Don't shoot your gun unless you have to. Even with a suppressor, it might be heard by the wrong people."

Everyone nodded. No one spoke. Benjie kicked a pebble on the sidewalk. Horne kept clearing his throat. Amelia hummed to herself under her breath, the same classical song she'd been repeating all week, her hands skimming over an invisible violin.

Several city blocks later, a shattered skyscraper jutted into the sky like the shards of a broken bottle. A small granite memorial stood in front of it. She remembered the shaky videos from the newsfeeds. The terrorist group Right Hand of God had bombed it two years ago. No one bothered to rebuild it. Why put money into a crumbling city already choked with violence and hopelessness?

"Today is my birthday," she said suddenly. She needed to tell someone. She needed to untangle the anxious knot twisting in her gut. She needed to talk, to laugh about something. Otherwise, this empty, gutted city was going to break her heart. "Happy eighteenth to me."

"Congratulations!" Finn's face broke into a delighted, lopsided grin. She couldn't see it beneath his mask, but she knew it was there. "Why didn't you tell me before?"

"Because...it didn't seem right. With everything." She gestured with both hands, encompassing the whole damn screwed-up world.

"Hogwash. Fiddlesticks. Balderdash!" Finn said.

Benjie giggled.

At 6'6", Finn towered above her, his meaty arms and legs like tree trunks. He was huge, an imposing, intimidating giant—until he grinned mischievously, flashing his gap-toothed smile. In reality, Finn was gentle as a teddy bear.

He peered down at her, his brows furrowed. "What's wrong?"

She sighed. For such a giant goofball, Finn was perceptive when he wanted to be. Too perceptive. The truth was, Zia was on her mind.

Instead of fading like one of those pre-digital photos, she grew even more vibrant in Willow's memory with each passing day. Her turquoise pixie hair framing her heart-shaped face, her nose always wrinkling up like a puppy, her exuberant laughter filling every corner of Willow's mind.

She never wanted to forget her sister, but she didn't know how much longer she could endure the pain and guilt. Today was yet another reminder that Zia would never have a chance to grow up, to graduate from high school, to transform from girl to woman. She would forever be stuck at thirteen, frozen in Willow's memories.

Zia would never turn eighteen, and it was Willow's fault.

How could she explain any of that? Besides, if she started to talk about Zia, she'd cry, and once she started crying, she might never stop. She had to be strong. For herself, and for Benjie. It was what her mother would want.

She was *Ate*, the big sister in her Filipino family, the one responsible for her siblings. She'd failed with Zia. She couldn't fail with Benjie.

"Nothing's wrong," she said with forced brightness. "Other than the obvious end-of-the-world angst. I'm fine."

Finn grabbed her hand and gave it a quick squeeze, letting go before anything got awkward.

Her cheeks flushed for no damn reason. She ducked her head, letting her thick black hair fall across her face.

Finn didn't seem to notice. He rubbed his hands together gleefully. "Now, what kind of cake would you like? I'm partial to red velvet, but I know not everyone's tastes are as refined as mine."

"Anything but chocolate," Benjie chimed from between them.

"What?" Finn said, aghast. "What could anyone possibly have against chocolate?"

"Lo Lo hates chocolate."

She managed a smile for Benjie's sake. "That's not true."

Benjie grinned sheepishly. "Okay, it's me. I don't like chocolate. But Lo Lo only wants a cake flavor that I want too, right?"

Finn shook his head in mock-horror. "How little I know thee. Obviously, you've never had the right kind of chocolate. We must remedy this, Sir Benjie." Lately he'd been calling Benjie "sir," telling him they were knights on a magnificent quest, to distract him from their harsh new reality. Benjie ate it up like a half-starved puppy.

"We both like white chocolate." Even though she hadn't had any since last Christmas. Her *lola*, her Filipina grandmother, had made faux candy canes with white-chocolate-dipped pretzels to go with *nilagang baka* and *pancit*. It had been a very special treat.

"White chocolate isn't real chocolate," Finn scoffed. "Everyone knows that."

A noise came from somewhere ahead of them, a clanking sound like a can being kicked across the road. Willow caught a flurry of movement out of the corner of her eye.

She seized Finn's arm with one hand and tightened her grip on Benjie with the other. "Shhh."

Jericho raised his right fist. Willow, Finn, Benjie, and Jericho ducked behind a bus parked crookedly across two lanes in the

26

middle of the road. Celeste, Amelia, Horne, and Micah found cover in a narrow alley between a shoe store and a coffee shop. Gabriel was behind them, covering the rear. Silas was scouting somewhere ahead of them.

Willow slipped her gun out of its holster. Jericho raised his finger to his lips and gestured for her to creep around the left side of the bus, while he checked out the right. She nodded and glanced back at Benjie and Finn. Finn gripped his hand and drew him close, dwarfing the small boy beside his bulk.

Satisfied Benjie was safe with Finn, she dropped into a crouch and inched around the side of the bus. There were too many cars ahead of her to see clearly. Keeping her gun up and her back pressed against the bus, she made her way forward.

Anxiety swirled in her stomach, but not fear or panic. She'd trained with Silas and Jericho daily—sometimes hours a day—for weeks. She was no expert fighter or marksman, but she felt more capable than she ever had. With every lesson, she was stronger, smarter, and better able to protect herself and Benjie.

There was another sound, like tin cans clanging against each other. Someone coughed and swore violently.

Her heart beating against her ribs, she knelt and raised her head over the nose of the bus. Less than twenty yards ahead of them, an old man stumbled out of a SmartFlex repair shop. He was frail, with a fringe of white hair rimming a bald scalp. He wore only a flimsy T-shirt and hospital scrubs.

But it was his face that drew her focus and stopped her heart. Blood streaked his mouth, stained his ears, and rimmed his eye sockets. His eyes bulged blood-red. His skin was gray as a filthy rag, the veins all over his body a reddish-black, standing out like a grotesque roadmap.

The man was infected.

He turned and looked straight at Willow.

Willow didn't move, didn't breathe. If they drew his attention, he'd charge them, coughing contagious blood and spittle. He was an innocent, suffering victim. She didn't want to shoot him, but she would if she had to.

He didn't see her. He doubled over and vomited a pink-tinged yellow sludge. He straightened, gripping his stomach with frail, trembling arms, and looked both ways, as if this were an ordinary day in an ordinary world.

He staggered into the street, weaving between cars, half-falling against a sedan, pushing himself up, then bumped into a rust-orange minivan and toppled to his hands and knees.

For a minute, Willow lost sight of him. She tracked his faltering movements through his groans. The old man appeared again as he crawled onto the sidewalk and into an office building across the street with a missing front door.

No one moved until the man's anguished sounds faded into silence. When the group gathered again at the rear of the bus, their faces were drawn, their expressions tense. They hadn't seen anyone infected with the Hydra virus so close in a few weeks.

Willow had thought the horror was seared into her mind. She was wrong. It was as shocking now as the first time.

"We should help him," Micah said in a low voice.

Jericho shook his head. "The only thing that will help him now is death. Is that what you want to do?"

Micah's bronze skin paled. "No."

Willow squeezed his arm. She knew how he felt, but there was nothing they could do. They needed to move on, and quickly.

A few blocks later, they came across several bodies lying in the doorway of a sleek, black-glassed, twenty-story building. They were piled on top of each other, almost as if they had been stacked there on purpose.

The top body moved.

"Lo Lo," Benjie gasped.

Willow saw it. Her gun was already in her hands.

But the movement wasn't human. Not this time. A dozen rats scurried over the bodies. Chewing. Feeding.

Willow's gut curdled. "Oh, gross."

"Stay away from them," Finn warned. "Or things will go from pudding to poop real fast."

Willow nudged the safety off her gun. "That's the understatement of the century."

But it was too late. Three of the rats raised their brown, furry heads. They sniffed the air, their nostrils quivering. Dread gripped her as the creatures turned as one toward them. Red stained the fur around their tiny jutting teeth.

The biggest rat scrabbled off the bodies and skittered a few feet toward them. The thing bristled with black fur, its tiny eyes beady, jagged incisors gnashing against each other.

It sat back on its haunches and sniffed, whiskers trembling. Sensing what? Their warm blood? Their beating hearts?

"We need to go." Several vehicles parked bumper to bumper blocked their immediate exit to the left. They could retreat or move on. Willow edged forward to pass the nasty vermin. "Benjie, come on."

But Benjie stood frozen, staring at the largest rat as it abruptly dropped to all fours and scurried straight toward him.

Willow aimed her gun, about to send the sucker to kingdom come.

"Don't shoot unless you have to!" Jericho warned. "A gunshot might bring even more trouble."

Willow grunted in frustration as she aimed a kick at the rat instead. It dodged but changed direction, coming at her and making a line drive for her ankle.

Willow jerked her foot free as the little beast clung to her ankle, its claws digging into her pant leg. It squeaked as it bounced to the concrete, found its footing, and charged her again. She nailed the thing with a vicious stomp. This time, it didn't get up. "What the hell!" Rats shouldn't act like this. They ran from larger predators. They stalked the corners and alleys and sewers of the night. They didn't attack aggressively during the day.

A second rat scurried for Micah. He batted it aside with the butt of his semi-automatic rifle. The other rats squealed, darting from the dead bodies and forming a disgusting little pack on the sidewalk —a dozen of them, skulking and twitching, their pink, scaly tails slithering behind them.

"They're like the dogs." She backed away in horror. "They're infected."

"Don't let them bite you!" Celeste cried.

Jericho slid the pulse stick from his belt, activated it, and swung it in a wide arc. One of the rats lunged at him. He danced back, narrowly missing the rat as it leapt for his left ankle. He stabbed the stick into the rat. The rat's body slumped—two brown, twitching chunks of meat instead of one.

"Gross," Willow said.

"Wicked!" Benjie breathed.

"Watch out!" Amelia flung a small brown rat off her shoe with a hard kick. The thing skittered toward the next closest person, Celeste, who barely suppressed a scream.

Hearing their cries, Silas raced back from wherever he'd been scouting. He plunged forward and swung his nail-spiked bat at the pack of rats. He took out three of them immediately.

Jericho took out another two, the plasma crackling and sizzling as it sliced through warm flesh. The remaining four scattered, skittering back through the gaping office door with a furious chattering.

"I suggest we all get bats," Silas said, hefting his.

"Those things are almost worse than the dogs," Amelia said, her face even paler than usual. "They're so fast and hard to actually hit."

Gabriel nudged at a limp brown body with his boot. "They're wily little bastards."

"Keep away from them," Willow said. "They carry the infection. A bite could be deadly."

No wonder Raven refused to enter the city. It was a maze of dangerous traps and dangerous people. And now this. Aggressive, infected killer rats.

Some birthday.

4

MICAH

The hairs rose on nineteen-year-old Micah's arms. Everything was eerily silent. A metropolis built for millions, now a mausoleum for the dead and dying. It looked like the world had just pressed pause, like any minute, some supernatural being would lean down, press the "play" button, and the noise and chaos and millions of insanely busy lives would start up again, just like clockwork. It was all here, just waiting for them.

Of course, when you looked closer, the cracks in the veneer appeared. The slumped forms in the cars weren't stuck in traffic. The small bent head in the backseat of the yellow SUV wasn't looking down at a doll or latest holo game on her SmartFlex. She was stuck there for all eternity.

The city was empty. Empty shops, empty offices, empty apartments and condos, empty streets—but for the dead bodies, the scurrying rats. The broken windows, the shattered storefronts, the boarded-up entrances and bullet-riddled holoscreen signs all spoke of violence, destruction, and catastrophe.

Last night, they'd tried nine different condo and apartment buildings in search of shelter, driven away each time by the massive numbers of bloated, decomposing bodies. The fetid, overwhelming stench churned his stomach and sent shock-waves of dizziness through his system.

Finally, with darkness hovering over their heads, they'd found shelter in a home goods store, padding the floor with chenille throw blankets and decorative frilly pillows embroidered with 'No place like home.' Benjie discovered a stash of Nerds and Finn's favorite sour-explosion Skittles beneath a checkout scanner. Celeste and Micah joined the two of them in a game of poker.

It had been a good night—as good as could be expected, anyway. Now they were out in the wild again, trudging through the silence and the rain. They drove off several more rats, but no large packs.

He glimpsed several furtive movements out of the corner of his eye. Once he caught sight of someone in a pine-green jacket ducking behind a shattered window. There were survivors here, but they remained in the shadows, avoiding contact with others. Maybe theirs was the wisest method.

They trudged past the old CNN building, Centennial Park, a brightly-colored children's museum. They passed what used to be the famous aquarium: the one the Earth Liberation Army had bombed three years ago. Now there was a forty-foot obsidian sculpture memorial featuring two entwined dolphins.

He'd never understood why a group so dedicated to animal rights could have murdered all those helpless sea creatures. In the manifesto repeated ad nauseam on the newsfeeds, the Earth Liberation Army claimed animals were better off dead than imprisoned. The world had been crazy for a long, long time.

After hours of walking, they took a break inside a deli called Flash Food. Micah and Gabriel cleared the place, checking for humans, animals, and bodies, and found nothing. There was a back exit to an alley down the hallway to the bathrooms, offices, and storage closet. This was as good a place to rest for lunch as any.

Gabriel stood guard by the shattered front doors while Micah and the others sat in the black chairs and unloaded the remains of their supplies from their backpacks.

On the left was a sleek gray smartwall with superimposed buttons to swipe for pizza, sandwich, pasta, fruit, or stir-fry. Once the printer robots behind the wall manufactured the meal from powdered ingredients, it would eject from one of several chutes. But without power, the wall was as silent and useless as everything else.

"We'll have to scavenge soon," Jericho said, chewing on a piece of faux-beef jerky. "I don't care to expose us to more danger than we have to. The only positive about the city is the millions of kitchens and pantries full of food no one's using anymore. There's not enough people left alive to empty it all out. Not yet."

"How long do you think it will take to get through the city?" Amelia asked.

"A few more days, if we're lucky. Maybe we can find some bikes or Segways, anything faster than walking. But honestly, with getting around the cars blocking the roads and the bodies and broken glass and debris on the sidewalks, walking might be the fastest."

"And the quietest." Micah dug into a jar of peanut butter with a plastic spoon. "We need to get in and out before anyone even knows we're here."

Jericho cracked his knuckles. "He's right."

"So no talking?" Benjie asked.

"Only whispers, like we've been doing."

They gathered their things, stood, and crowded around the entrance. "I'll make sure it's clear," Gabriel said. "Then I'll take up the rear."

Outside, a light drizzle spat from the gunmetal sky. Several blocks away, a short, squat building was on fire, black smoke pouring into the air.

"Hey," someone said. A voice he didn't recognize. A stranger.

A chill zipped down his spine. Micah whipped around, along with Silas, Gabriel, and Jericho, their guns up and aimed at the threat.

Two men stumbled down the street. They wore dirty cargo pants, camouflage jackets with hoods, and masks and gloves. The first, larger man had a ragged gray beard. His arm was slung around the smaller man's waist, propping him up. "Help us!"

Gabriel leveled his rifle. "Don't come any closer!"

"It's a trap," Silas hissed.

"We don't know that," Micah said. The men looked unarmed. Neither held weapons or wore gun holsters that he could see.

"No closer!" Gabriel said again, flicking off the safety of his gun.

Jericho turned to Gabriel. "I thought you said it was clear!"

"It was." Gabriel's voice was tense, his eyes flashing. "They must have slipped through an alleyway or exited one of the buildings."

"He's hurt," Gray Beard called out in a rough baritone voice.

"Get behind us," Micah said to Amelia, Celeste, and the others. Finn pushed himself in front of Benjie. Willow joined Micah, Silas, Gabriel, and Jericho, who all stood in a line in front of the rest of the group, protecting them.

"Go back in the store, nice and slow," Gabriel said. "Find something large and dense to hide behind, just in case."

"Okay," Amelia said.

Micah sensed movement behind him as Amelia and the others followed instructions. The tension in his gut eased a fraction. At least they were safe for the moment. If things went south, they could slip out the back exit and make a run for it.

"Please, we just need a little food and water," Gray Beard repeated. He dragged his partner another step closer.

"Stop!" Gabriel shouted. "I'm warning you!"

"We will shoot," Jericho said.

Micah lowered his gun, though he kept his finger on the trigger. "They're hurt. We can help them."

"They're tricking us," Silas spat. "Use your brain for once. Where did they come from? They just appear out of nowhere, needing our help? Needing *our* food and water when there's still plenty to scavenge?"

Micah hesitated. "I don't know, but we should ask rather than shoot them."

Silas gestured with his gun. "I would if they'd back the hell up."

"Don't do anything rash, Silas," he said.

"Tell them that," Silas said, his voice rising.

"Stop right now!" Jericho demanded. "You could be infected! Stay at least ten feet away!"

"We're not infected," Gray Beard said, wiping sweat and dirt from his brow with his free hand. "I promise you that."

"I'm sorry, but we can't take you at your word." Micah blinked the rain out of his eyes. His glasses were fogged and misty. He squinted at them, trying to make out the details of their faces, to read the intent behind their eyes. "Just stop for a minute. We'll toss you some cans of food and a couple bottles of water. We've got some bandages, too."

"There are bad people after us. We need shelter. We can't stay out here." Gray Beard kept repeating his plea. As he spoke, he kept advancing, dragging his wounded friend with him.

They were closer now, less than ten yards away. Micah rubbed his fogged glasses with the jacket sleeve of his free hand. Blood stained the wounded man's pant leg from his thigh to his ankle.

But it could be fake. Both Harmony and Raven had warned them of the dangerous gang prowling the city. Silas could be right. They might be preying on the innate goodness of others, waiting to get close enough before they struck.

What was the right decision? What if they made the wrong choice? The consequences for getting it wrong would be devastating.

He bit the inside of his cheeks. *Be brave. Be good.* Always do the right thing, his mother told him before she died, Catholic prayer beads wrapped around her gaunt fingers. They couldn't shoot unarmed men. "Put your guns down. They'll stop if we lower our weapons."

"Like hell, they will," Silas said.

His stomach knotted in dread, every sense heightened. The cold rain drizzled against his face. The reek of smoke and ash and the fetid, stomach-roiling stench of death stung his nostrils. His heart-beat jack-hammered against his ribs, his breath loud in his ears.

The men staggered closer, dirt on their faces, panic in their eyes. Silas pointed his gun, his outstretched arms steady, his finger twitching on the trigger.

"They're not stopping," Willow said.

Gabriel punched off a few shots at the men's feet. Chunks of concrete sprayed their legs. Gray Beard fell back, but as soon as the bullets ceased, he took another step. "Please, we can't stay out here. I know you're good people. I know you won't shoot."

Now they were five yards away, nearly breaching the ten-foot infection safe zone. The wounded man reached for something in his pocket.

"Don't move!" Willow cried.

Silas fingered the trigger. "To hell with this."

Micah whirled toward Silas. "Don't—"

But it was too late.

Silas squeezed the trigger twice in quick succession. A single bullet punched into the bigger man's chest. The second bullet struck the smaller man in the head.

They both crumpled without a sound.

5

AMELIA

Amelia huddled with the rest of the group behind the counter of the Flash Food place. Glass littered the black-and-white checkered floor. Dozens of Styrofoam coffee cups had toppled over the cash register screen.

Celeste clutched one in her hands, frantically tearing it to shreds. She stared at Amelia with huge, wild eyes. Horne crouched in the furthest corner, his hands over his ears, his head down, murmuring some useless meditation over and over. Finn hunched next to him, Benjie trembling in his arms.

Amelia hated this sense of helplessness, not knowing and not being able to do a thing to help. She couldn't shoot a gun or throw a knife or break a man's neck with her bare hands.

She wasn't like Silas, who took to fighting like a dog to water. In this new, dangerous world, the social graces she'd so carefully honed were useless. As useless as her years perfecting her skills as an accomplished violinist. There were no orchestras in the apocalypse.

Two gunshots blasted in quick succession. Even with suppressors, the shots were impossibly loud in the echoing silence. She cringed. Her mouth went impossibly dry.

For a long moment, no one moved. Who'd taken the shots? Who'd been hit? Everyone she cared about was a possible target— Silas, Micah, Jericho, even Gabriel if she allowed her heart a choice in the matter.

Benjie whimpered.

"Stay here," she whispered urgently. She refused to remain there a second longer. She needed to know.

Celeste ripped off a chunk of Styrofoam and let it drop to the floor. "You don't know what's out there. It's too dangerous. Jericho said to wait—"

"It's dangerous to wait here like sitting ducks. I'm going."

"Be careful," Finn said.

But she was already up and creeping around the front of the counter. She couldn't see anything through the front windows and shattered glass door but empty sidewalks, silent cars, still buildings. No movement but the cold, gray rain.

She slipped outside. Silas stood stiffly on the sidewalk a dozen yards away, staring at the two bodies at his feet.

She raced down the sidewalk, pushing between people, counting them in her head even as she shoved them out of the way. Micah, Jericho, Willow, Gabriel. None of them hurt.

Relief flooded her. Her knees wobbled. "What happened?"

Jericho grabbed her arm to hold her back. "Silas shot two people."

She wrenched free from his grasp. Jericho was like her mother, always trying to protect her. She didn't need protecting from this. She might not be an expert marksman, but she was strong enough to handle death.

She went to her brother. "Silas."

Silas didn't move or speak. He hunched his shoulders, one hand shoved in his pocket, the other gripping his rifle with white-knuckled fingers. Rain ran down his face, matting his short brown hair to his skull.

She glanced at the bodies crumpled at their feet. They were both dead. Her stomach lurched. She took a deep, steadying breath and placed her hand on her brother's arm. "Did they threaten you?"

"Yes," he said in a dull voice.

"No, they didn't." Micah squatted beside the bodies. He lifted the men's jackets with gloved hands and patted them down. "No guns."

"That one was reaching for a weapon." Silas pointed at the smaller man. "It was a trap. They were pretending they needed help to get close enough to attack."

"He was hurt." Micah gestured to one of the bodies. The smaller man's hood covered the top half of his face, the lower half hidden by his face mask. Both men's clothes were dirty, but the smaller one's right leg was stained with blood.

"A trick," Silas spat.

"It's easy enough to check," Amelia said with a calmness she didn't feel.

Micah pulled out his knife and ripped open the man's tan cargo pants. A long, ugly gash marred his thin, almost hairless leg from the thigh to the shin. His sock and shoe were crusted and clotted with blood. Red swirled in the rain puddling on the sidewalk.

Micah's face blanched. "We just killed two innocent people."

"Not us." Willow glared at Silas. "Him."

Silas staggered back. "They weren't innocent. They wouldn't listen. They wouldn't stop. We warned them."

"He's right about that at least," Gabriel said. "They refused to stop. They could've been infected."

"You should have waited for orders," Jericho said.

"I did what I had to do, what none of you were willing to do! That's what a soldier does. He protects his own."

41

Jericho's voice was hard as steel, his eyes a dark, glittering obsidian. "You're no soldier. You're an impudent, reckless child."

Silas flinched like he'd been slapped. "At least I'm not a weak, indecisive pussy. You're going soft, Jericho." He pointed at Micah with a shaking finger. "Just like *him*."

Micah's nostrils flared. "We can't just go around killing every person we feel threatened by!"

"Wake up, Micah!" Silas snarled. "This is a kill-or-be-killed world. That's exactly what we need to do!"

"If one of them was hiding an M16 beneath his coat," Gabriel said evenly, "we wouldn't be having this discussion. Silas would be a hero."

"I highly doubt that," Horne said.

Silas lunged at Horne, but Gabriel and Jericho pushed him back.

Amelia kept staring at the wounded man's leg. Something wasn't quite right. It was too thin, too hairless. Too young.

She bent down and tugged off his mask. But for a smattering of pimples around his chin, his face was round and smooth. It wasn't a man, but a boy, maybe thirteen.

Horror stuck in her throat like a hook. A low buzzing filled her ears. Numb tingling started in her fingers and crawled up her arms. It was just a kid. Her brother had killed a kid.

Silas swore and reared back. His mouth contorted, anguish shadowing his features. He masked it with a contemptuous grimace, but she saw it. Dismay vibrated through his entire body.

"He's just a boy," Micah said, shaken.

Silas recovered swiftly. "That doesn't change anything," he sneered. "He still could've killed us all."

"He was unarmed. They both were," Micah said.

"He knows, Micah." She could see it in the quiver of his lips, the flare of his nostrils, the sharp panic in his eyes. He regretted his actions, but he couldn't admit it. He'd never admit it. She felt dazed, shaken, unsure what to do. She wanted to wrap him in her arms and slap him at the same time.

Overhead, the sky darkened like a stain. The dull gray light drained all the color out of the world. Cold, dreary rain spat against her face. Her wet hair plastered against her head. She shivered, wrapping her arms around herself as the first beat of pain pulsed against her temple. A headache, possibly a migraine. Maybe worse.

Finn pointed at the boy's neck. "There's something else."

Micah nudged the boy's coat aside and revealed a tattoo of a flaming skull beneath his left ear. Amelia checked the older man. His neck sported the same tattoo.

"What is it?" Celeste asked.

Finn peered over Micah's shoulder. "It's a gang sign."

"Are they Pyros?" Willow asked, shaken.

"Maybe." Gabriel bent down and examined the tattoo with gloved fingers. "Probably."

"What does that mean?" Celeste asked, her voice edged with rising hysteria.

Micah took off his rain-slicked glasses and wiped them on the shirt beneath his jacket. A single curl was slicked against his forehead. "We're in even greater danger now."

"Let's just face the facts here." Horne jutted his chin at Silas. "That boy is reckless and violent. He's a stone-cold killer. He needlessly killed two innocent souls who may now bring the wrath of a ruthless gang down upon all our heads. He's a danger to us all."

Amelia whirled on him. "Just what are you suggesting?"

"I vote we kick him out."

"I don't know," Finn said uncertainly, glancing between Willow and Silas. "That seems harsh, but he killed a kid. We can't just act like it didn't happen."

"This isn't the Boy Scouts or a book club," Willow said. "We don't just kick people out."

43

Horne gave a scornful shrug. "Then banish him. Use whatever terminology you prefer."

Celeste crossed her arms over her chest. "I vote for banishment."

"Absolutely not." Amelia fought down the anger and fear clawing her insides. They didn't understand. They didn't know Silas like she did. He was a lot of things, but he wasn't a stone-cold killer. "I can't believe you people."

"Your brother's going to get us all killed," Horne snapped.

She whirled on him. "He protected you!"

"He's a trigger-happy sociopath."

She expected Silas to swear, rage, and insult everyone. Instead, he just stood there, his features etched in stone, his fists bunched —taking it.

"He's a monster," Horne hissed through clenched teeth, his face turning blotchy and ugly.

"Maybe," she conceded. "But he's *my* monster."

She was scared and horrified and sickened, but she couldn't turn on him. He was her brother, no matter what. No one else understood him. No one else knew what they'd both been through, the things they'd endured.

Silas had defended her, protected her, willingly suffering the wrath of their father. It was Silas who put his body in front of hers as she cowered, trembling in fear. Declan had never struck her. The same couldn't be said for Silas. Could you ever escape violence when you'd been raised in it? It got in your blood, grew in your bones. She couldn't blame him for any of it.

Her mother was gone. She'd never had a real father. She wasn't going to lose her brother, too. She stepped in front of Silas. "Go ahead and banish him. But I'm going with him."

"You can't do that," Jericho said tersely.

She glared at him, blinking the rain out of her eyes. "Watch me."

"You may have the cure in your blood, Amelia," Micah said.

"You are the most important person in this group, maybe anywhere. Our number one mission is to get you safely to the Sanctuary."

"I'm aware," she said hotly. "That doesn't change anything."

Gabriel ran his hand over his stubbled jaw with a frown. "You don't have a choice. I won't let you leave."

"You won't let me? What are you going to do, tie me up and carry me over your shoulder like a sack of flour?" It felt good to let the anger out, to say exactly what she thought and felt. She'd spent a lifetime hiding anything that made her flawed, that made her ugly. But she didn't care about being ugly now.

"I will not leave my brother willingly. I'll fight you every second." She shot a look at Micah. "You've seen what I can do with a syringe. Just imagine what I'll do with a knife."

A ghost of a smile flickered across Silas's face, then disappeared.

Gabriel studied her with his dark, penetrating gaze, with those eyes that could reach deep into her soul. He was searching for weakness. He'd find no weakness here. She squared her shoulders. She did not flinch or look away.

Gabriel nodded to himself, as if deciding something. "If she goes," he said, "so do I."

Amelia flashed him a grateful look.

Horne threw up his hands. "Good riddance is what I say. Let's rid ourselves of the terrorist and the murderer in one fell swoop."

"And two of our best fighters." Jericho turned to Micah, his jaw working. "Say your piece. I know you have something to say."

Both Micah and Amelia looked at him, startled. Jericho never asked anyone for advice. He was the leader. His word was law. Anyone who didn't like it could leave. But he'd kept them all alive a dozen times, so everyone accepted his rule, however grudgingly.

Micah cleared his throat. "We're not savages. We can't live like that. I refuse to live like that, killing before someone else kills me.

We could have shot at their feet again. We could have wounded them if we had to, without killing them.

"Silas behaved recklessly. This boy is dead because of him. We killed two people. I can't imagine there won't be consequences." He met Amelia's gaze, his expression pained. He looked guilty himself, as if he were taking the weight of shame as his own. "We will deserve it."

"Would you banish him?" Jericho's voice was even, his face expressionless. It was impossible to read him, to know which way he would go. Jericho was tough, merciless when he had to be. But he also cared for Silas. Amelia didn't know what he would do.

Micah glanced at Amelia again. She pleaded with her eyes, begging silently. But she didn't say anything more. Her words were nails in her throat.

Micah sighed heavily. "All that being said…no, I wouldn't."

"Then I won't either," Jericho said briskly. "It's decided, then."

Amelia let out a breath. She was willing to leave them behind for Silas if she had to, but she felt immense relief that her challenge wouldn't be put to the test.

Silas growled deep in his throat, the only sign that he'd even heard them. He smiled hard, his teeth pulled back from his lips, his eyes empty. His body was present, but his mind was somewhere else, somewhere none of them could reach.

"You're just going to let Micah decide?" Horne whined. "Is he in charge now?"

"I'm in charge," Jericho said. "And I say we need every able-bodied fighter we have to defend ourselves. We've dallied for too long already. It's time to move."

Silas turned and stalked down the empty street, his rifle over his slouched shoulders, one hand shoved deep in his pocket, leaving the group behind without a backward glance.

"He didn't even say thank you," Celeste said.

"He was never one for manners." Amelia repressed a small, sad smile. This wasn't the time for humor, not with two dead bodies at her feet. But Silas was Silas. He never changed, not even for the apocalypse.

Finn took Benjie's hand. "Where's he going, anyway?"

"Probably to tear the wings off some butterflies," Finn muttered.

"I know what he's doing," Willow said. "I can keep an eye on him. We'll scout a shelter for the night."

Jericho nodded. "And food."

"We need thick leather boots," Amelia said. "To protect against the rats."

Willow kissed Benjie's head. "Stay with Mister Finn. I'll be back." She pulled Benjie's inhaler out of her cargo pocket and handed it to Amelia. "Will you watch this for me?"

"Of course—if you'll watch my brother for me." She wanted to run after him herself, but he wouldn't talk to her. She knew he wouldn't. He'd only shut her out. Maybe Willow could reach him in a way she couldn't.

Willow met Amelia's gaze and nodded. "That's what I aim to do." She shouldered her rifle and jogged after Silas, a gray shape disappearing into the rain.

Amelia watched them go, foreboding settling in the pit of her stomach like a block of ice. The group was still intact, but they weren't out of the woods.

Whether he'd meant to or not, whether he'd acted rashly or not, Silas had killed two Pyros. Somehow, some way, that was going to come back to haunt them.

6

WILLOW

"This place is as good as any," Willow said.

She and Silas had spent the last two days scavenging and scouting. As the sun began to sink between the skyscrapers, they'd discovered a huge, abandoned mall. It was mostly free of infected bodies, contained a food court with some packaged and canned goods in storage cabinets, and had clothing stores galore. Best of all, there were no rats in sight.

They'd circled the massive structure, circumventing smaller shopping centers, a huge, mostly empty parking lot, and a residential street of tenement housing filled with cars to provide cover. They approached from the back. There were a few semi-trucks, one parked in front of an open loading bay.

They clambered inside and passed through the darkened warehouse into the main mall. Pale, watery light filtered through the transparent, domed roof. Shadows crouched in the dim corners of the windowless shops. The mall was vast and empty, even their whispers echoing down the silent corridors.

She caught a glimpse of herself in a trio of mirrored spheres hanging outside of a high-fashion smart jewelry boutique—necklaces that predicted your stroke risk, bangles that monitored circadian rhythms. Her knotted, ratty hair was plastered around her drawn face, a streak of dirt marring one cheek, her eyes sharp and cunning as a wild animal's. She looked away quickly.

She shivered, her clothes soaked, glad to be out of the wet and the cold. Her scalp itched. She ran her tongue over her furry teeth, disgusted. They brushed with manual toothbrushes they'd scavenged from a convenience store, but it wasn't enough. She would've traded her meager life savings for a single night of modern amenities. "I bet they have boots. And I'm dying to change my underwear."

"It's time to get the others," Silas said, ignoring her lame attempt to get some kind of rise out of him.

"Not yet." They'd barely spoken in the two days since she'd joined him, since he'd killed the boy and the old man. Willow was pretty terrible about talking about feelings, but then, so was he. The more time they spent together, the more comfortable they became with each other's silence.

Bizarre as it was, she felt a connection to Silas. He was a world-class asshole, but he'd also taught her how to fight, how to win, how to stay alive. They'd both had to kill. They both lived with guilt like a cancer eating away at their insides. "Fight me."

His mouth curved in its usual smirk, but his eyes were sharp with regret and guilt, emotions Willow knew all too well. Silas knew he'd screwed up. He didn't need Willow to tell him that. She knew better than anyone how it felt to fail so horrifically. He just needed someone to be near him, someone who understood.

"Now?" he asked. "You look like a drowned poodle."

"You look worse, believe me." She shook out her arms and tucked her chin, getting into her fighting stance. "Give me your best shot."

Silas circled Willow slowly, throwing a few warm-up jabs.

Willow deflected his blows easily. She threw a counterstrike, nailing his shoulder.

She faked another jab, intending to come at him with a cross, but he knew her too well. He blocked it and kicked simultaneously, sweeping her legs out from under her.

She went down hard, the air knocked from her lungs, sharp pain striking her elbows and tailbone. Thank goodness for the extra padding on her behind that wouldn't go away, apocalyptic starvation diet or no.

She leapt up before he could catch his breath. She jabbed an uppercut at his face, her fist glancing off his chin.

He staggered back.

She flexed her fists as she stared at him. His face was still tense, his eyes drowning in

darkness. She needed to say something. This time, silence wasn't enough. "What happened sucked."

He only grunted.

Willow had killed a Headhunter at Sweet Creek Farm. She'd stabbed him, felt his warm lifeblood gushing over her hands. A part of her had hated it. Another part of her had relished the power of taking a life. She could do it again. She would do it again if she had to, in order to protect those she loved.

It would feel awful to accidentally kill a kid. But her finger had been twitching on her own trigger, too. It could just as easily have been her. "They didn't stop. You did what you had to do."

For a long moment, he just stared at her, breathing hard.

"I would have done the same thing. I would've felt guilty as hell. But our people come

first. They have to."

He cocked his head, studying her with that cutting gaze, sharp as stone. "You really believe that?"

"Hell, yes, I do. We survived the Headhunters. We've heard the rumors about the Pyros. What they're capable of. We know what kind of people are out there. We have to protect our own. That's what you did."

Finally, he nodded. It wasn't in him to show gratitude or apologize. She didn't expect

it. But when his smirk returned, it seemed happier, lighter somehow.

Which is when she attacked. She surged forward, feinted to the left, and landed a hard punch to the right side of his jaw. He stumbled back, reeling.

For a second, his expression was a mix of pained and furious, then the shadows cleared. He rubbed his jawline and spit a glob of blood on the floor. "Damn, Cupcake. I guess I'm one hell of a teacher."

She shook out her hand, flexing her stinging knuckles. "No, I'm one hell of a student."

His hunched shoulders relaxed. He gave her a smile—a real one, one that reached his eyes for maybe the first time since she'd met him. She smiled back.

She pointed at a department store to their left, where dozens of shiny white mannequins gleamed—their limbs contorted, their slim, flawless bodies draped with the latest fashions. They were the old-fashioned kind made of molded plastic, not the new holograms that writhed seductively, purring your name as you passed.

There were at least a hundred on this floor alone. They stood, silent monuments to...something. Rampant consumerism? Arrogant cultural something or other? She didn't know. It didn't matter. She just wanted to bash their perfect plastic heads in.

She grabbed a pair of diamond-studded sunglasses off one of the mannequins and stuck them on her head. "Ready to destroy something?"

"Always so demanding, Cupcake." He flashed her a wicked grin, already reaching for his pack to seize the nail-studded bat. "But I aim to please."

WILLOW

"**W**hat about these?" Willow asked, kicking out her leg to show Amelia her new shin-high brown leather boots.

"They look lovely." Amelia laced up her own sleek black pair with a rim of gray fur at the knees. It was the apocalypse, and yet somehow, Amelia still managed to look spectacular.

Willow stifled a scowl. She was only five feet tall, with a shoe-size to match, but she was cursed with her dad's thick calves. The brown boots were the only ones that fit her. Something so stupid and insignificant shouldn't have bothered her, but it did.

Since the world had ended in early September, fall styles were on display, but most of the heavy winter stuff hadn't arrived yet. But there were plenty of boots, jackets, scarves, and thin cotton or leather gloves to choose from.

Benjie was off shopping with Finn and the guys, giddy at being included with the adults. She felt only a slight anxiousness at not having him at her side. She trusted Finn and Micah. And Jericho,

Silas, and Gabriel were excellent fighters. Benjie was safer with them than with her.

Though she was working on that. She and Silas continued to train and spar every chance they got. Every day, she grew in strength and skill and prowess. With every fading bruise, her body grew harder, more resilient. She could take a punch in the face and bounce back up again, spitting blood and ready to return the favor.

She was still short and chubby; still plain, invisible Willow. But she was tough. She could fight. She could shoot. She could kill a man if she had to. And that made all the difference.

Amelia held a cranberry-colored cable-knit sweater to her chest, frowned, and discarded it. "Where's Celeste?"

Willow glanced around the large department store. Celeste had disappeared. They'd all been together the last few hours, wandering the stores, collecting jackets, sweaters, a change of clothes for their backpacks, and new underwear, bras, and socks.

She'd picked out a bright turquoise scarf in honor of Zia. She fingered the luxurious, velvet-soft fringe, a sudden shard of grief sliding between her ribs. Some days, everything made her think of Zia. Some days, everything hurt.

She needed a distraction. "I'll find her," Willow offered.

She wandered between the racks of designer clothes, purses, and sunglasses, her eyes stinging. Thoughts of her family flashed through her mind: Zia dancing and singing karaoke at the top of her lungs, doing her donkey-bray laugh; Benjie and Zia decorating each other's hair with a bunch of tiny butterfly clips, Zia's turquoise-tipped pixie hair standing up all over her head; her mom sipping a margarita and smiling in relaxed contentment on the *Grand Voyager*, the last time Willow ever saw her.

She shoved those thoughts out of her head. Zia was gone now. Her mom was gone, too. There was no time for tears while the world fell to pieces all around you. The only thing left to do was survive. And surviving, at least, she was good at.

Willow finally found Celeste behind the customer service and administrative offices, in the women's bathroom. The large, upscale bathroom was decorated with gray slate tile and shiny chrome counters. Everything was rimmed in a film of dust.

Celeste had stripped off her pants and shoes and was balancing her leg on the lip of the sink, a razor in one hand and a bar of hand soap in the other. A half-full bottle of water sat on the counter next to her.

Willow fisted her hands on her hips. She cleared her throat loudly. "Nice underwear."

Celeste rolled her eyes. "Thanks."

"What are you doing?"

"What does it look like? I'm practicing personal hygiene." She gave a haughty sniff. "Which the rest of you have obviously forgotten."

Willow touched her snarled, ratty hair. Now that she thought about it, her scalp itched like crazy. Her whole body felt grimy. "There are kind of more important things to do in the apocalypse. Like staying alive."

Celeste poured a bit of water over her shin, scrubbed with the soap, and dragged the razor across her leg. "Speak for yourself."

Part of her wanted to get out of there and return to shopping, which was actually kind of fun in a weird, disconcerting way. She'd never in her life picked out an item of clothing without regard to cost. Now she could choose anything and everything. She'd never cared about fashion, but Zia would have loved it.

She should probably leave. Celeste represented everything she despised in the elites: spoiled, clueless, self-absorbed, vain. Celeste was model-beautiful, with flawless brown skin, curved cheekbones, and perfectly arched brows. She'd grown up in luxury, in a world apart from the one Willow knew, where everyone was desperate and hopeless and starving.

Celeste always seemed to bring out everything she despised the most about herself, all the envious, petty, insecure parts. That old fear prickling at her that she would never be good enough, pretty enough, smart enough. Simply, enough.

She turned to leave. There was no reason to torture herself in Celeste's presence. But something made her hesitate.

Celeste's face reflected in the mirror was drawn and forlorn, wounded somehow. She looked lost. Vulnerable. Willow's mind flashed back to the *Grand Voyager*, when they'd been trapped together in the water beneath the bridge. Celeste's eyes had that same haunted look now.

Oh, hell. She crossed her arms over her chest. "No one cares if you're a hairy ox, you know."

"*I* care!" Celeste sniffed again and rubbed the back of her arm across her face. Her eyes were rimmed with red, dark circles smudged beneath them.

"Wait, are you crying?"

Celeste glared at Willow in the mirror. Her lower lip trembled. "I get it, okay? You're the strong, fierce one. Amelia is the stoic ice queen. Where does that leave me? Nothing in my life has prepared me for *this*." She waved her arms, encompassing everything, the whole damned and ruined world.

Willow shrugged, taken aback by the outburst and not sure what to say. She shifted uncomfortably. "It's not easy for any of us."

Celeste lowered her leg. She hunched her narrow shoulders and gripped the counter with both hands like she wanted to rip it out of the wall. "I'm not like you. I don't belong."

Willow fought down a hot spark of anger, but she couldn't keep the sarcasm out of her voice. "Please tell me more about how it sucks to be you."

"Never mind." Celeste wiped furiously at her eyes. A single tear slid down her flawless cheek. "My life wasn't perfect, you know, whatever you think."

Willow felt a pang of sympathy. She did her best to ignore it. Damn it. She couldn't. She leaned against the cold bathroom wall and sighed. "Try me."

Celeste glared at her for a minute beneath her long lashes, probably deciding whether to simper some stupid nonsense or actually say something real for a change. She picked up the razor, put it down again, then finally took a deep, shuddering breath. "Okay, fine. My mother was the CEO of a huge biotech company, before— before the *Grand Voyager*. It was a big deal, even in this day and age, you know? An African-American *and* a woman? She was a workaholic and a perfectionist, and she still believed they'd rip that title away from her the first chance they got."

Celeste took a swig from the water bottle and wiped her mouth primly. "You'll probably think this is crazy, but some of the wealthiest families are—were—using marriage to consolidate their power. My mom hired this match-maker, had me all set up to marry Jefferson Kellogg, the son of the BlueTech holoscreens founder. It would be this young-love, fairy-tale wedding. All pre-planned for maximum reach and media coverage, of course. The vloggers would eat it up. More importantly, it would fortify our family's future, create a tech dynasty."

Willow frowned, understanding dawning. "But aren't you—"

"Gay? Yeah, I am." Celeste pulled on her tight, forest-green suede pants and tugged on a pair of white silk socks. "But that didn't fit into my mom's plans."

"Why didn't you just say no?"

"Have you ever met my mother?" She glanced at Willow, as if remembering who she was talking to. "She would've cut me off.

From my credit accounts, my share of the company, the inheritance. Everything."

It would be hard for someone like Celeste to even consider such a possibility. Willow wouldn't be poor if she had the choice. No one would. Worse, the pressure from a parent to be something you weren't, to sacrifice an essential part of your identity for their own selfish gain...that would suck. No matter how much money you had.

Willow didn't know what to say. Things were easier when everything was black and white, when the elites were rich bitches, not real people with real problems. She shoved her bangs out of her eyes. "At least now you can be whoever you want to be."

Celeste turned back to the mirror. "Yeah," she said slowly, "I guess I can."

Willow pointed to Celeste's boots, a pair of white designer stiletto heels. "I hope you weren't planning on wearing those."

Celeste huffed. "There's no reason to be ugly."

"No, but there are several very good reasons to be able to run."

~

Thirty minutes later, Celeste had a practical but attractive pair of thick leather knee-high boots sans heels. They met up with Amelia in the makeup section of the department store.

Amelia held up an expensive-looking, curved glass bottle. "Perfume!"

"Hallelujah!" Celeste said.

"Try some, Willow." Amelia held out the spritzer. "You'll forget for half a second that we all smell like a pig sty."

But Willow had stopped paying attention to them. The exterior window adjacent to the mirrored perfume counter was broken in the left corner. Safety glass kept most of it intact, but there were a few holes—bullet holes, her mind registered numbly.

A faint scream filtered through the window.

She raised her finger to her lips. "Shhh!"

Celeste and Amelia immediately fell silent. Willow dropped into a crouch, crept to the window, and looked out.

A shopping plaza was located across the massive parking lot. Dozens of bodies were piled in front of a sporting goods store. Five figures emerged from the darkened entrance of the building. They were dressed from head to toe in personal protection gear—yellow pressurized suits and helmets. Two of the figures carried a body between them and tossed it on the pile.

Willow sucked in her breath, fighting down revulsion mingled with fear. What the hell were they doing?

Another scream echoed through the air. Two more yellow-suited figures strode from the store, dragging a woman between them by her arms. Her blonde hair was short. She wore a long polka-dotted skirt and a ratty jean jacket with red patches. She struggled to stand, to wrench herself away from her captors. They tightened their hold and dragged her to her knees, turning her so she faced Willow. She looked up at her captors, her mouth open as if begging for her life.

The red patches and polka dots weren't designs. They were blood. Blood leaked from the woman's ears and trailed down her neck. Blood smeared her eye sockets and rimmed her mouth.

"She's infected," Amelia breathed beside her.

"Stay down," she hissed.

"What are they doing?"

"I—I don't know."

One of the figures tossed something on the pile of bodies. It ignited in a whoosh of flame. Another one shook a can of paint and sprayed several red X's encased in circles over the doors and exterior walls of the sporting goods store.

The woman screamed louder, writhing in an attempt to escape. A third figure held a syringe. He strode up to the woman and jammed the syringe into her neck. Within seconds, she slumped forward, her head hanging limp.

The two people who'd forced the woman to her knees picked up her body like a piece of trash and threw it on the pile of burning bodies.

Amelia gasped. Celeste covered her mouth with her hands. Willow continued to watch, numb and disbelieving, unable to look away.

Celeste moaned. "Why did they do that?"

"They're clearing buildings," Willow said. "Disinfecting."

Amelia leaned back against the wall. She was breathing hard. "They didn't have to kill her."

She hated even thinking it, but it made a dark, twisted sort of sense. "In their minds, that woman could continue to spread the infection as long as she was alive. There was no hope for her anyway."

"Maybe—but the way they're doing it is...barbaric."

Her stomach churned. Acid burned the back of her throat and she gagged. The acrid stench of charred and burning flesh filled her nostrils. Human flesh. Human bodies. They were real people, with families and lives and dreams and...her brain stopped.

"Do you think those are the Pyros?" Amelia asked.

Willow backed slowly away from the window. Did those people have flaming skull tattoos on their necks, too? She hoped not. She prayed to every deity under Heaven that they never ran into those people. "Whoever they are, we should stay very far away from them."

8

MICAH

"We should sleep here." Micah gestured to the rows of designer sleep pods in the Dream Sleep store located on the second floor of the mall. "Too bad these things need electricity and a net connection to work."

"You ever slept in one?" Gabriel asked as he cleared the large store, checking around and beneath each pod, the dead holo display ports, and behind the counters. This store had no external windows, the shadows dark and deep.

"Nah, but I always wanted to try the floating-in-outer-space feature."

"Me too."

Micah's new boots squeaked on the tile floor. He opened the fanciest pod—a sleek, egg-shaped Dream 3000 model. "Never mind. They don't even have mattresses."

"It's all in the haptics, I suppose."

"I guess. But I'd still take a real mattress any day."

Gabriel grinned. "Me, too."

Micah had worried it would be awkward between them when

Gabriel suggested they pair up to clear the top floor of the mall. But they had slipped easily back into their old rapport. Micah still wasn't sure if that was a good thing or not.

He missed his brother like a hole inside his chest, like a phantom limb that still ached long after it had been severed. In times like this, when he suddenly felt close to the brother he hardly knew anymore, it made the ache pulse with fresh agony.

"Hey, look at this," Gabriel called from across the store. He stooped behind the counter and held out an oblong-shaped object in his gloved hands. Micah couldn't make it out in the dim light until he was closer.

He brightened, his face breaking into a smile. "No way. A violin."

Gabriel clutched it almost reverently. It was old; the wood was dull with scuffs and dings, but all the strings were there. Nothing looked broken. "I found it beneath this old blanket. There's a pillow, sleeping bag, and a few cans of beans."

"Maybe you shouldn't touch it. It could carry the virus."

Gabriel shook his head. "Whoever left this stuff hasn't been back in a couple of weeks. There's dust, see?" He wiped his finger over the neck of the violin and showed Micah the print he'd left behind. "The bow is here, too."

Micah thought of Amelia, the permanent indentations on her fingertips from her years of playing, how she still practiced when she thought no one was looking—her hands fingering imaginary strings, her chin cupping an invisible instrument. "Amelia will love it."

Gabriel hesitated, then thrust the instrument toward him. "You should give it to her."

"Why? You found it."

"She wouldn't want it from me."

Micah just stared at him.

A pained expression crossed Gabriel's face. "I don't want this tainted for her in any way, you know? It's the one thing she loves. It'll be better if you do it."

Micah took the violin, wrapped it in an extra sweater, and tucked it gently into his pack. "Thanks."

Before he zipped his pack, he took out his copy of Jack London's *The Call of the Wild*. He felt like the dog, Buck, thrust from the life he knew and hurled into a harsh, brutal world where danger lurked everywhere, every moment filled with peril. *They were savages, all of them, who knew no law but the law of club and fang.* Was that the world they lived in now, where morality was a handicap? Where the struggle to survive meant only the ruthless survived, the ones willing to kill before they were killed first?

"What's that for?" Gabriel asked.

Micah smoothed the pages and placed it on top of the sleeping bag. He didn't believe that. He wouldn't. They were humans, not animals. "We took something. In case anyone comes back, we should leave something in return. Otherwise, it feels like stealing."

"You and your books," Gabriel said, his voice suddenly gruff. He cleared his throat. "This store is cleared. Let's go check the next one."

They moved carefully, always alert, clearing each store, checking each new section of clothing racks, shoe, purse, SmartFlex displays, and jewelry counters. In one department store, dozens of mannequins had been knocked down, their molded heads bashed in.

When they were finished, Jericho gestured to them from the first-floor atrium. In the center of the mall was a tall open area featuring a zero-grav zone play area for kids. Three stories of balconies were connected by slim escalators crisscrossing each other.

"We're sleeping in the furniture store called Fieldwell's," he called up to them. "Enough sofas for everyone. I've already instructed everyone else, but if things go sideways, first rally point is Peachtree Suites, a smaller hotel located ten blocks behind the Westin Peachtree Plaza."

Micah nodded. He remembered passing the glittering, cylindrical skyscraper. Every time they bunked down for the night, Jericho always gave them an emergency rendezvous point, just in case.

By the time they reached the furniture store, the sky had darkened. The drizzling rain had turned into a downpour, battering the roof above them with a steady roar. Outside, the wind howled.

Celeste sauntered in at the same time, her face contorting in disgust as she took in their surroundings. She smoothed her hair as she jutted her lower lip. "We're staying here? The decor is so...common."

Silas shot her a withering stare. "I apologize if the accommodations aren't up to your standards. Would you rather have the presidential suite? How else may we serve you? Turn-down service? A chocolate on your pillow, m'lady?"

Celeste snorted. "Oh, go to hell."

"I think we're already there, princess," Silas drawled, smirking.

Celeste sighed extravagantly and flopped onto the closest leather sofa, her arm over her face. "I just want one night in a real sleep pod. Is that too much to ask?"

Micah ignored their squabbling and moved further into the room. Fieldwell's was an enormous, rectangular building with an airy, three-story ceiling. Clusters of fancy furniture formed sections with narrow marble pathways snaking between them. The entire back wall featured retrofit SmartHome features.

He picked up a digital brochure, somehow still working after all this time. It hadn't even been four months, he realized with a jolt.

He turned the brochure over in his hands. The words 'Imagine Yourself Home' glittered across the front flap. There was a scanner to scan customers' SmartFlexes so the giant holo ports on either side of the display table could project your own avatar—pulled from your own stored photos—maybe of you waking up and stretching to a refreshing sunrise over a glittering ocean, or of you lounging with smart, sophisticated friends, a cocktail in your hand, a beatific smile on your flawless face.

In newer buildings designed within the last few decades, every aspect—floors, walls, ceilings, appliances, entertainment systems— was carefully calibrated to the homeowner's preference. Visual, auditory, and sensory entertainment in every room of the house, at your fingertips or voice command. The shades raised automatically when the user sat up in bed, the coffee already percolating, the food printer hidden discreetly within the fridge busy scrambling recon- stituted eggs and spitting out perfectly browned toast.

The SmartHome ordered groceries before you needed it, auto- mated its own maintenance, self-cleaned, scheduled transports for morning and evening pick-up and drop-off, and coordinated your outfits with the SmartCloset add-on.

What the SmartHome couldn't do, the included service bot could, also customized to any preference—blonde or brunette, male or female, black or Asian or Latino. All of which so disturbed him, he threw the brochure on the floor like it were on fire.

Only the wealthy elites could afford any of this. The studio apartment Micah had shared with a friend before joining Gabriel on the *Grand Voyager* was dull and dingy, no matter how many times he'd scrubbed everything until his fingers were raw. The ceiling leaked. The power sputtered on and off, and in the summers the heat was overwhelming, the ancient, groaning air conditioner unable to keep up.

He wandered through the maze of furniture. The sofas boasted discreet fingerprint identifier pads, the posh cushions calibrated to individual comfort preferences—thick or thin, dense or feather-bed soft. He couldn't help thinking of Goldilocks.

But this world of glitz and glamour was over now. The Hydra virus didn't care how rich you were or who your parents were. It didn't care whether you were barely scraping by, half-starved, or the owner of three private jets. It destroyed everything and everyone in its path.

Well, not everyone. They were still here. He felt the weight of the violin in his pack and smiled to himself. Someway, somehow, they would create the world anew. They would start with people, not things. And they would do a better job this time.

Micah found Amelia heating pouches of pasta over a small gas stove they'd found in their scavenging a few days ago. She'd placed the stove on top of a cut-crystal coffee table worth more than a year's wages on the *Grand Voyager*. It seemed fitting, somehow.

She tucked a short, ragged tendril of hair behind her ear as she looked up at him. Shadows smudged the fragile skin beneath her eyes. "Hey."

"Are you feeling okay?"

She hesitated, as if debating whether to tell him the truth. She pressed her fingers over the bridge of her nose and winced. "Headache. I'm hoping it won't turn into a migraine. I'd be pretty useless for a while."

He swung the pack from his back and squatted next to her. He shoved his glasses up the bridge of his nose, clearing his throat nervously. "I can't make it go away, but I do have this."

She gasped when he pulled out the violin. She tugged her mask down and grinned at him in delight. "Where in the world did you get it?"

For half a second, he debated whether to tell her that he'd found it. The way she was looking at him, her tired eyes shining, her face lit up with pure, unadulterated joy—it did something to his insides.

His heart beat a little harder in his chest. He wanted her to keep looking at him. He could gaze at her forever.

But he couldn't lie. And she was stronger than Gabriel gave her credit for. She didn't need protecting, not like that. He bit the inside of his cheeks. "Gabriel found it and thought of you."

Her smile dimmed, but only slightly. "He asked you to give it to me instead."

He nodded.

She ran her hands along the delicate neck, the curved body, each individual string. She sighed and held it against her chest, her eyes closing in pleasure. "When I was sick, I thought I'd never get to play again. Thank you."

"Thank Gabriel."

She opened her eyes. "I will. But I can thank you if I want to."

He flushed, his cheeks warming. "Will you play for us?"

Around them, people were setting up their sleeping quarters, cleaning and checking weapons, and scrounging up cans, pouches, and tins for dinner.

"What about noise?"

Micah pointed up. The rain pounded the roof. The wind shrieked and moaned. "No one will be out in this. The rain will drown out the sound. You should play."

A slow, delighted grin spread across her face. "Okay, I will."

Amelia drew the bow across the strings. The first exquisite notes floated through the air, flowing over him, around him, through him. The song was sensuous, dark, and soulful. He recognized it but didn't know the composer—Dvorak or Tchaikovsky?

The tension in Amelia's jaw and around her eyes faded as she played. She closed her eyes, lost in the concentration of her art, her fingers moving with a beautiful fluidity and grace.

He couldn't take his gaze off her. His heart filled with a contentment like he hadn't felt since before the *Grand Voyager*. This was peace. This was everything right and beautiful and good.

The music swelled through the room, deep and sonorous and lilting. It was a song full of hope and dreams and love and every good thing that inspired people to feel, that made them human.

It was a song to break the world. It was a song to remake it again.

9

AMELIA

For the next two hours, Amelia played movements from Brahms' Sonata Number 3, Bartok's Concerto Number 2, and Shostakovich's Concerto No. 1 in A Minor. Her fingers trailed the violin's delicate stem, the chipped and battered wood.

The greatest violins were temperamental, moody and high strung as a human being. This one was old and cheap. It wasn't her 18th-century Guarneri, but she didn't care. She coaxed out the notes, the sound sliding from the strings bright and vibrant and full and more beautiful than she could stand.

The headache was building behind her eyes, but she refused to let it steal her pleasure. She refused to worry about migraines and seizures. For the first time in months, she was doing what she was meant to, what she was born for.

She switched to Bach's Chaconne from Partita No. 2 in D Minor, her favorite piece. She swept the bow across the strings and focused on the music until it flowed through every inch of her, filling her up, thrumming through her fingertips. Until there was nothing else. Her music filled the room, trembling in sweet and bitter tones.

It was too easy to forget that there was anything but chaos and violence and fear and death. They were all survivors, though they were dirty and exhausted and traumatized. But there was more, so much more. Life was more.

They could find it again. They would reach the Sanctuary. They would reach safety. They would find a place for music and beauty and love.

It existed. She knew it in her heart and soul.

Amelia opened her eyes as the last haunting note faded. It was completely dark except for the glow emanating from the Smart-Flex Micah had set up for her. The rest of the group had fallen into exhausted sleep as soon as their bodies hit the cushioned sofas.

Willow and Finn had pulled two sofas together, sharing the cushions with Benjie nestled between them. Celeste had a leather couch as far from Horne as she could get. Micah was still reading by flashlight.

Jericho took first watch at the main mall entrance. Silas took the west exit, which opened up to another shopping plaza, the one with the sporting goods store and the dead, burning bodies.

Gabriel guarded the south exit leading to a massive parking lot. To the left of the south exit were the bathrooms, a suite of administrative offices, and a steel door connecting the store to a large storage warehouse full of plastic-wrapped furniture waiting to be delivered.

Amelia tucked the violin inside a cashmere sweater she'd found in one of the designer boutiques. She should sleep. She was bone-weary, but her dreams were still capricious, treacherous things. There were nights that Kane still haunted her—his awful hands scrabbling over her skin, his beady eyes and bristling, leering grin.

She'd wake thrashing and moaning, horror-stricken, weak and terrified all over again.

It wasn't every night, or even every other night anymore. Slowly, inexorably, she was ridding herself of him. He held no power over her anymore, dead or alive. Soon, she wouldn't dream of him at all.

She sighed and made her way to the bathrooms in the darkness, using the blue glow from her SmartFlex for light. It had rained so much, Jericho's solar charger was nearly useless. Her SmartFlex battery would be drained by tomorrow.

She tried to tell herself she didn't care. But still, there was something comforting about the blue glow of the interface, the time and date features that still worked even though little else did. It was 10:15 p.m. on Wednesday, December 13th. As if that made a difference. But somehow, it still mattered.

"Watch your step." Gabriel's voice came out of the darkness, just as she narrowly avoided scraping her shin against an end table jutting awkwardly into the walkway between furniture groupings.

Gabriel flicked on his battery-operated flashlight and lit her way. She paused outside the bathroom doors. The storm had stopped, though only the faintest light filtered through the south exit's glass doors on her right.

Thick clouds covered the stars. The empty parking lot and a few barren trees glimmered wetly. "Do you think it will freeze tonight?"

"It will soon enough."

Pain pressed against the backs of her eyelids. She pressed her fingers against her forehead, willing it to go away. She hoped it wasn't a migraine, but at least they were in a safe place, for now. But a migraine wasn't the worst thing.

When would the next seizure come? Would she feel a warning, or would it bear down on her like a roaring train? How much damage would it do? What parts of herself would it steal? Her memories? Her ability to walk and run? Her music?

71

"Is something wrong?" The kindness in his voice brought another kind of pain, a sharp twist deep in her soul.

"I'm fine." She could barely see his face, only the outline of his features, his eyes a pale glisten in the dark. Her stomach tightened against her will. "Thank you for the violin," she said quietly.

Gabriel sighed. "My brother, the truth-teller. I should have known."

Amelia smiled tightly, though he couldn't see it. "He's consistent, you have to give him that."

"He's a good guy."

"Yeah, he is."

They fell into an uneasy silence. Could he hear the rapid, unsteady beat of her heart? This was the first time they'd really been alone since the *Grand Voyager*. A rush of memories flooded her. She nearly staggered beneath their weight.

A flicker of pain pulsed beneath her eyes. She sucked in her breath, her vision wavering. She swayed slightly.

"Hey. You okay?" He reached out and steadied her.

His hand brushed the bare skin of her wrist, sending a cascade of sparks through her. She sucked in her breath and pulled away.

"I'm sorry," he said quickly, taking a step back. He sounded earnest, his voice full of remorse. "I don't want to make you uncomfortable."

She rubbed her arm. "It's—it's okay."

"I'm sorry, you know," he said suddenly. His words came out in a rush. "I'm sorry for everything. I know you probably don't believe me. I wouldn't believe me. But every second of every day, I think about what I did to you. It must be hard for you to be near me, after what I did…"

She stiffened. She hadn't planned to have this conversation now. She wasn't prepared. She felt exposed, vulnerable. "What do you expect me to say?"

"You don't have to say anything. This isn't easy for me..." He cleared his throat. "I'm probably saying it all wrong."

A flare of anger flashed through her. It made no sense, but she couldn't help it. She hadn't wanted to speak to him, so why did she suddenly feel such ire that it had taken him so long to speak to her? "It's been months. You could've said something earlier."

She felt his shrug. "I was a prisoner in handcuffs. You were dying of the Hydra virus. It wasn't a good time."

She laughed. It was sharp-edged and painful, but it was still a laugh. The darkness surrounding them felt freeing somehow. Like they were in a world apart. Like she could say anything, finally speak the words she'd been thinking for months. "I forgave you for being a terrorist, you know. But once you knew the truth..."

"I know," he said, his voice thick.

"You betrayed me."

She waited for him to make an excuse, to claim brainwashing or that Simeon had forced him to give her up, to diminish what he'd done in some way. *It was Kane and Simeon who did the real damage, who were the real monsters...*but he'd said none of those things.

"You took a chance on me," he said instead. "You trusted me. We —we had a moment. More than that. What I felt for you, that was real. That's what I need you to know. I didn't fake it. Not—not any of it."

Emotions roiled inside her. Tears sparked the backs of her eyelids. It was a good thing, hearing him say it. He knew what he'd done. How much he'd hurt her. Her heart still felt like a ball of fire inside her chest. "Okay," she managed.

Her eye adjusted to the darkness. She could make out his arms flexing as he curled his hands into fists at his sides. "It's not okay. It wasn't then and it never will be. I took your trust and shattered it into a thousand pieces."

"You did." She lifted her chin. She held the words on her tongue

73

carefully, like they might break in her mouth. "You broke my trust, but you didn't break me."

He was so close she could hear his breathing, the hitch in his chest. Heat radiated from his skin. Her heart beat faster.

"You're stronger than I was," he said softly, "than I am."

She rubbed her charm bracelet beneath her sweater. Pain pulsed behind her eyes, but she ignored it. "You could have told everyone what my father did, that he was the one who engineered the Hydra virus. You could have claimed your innocence. But you didn't. Why?"

Gabriel shifted, leaned against the wall. The outline of his profile was sharp in the dim shadows. He was still as handsome as ever, strong and fierce as a hawk. "They would have suspected you and your family by association. They would've interrogated you, imprisoned you, or worse."

"You let your brother believe you were a monster rather than rat me out."

"I was already a monster," he said heavily.

For a long time, neither of them spoke. She didn't know what she was supposed to think or how she was supposed to feel. He had committed truly awful acts. He'd acted monstrously. Did that still make *him* a monster? "Micah says there's hope for everyone."

He shifted in the dark. "So did Nadira."

Her heart twinged at the thought of Nadira. She had been genuinely kind and tenderhearted. The world was a bleaker place without her. Nadira had believed there was still good in Gabriel, that even a terrorist could be redeemed. Was it possible? Did she want it to be true?

He peered at her intently. "You told Micah the truth yourself."

She didn't tell him how trust was a brittle but precious thing. When it shattered, it shattered her heart, too.

But she couldn't stay broken. She refused to stay broken. She wouldn't let Kane or Simeon or her father win. She needed to trust someone. It was part of rebuilding herself, one shard at a time.

But he didn't need to know that. "It was the right thing to do." They stared at each other for a long moment.

She held his gaze a beat too long before dropping her eyes. "Well, I'm thankful."

His lip curled, revealing a flash of white teeth. "See, we can be civilized."

She couldn't see the dimple in his left cheek, but she knew it was there. She swallowed, her mouth suddenly dry. She needed to get out of there.

A wave of dizziness rushed through her, not just from Gabriel's presence. Her headache still throbbed against her skull. She needed to lie down, and soon. She moved toward the bathroom. "I need to go."

He moved out of her way. "Of course."

She opened the door into complete blackness. She held out her SmartFlex, the blue glow illuminating a circle of the cement floor. Before her mind could register that cement was an odd choice for an upscale department store bathroom, something erupted out of the darkness.

She glimpsed a snout and teeth and tiny black eyes. A small, furred creature lunged at her. She gasped and stepped back, leaving the door wide open.

A brown rat skittered out of the doorway. It rose on its haunches less than a yard from her feet, squeaking angrily.

Amelia kicked at it. It turned and fled back into the darkness.

"What the hell was that?" Gabriel asked.

"A rat. It came from in there." She pointed at the door to the storage warehouse. Warily, Gabriel stepped into the doorway and flicked his flashlight inside, illuminating the shadows.

Amelia froze. Dread coiled in her stomach as the shadows separated into distinct shapes. Wriggling bodies. Shiny black eyes. Flat, wide teeth. Sharp little claws.

A dozen. Then several dozens. A hundred. More than she could count.

They gathered along the armrests of plastic-wrapped lounge chairs, perched on table tops, skittered from sofa cushion to sofa cushion. They amassed atop coffee tables and end tables. They crouched a hundred deep within every corner like thick, bristling shadows.

These were not the cute pets used to sawdust and cages. Their eyes glittered with malice. Their tiny, bone-sharp teeth gnashed, the fur around their jaws damp with a yellowish, foaming saliva tinged red.

They were infected. The virus raged through them, twisting their brains with blood-lust until they were savage little monsters, only longing to spread the virus through bites to as many victims as possible.

A huge black rat emerged from the shadows a dozen feet from the door. It crept stealthily toward her. Gabriel swung the beam of the flashlight, the light reflecting in its tiny eyes. It sat back on its fat haunches and chittered angrily, whiskers twitching.

One by one, and then in clumps, the rats behind it slipped from chairs and sofas and tables and dropped to the cement floor.

"Gabriel..."

"I see them. Don't move. Don't startle them." Gabriel edged closer, moving in front of her protectively as he stretched for the door handle.

The fat rat charged. Instantly, the rest followed. A living tide of brown, writhing bodies rushed toward them.

"Shut the door!" Amelia screamed.

"What's going on?" a groggy voice blurted from the darkness. But there was no time to answer or call for help.

The rats scurried across the floor, hundreds of bristling, hunched backs and slithering pink tails, a thousand claws scrabbling against cement.

Gabriel dove for the handle and slammed the door shut. Two rats squeezed through. They lunged at Amelia's feet, both of them clawing up her leg. One bit down hard over her shin, its teeth catching in the thick leather of the boots she still wore. Thank goodness for small mercies.

"Don't move!" Gabriel swung his rifle like a bat, connecting with the biting rat and sending it flying. It landed a few feet away, deep in shadow, but Gabriel pummeled it with the barrel of the gun.

The second rat scampered up her thigh, its scrabbling claws finding purchase on her pants. She shrieked, frantically batting at it.

She was immune from the virus passed by human transmission, but she didn't know about animals. The virus could be a mutation. She had to assume this rat was as deadly a threat to her as it was to everyone else.

She wasn't wearing gloves. If she tried to grab it and it bit her hand...but she had no choice. The thing would gnaw through her pant leg and bite her thigh in half a second if she didn't do something.

She could barely see. Gabriel's flashlight swung wildly, the beam of light skittering in all directions. The shadows shifted like liquid oil, tricking her eyes.

She could feel the thing like a weight hanging from her leg. If she missed, if her aim was off by even a fraction...

She caught a flash of tiny shining eyes and a black bulge on her thigh.

Amelia seized the rat around its middle. It felt like a thick, terrycloth towel. A towel that was dense and coarse and bulged grotesquely beneath her fingers.

She screamed and flung the creature as hard as she could against the wall. It struck with a wet thump and slid to the floor. It writhed, twitched, and fell still.

Gabriel leaned against the door, his chest heaving. She sagged next to him, her shoulder only inches from his. They stared at each other in shocked horror.

"Are you okay?" Gabriel asked. "Were you bitten anywhere?"

"No," she gasped. "You?"

He shook his head.

Micah and Finn stumbled toward them, wiping sleep from their eyes. "What just happened?"

There was a scratching sound against the door. Like an old-fashioned key scraping against metal. Like tiny scrabbling nails.

The rats were trying to get out.

The blood drained from Amelia's face. "Whatever you do," she said, "don't open that door."

10

MICAH

Micah awoke to the sound of shattering glass. The stench of smoke filled his nostrils. Not the distant smoke that swirled constantly in the air, but the intense, fetid smoke from a nearby fire.

A fire so close, he could feel the heat of it on his skin.

He opened his eyes, expecting complete darkness. Instead, everything was orange, flickering shadows.

"Fire!" someone cried.

Micah staggered to his feet, blinking sleep from his eyes. He shoved his glasses on, jerked on his pack, and grabbed the rifle resting on the cushion beside him. He seized the flashlight from his pocket and flicked it on.

The glass doors of the west entrance were shattered. Little fires surged from a half-dozen places. A brocaded sofa whooshed into flames. A coffee table blazed.

Another line of fire trailed from a broken bottle. Several bottles were scattered near the west entrance, flaming rags stuffed inside. Molotov cocktails.

They were under attack.

"Everyone out!" Micah shouted.

"Get up!" Silas cried, charging between the sofas. He gripped Willow by the shoulders, yanking her from her cushions and blankets and weary dreams. "Wake up!"

Celeste and Horne rose, coughing and pulling on their masks. Jericho stumbled toward them from the west entrance, smacking at his sparking, smoking pants with a sofa pillow.

Finn grabbed Benjie with one arm and hauled the boy over his shoulder. Willow grabbed Finn's hand and dragged them toward the double doors of the south exit, the closest escape.

Ribbons of smoke writhed through the thickening air high over his head. Thank goodness the ceiling was three stories high. It would give them the few precious moments they needed to breathe —though he could already feel a tightness in the back of his throat.

Micah brought his shirt up and covered his mouth, though he already wore a mask. He swung his flashlight, searching frantically for Amelia and Gabriel.

She was slumped against a sofa armrest twenty feet from the bathrooms and office suite. Gabriel leaned over her, his hand on her shoulder. She bent her head, her hands pressed over her ears, her chest heaving.

Something was wrong with her. A migraine or ...worse. He staggered toward them. His shin struck the corner of a coffee table, sending pain jolting up his leg. "Amelia! Go, go!"

Then he heard it. A melodious, sing-song voice cut through the coughing and shouting. "Come out, come out, wherever you are!"

Micah stiffened. Dread solidified in his gut like a block of ice. He exchanged a horrified look with Gabriel.

The Pyros had found them.

"We know you're in there!" the voice came again.

Micah whirled, raising the muzzle of his rifle. The bulky forms of sofas, chairs, tables, and buffets could hide anything. To his left, the flames danced higher, licking the walls, leaping from object to object, feeding on wood, carpet, stuffing, and fabric, bathing everything in a wicked orange light.

Four shapes materialized out of the smoky shadows, striding into Fieldwell's from the main mall entrance. They wore fitted respirator masks over their mouths and noses, thin tubes trailing from their masks to cylindrical oxygen tanks hooked to their backs.

The first man stepped onto an ornately carved coffee table. A billowing black trench coat swept to his knees. He wore thigh and hip holsters and gripped a pulse gun in each hand. When he spoke, his voice was lilting and musical, only slightly distorted by the mask. "Little piggies, little piggies, let us in."

Celeste screamed.

"How'd they get past our watch?" Micah gasped, stunned. It still felt like some horrible dream he could wake up from.

The air to his left shimmered with heat, everything distorted like a desert mirage. Only the leaping flames were no mirage. And this was no dream.

Silas came up beside him, swearing profusely. "I was guarding that entrance, but when I smelled smoke, I ran to warn the others. The bastards were waiting. They snuck in behind me."

Micah coughed into his arm. "They're trapping us."

"What do you want?" Horne yelled. He cowered behind a purple loveseat. "I'm certain we can work something out to our mutual benefit."

Horne believed he could smooth-talk their way out of everything. But this plan was too well orchestrated. These people wanted something, and they expected to get it. The sickening feeling in Micah's gut told him he already knew what it was.

The trench-coated man's face was leathery and well-lined, like the spidery cracks in a window. The part of his nose not hidden by the mask was misshapen from being broken too many times. His eyes were quick and pale, a deadly coldness to them. "You killed the wrong kid, my friends."

Beside Micah, Silas stiffened.

Micah's mouth went dry. "That was an accident." He'd feared consequences for Silas's rash actions. Violence never occurred in a vacuum. There were always repercussions, like waves rippling out from a rock hurled into a placid river. There was a cost for everything.

The man only laughed. As if he could read Micah's thoughts, he said, "There's a pretty price on your heads. And we're here to collect."

The second man, a short, heavy Latino wearing a cowboy hat, a gold chain around his neck and fat gold rings adorning his gloveless fingers, gestured at them with his semi-automatic. "Put your weapons down. Make your way in a line toward those doors behind you, nice and easy now."

"I wouldn't take too long," the third one said. She was a muscular black woman with the sides of her head shaved, her mohawk dyed blood-red. "This whole damn place is going up in flames."

"There's no need to hurt anyone," Finn said. "We can explain what happened—"

Mohawk aimed her rifle at his feet and let off a volley of bullets. A glass coffee table shattered. Benjie cried out. Finn leapt back, pressing Benjie to his chest.

Willow's face contorted in fury. "You could've killed my brother! He's just a kid!"

"A kid's life for a kid's life, eh, Sykes?" Cowboy said to the man with the black trench coat.

"Seems fair to me," said the man called Sykes.

"Moruga gets to decide that, Alvarado," the fourth attacker said to Cowboy. He was shorter and slender, maybe nineteen, with blonde hair shorn close to his skull, an eyebrow ring, and tattooed stars below each eye. A second tattoo peeked over the collar of his jacket—a flaming skull.

"You're Pyros," Micah croaked. He blinked and coughed, the first tendrils of smoke worming into his throat.

Tattoo Boy sneered. "Excellent deduction. What was your first clue?"

Sykes gestured at the boy. "You can handle this, Nicolas."

Nicolas aimed his gun at Micah's face. "Now put the guns down or I shoot you first."

Reluctantly, Micah lowered his rifle. His jacket covered his side holster. He risked keeping it. Slowly, the others did the same. Silas threw his weapon to the floor with a growl.

The fire hissed and sparked. The flames grew larger, more ferocious, smaller fires joining to form a blazing wall. It chewed through furniture like toothpicks. Smoke billowed over their heads, still near the top of the high ceiling, but slowly descending like a black shroud of death.

Heat singed Micah's skin through his clothes, seared his throat. He prayed silently, his lips moving in a desperate plea.

They were trapped between ruthless killers and a wall of fire. There was no way out. No escape. Only a miracle could save them now.

11

AMELIA

"Hands up!" shouted Nicolas, the boy with the tattoos.

Amelia raised her hands. She blinked stinging tears out of her eyes. Pain sank vicious claws into her brain. Her vision blurred, the flames sparking and shimmering like holos.

She took a step and faltered, dizziness spiking through her. Micah grabbed her arm and steadied her. "Cover your mouth with your shirt. Breathe through your nose!"

Amelia obeyed, lifting her thick knit sweater and pressing it to her mouth and nose. She inhaled several frantic, panic-stricken breaths. The smoke intensified her headache until it was a crescendo of agony pulsing against her skull.

She prayed it was only a migraine, that the smoke wouldn't trigger something worse. A seizure now would be a death sentence.

"I said get in line!" Alvarado shouted as he adjusted his cowboy hat, the semi-automatic still aimed at Amelia. The Pyros jostled them toward the south exit and the parking lot. A black van waited for them in the rain, the rear doors open. Who knew what lay in store for them after that?

These people were going to kill them slowly. She could see it in the vicious set of their faces, the coldness in their eyes. They wanted revenge. Torture. Suffering. Death. And they were going to enjoy it.

Amelia had to find a way out. They had to escape.

She stumbled past the office doors, the bathrooms. The storage warehouse.

She had only seconds to decide. The fire raged to their left, popping and spitting and roaring like a ravenous dragon. The Pyros were well armed, but if they were distracted, Amelia's group might have a chance. They could escape the fire and run out the exit, or back into the mall, where a thousand nooks and crannies offered hiding spots, shelter from bullets, and improvised weapons they could use to fight back.

Even if it was only a slim chance, it was better than none. Her vision blurred, shimmering with bright, scintillating colors, then darkened. Pain struck her skull, splitting it open like an axe. She had to act while she still could. She had to move now.

She lunged for the warehouse door and wrenched it open.

A black mass poured from the doorway, a swarming, seething carpet of bristling bodies and slithering pink tails. A thousand tiny nails scrabbled over concrete, the awful sound raising the hairs on her arms.

"Rats!" she shouted in warning.

Chaos erupted. Celeste screamed in horror. The Pyros yelled curses. A gun went off.

Gabriel sprang at the nearest attacker, Nicolas, who stood frozen in shock. Jericho sprinted past her, kicking at the small squirming bodies as he lunged for the armed woman with the mohawk.

A rat skittered up Micah's ankle.

"Watch out!" Amelia cried.

He slammed his foot against the wall, knocking it off.

Amelia staggered, nearly falling. Micah grabbed her upper arm. "Run!"

The swarming rats blocked the exit. The only way was back through the furniture store, bypassing the fire to reach the mall. She turned and fled, pain exploding inside her skull, her lungs burning.

She faltered, stumbled again. Micah dragged her to her feet.

Silas, Willow, and Finn sprinted beside her, Benjie still in Finn's arms, Finn holding his shirt over Benjie's nose. They wove between armchairs and coffee tables. The fire blazed on their left, blasting heat solid as a wall, threatening to cut off their path to the mall entrance.

The boiling cloud of smoke descended over their heads. Amelia struggled to breathe, her throat seared. Stars exploded across her vision.

They should be crawling on their hands and knees, dropping low to escape the smoke, but they couldn't. If they slowed down even a fraction, death would get them anyway.

Behind them, the rats squealed as the heat blasted their tiny bodies. They shifted like a wave, fleeing the fire and instinctively heading in the same direction as the escaping humans. The rats spread like an oil slick, a writhing mound of bristling fur and lashing claws, gouging jaws and snapping, razor teeth.

Beside her, Silas skidded to a halt. He bent to pick up his discarded rifle. He spun and took aim at the rabid vermin.

"Silas!" Amelia cried. "Come on!"

"Just go!" Silas shouted.

Micah jerked her arm. She had no choice. They raced through the mall entrance into an enormous three-story atrium. She doubled over, coughing and choking, desperate to inhale mouthfuls of precious oxygen.

Her skull felt like it was fracturing, tectonic plates crashing into each other. The pain almost knocked her off her feet. *Not now, please not now.*

She struggled to stand, wiping her eyes, searching frantically for an escape. The escalators leading to the second and third floors were directly ahead of them. To the right, a bath store and a gift shop. To the left, a corridor lined with designer boutiques.

"Come on!" Micah rasped, pulling her again.

Amelia risked a glance behind them. Her heart seized in her chest.

Silas sprinted toward her, gesturing furiously as hundreds of rats flooded out of Fieldwell's. The rodents squealed in terror, scrabbling to escape the roaring fire licking at their tails.

"The escalators!" Finn shouted. "Go up!"

Silas sprinted by her. He and Finn raced up the escalator three steps at a time, Benjie still clutched in Finn's arms. "Come on! Hurry!"

Light blinded her, an aura shimmering before her eyes. A tingling sensation spread from her belly and flooded her body with weakness. Her muscles trembling, turning to water. She slumped to her hands and knees.

Not a migraine. Worse.

No! Not now! But she couldn't stop what was coming. She was utterly helpless. She didn't have her auto-injector. She didn't have her meds. She couldn't stop this defective, monstrous thing inside her from destroying her body from the inside out.

"Amelia!" Micah paused at her side. He tried to lift her, but she was dead weight. Her limbs wouldn't move, wouldn't obey her commands.

It was too late. The river of rats reached them. Amelia cringed, bracing herself for the pain and horror.

But the rats ignored her. They flowed around Amelia and Micah like a current and swept up the escalator stairs. They dodged

Willow, who stiffened a few steps from the bottom, her face a rictus of terror.

The rats feared the fire. Their survival instincts were still stronger than the virus's compelling urge to spread itself. But it wouldn't last long. They might only have seconds before the rodents remembered their ravenous, unnatural hunger.

She vomited once, then again. The pain flared, peaking in a shattering explosion of pain. She collapsed. Her brain was melting, her bones breaking, her skin shattering.

Finn and Silas stared down from the second-floor landing. "Help Amelia!" Finn shouted at Willow. "I've got Benjie. We'll find you!"

Willow waved them on, her body racked in a coughing fit. They ran.

"Wait!" Willow cried suddenly. She thrust her hand into her pocket, her expression stricken. "I have Benjie's inhaler! He needs it. The smoke will—"

"He'll be fine," Micah croaked. "We need your help."

Willow hesitated, torn.

She wouldn't blame her for leaving, Amelia thought distantly. Willow owed her nothing. She should save herself and her brother. Micah should save himself. She would only slow them down. She forced the words out. "Leave...me..."

"Willow!" Micah cried desperately.

Willow swore. She leapt the last several steps, kicking two rats out of the way as the rodents slithered up the escalator, their tiny claws clicking.

She bent over Amelia. Her shadow sparkled with brilliant colors. "Get up!"

Amelia heard them speaking, but they were very far away. She was underwater, and they were calling to her from a great distance. She worked her mouth, but no sound came out. She couldn't speak.

Her vision swam with light and dark spots. Her muscles were stiffening, seizing, her jaw rigid, her tongue thick and useless.

Her body was no longer hers. Her mind was no longer hers. It belonged to something else now.

"Seizure," Micah said from the other side of the world, the other side of the universe.

"Oh, hell," Willow said.

And then it came: the shaking, trembling, roaring darkness.

12

GABRIEL

Gabriel coughed violently, his lungs burning in the smoke-clotted air. He struggled to breathe through his mask. Heat shimmered all around him, oppressive as an oven.

Out of the corner of his eye, he glimpsed Amelia and Micah fleeing through the store, heading for the mall entrance. On his right, Celeste and Horne raced past him toward the parking lot exit.

He had to give them time to escape.

Nicolas, the young tattooed Pyro, was a statue, staring in horror at the writhing horde of rats pouring from the warehouse doorway. Past the rats, the main section of the furniture store erupted into flames. The fire was a crackling, popping cacophony, a pulsing roar in his ears. There was only one way out now.

He took a ragged breath and lunged at Nicolas.

He seized the gleaming pulse gun in the boy's hands with his right hand. With his left, he ripped off the boy's respiratory mask. If Gabriel was choking to death on smoke, this kid could experience the same pleasure.

Nicolas blinked to life with a growl and jerked back. He coughed, sputtering and hacking, but refused to release his grip. They wrestled for the gun.

"Give it up and I'll let you go," Gabriel grunted. The Pyro was just a boy, too young for this. He didn't want to kill him. "I won't hurt you."

Nicolas spat in his face.

Up close, the boy's skin was mottled with acne, his upper lip filmed with fine blonde hairs. But he had the cold, blank eyes of a killer. There would be no appealing to his better nature.

"Have it your way." Gabriel headbutted him.

Nicolas stumbled, mouth agape, but he didn't let go. He managed to regain his feet and tried to force the barrel of the pulse gun into Gabriel's chest. A single electrified blast from the weapon would melt his heart inside his body.

A squealing rat scurried onto his foot. Another leapt onto his calf, its claws digging into his boot. He kicked them off, almost losing his grip on the gun.

The fire raged behind him, roaring ever closer. He heaved, coughing violently, eyes bleeding tears. He was running out of time.

But he needed the gun. Jericho had gone after Mohawk with nothing but his pulse rod. Celeste and Horne were unarmed. If Gabriel didn't get this weapon and fast, they were all dead.

He changed tactics. Instead of yanking back as the Pyro expected, Gabriel shoved, hurling his weight into the boy's chest. Already pulling back and taken by surprise, Nicolas lost his balance and staggered.

The boy released the weapon. His arms windmilled wildly as he fell, toppling backward onto the wriggling carpet of rats.

The rats swarmed the boy. They scuttled along his arms and legs. Teeth jagged as shards of bone sank into his hands and the exposed skin of his face and neck. He flailed at them, rolling and kicking, knocking a handful off him but two dozen more instantly took their place.

He shrieked in agony.

Horror clawed Gabriel's throat. But he couldn't help him even if he wanted to. To wade into that writhing mass of infected teeth and claws was a death wish.

Four fat black rats raised themselves on their haunches, snouts twitching. As one, their heads swiveled toward him.

Gabriel fled for the exit, the boy's anguished wails echoing in his ears.

He took cover behind the wall to the right of the glass doors, the pulse gun clutched close to his chest. On the other side of the doors, Celeste and Horne cowered behind a potted plant.

"Why are you still here?" Gabriel hissed. The air was blurry, his eyes stinging so badly he could hardly see. He rubbed his face with the back of his arm. "Get the hell out of here!"

Celeste silently pointed outside, her pallor ashen.

He peered around the corner, sweeping the parking lot. It was difficult to make out anything through the sheets of freezing rain. The sky was black, the moon and stars hidden behind thick clouds. There were no other ambient lights, the city dark but for a few sputtering fires in the distance.

He took in the scene in an instant: a black van in the parking lot a few dozen yards away, three hostiles, their respiratory masks removed. Two stood apart; the third was engaged in combat with Jericho.

Alvarado, the Latino with the cowboy hat and the gold rings, was closest to Gabriel's position. His back turned to the mall, his pulse gun aimed at the grappling bodies, but he wasn't shooting. He was watching the fight. The female Pyro with the red mohawk stood ten feet past Alvarado on his right. She simply watched, her semi-automatic aimed at the pavement.

Jericho tangled with Sykes in close, hand-to-hand combat. Jericho had managed to saw the Pyro's automatic rifle in two pieces with his pulse rod—which now lay a dozen feet from him, the length of it crackling and spitting with bluish lightning.

Gabriel could shoot through the glass and take out Alvarado, but that would release the rats. He and Jericho wouldn't survive another battle fighting two enemies at once. And Celeste and Horne needed a clear path of escape. The rats had to stay inside.

He'd have to gamble that he could slip through the door and disarm the first Pyro undetected, that the hard rain pounding the pavement and the howling wind would hide his movements. Then Celeste and Horne could make a run for it.

He smashed one last scrambling, squealing rat with the butt of his rifle. He risked a glance back at the boy. He was no longer moving.

Micah and Amelia should have already made it out. He would hunt down every damned Pyro in this entire ruined city if something happened to them. But he couldn't think about that yet. These two were his responsibility now. "I'll take care of them out there. But you can't lose it. You've got to be ready to run."

Horne was a trembling, sniveling mess. Celeste stared at him, her cheeks streaked with soot and tears, but her eyes were clear. "I'm ready."

The furniture store was engulfed in flames, everything blazing, burning, sparks flying, the smoke a dark, writhing cloud. A terrible roar filled his ears, the sounds of wood popping, things splintering, the building heaving, caving in on itself.

His lungs burned. He coughed, choking, his lungs seeking oxygen that suddenly wouldn't come. But the fire wasn't the greatest threat.

Dread filling him, Gabriel lowered his gaze to the sea of bristling fur, tails, and teeth flowing down the hall toward him.

Time was up.

13

WILLOW

"Pick her up!" Willow cried. "Hurry!"

"We can't!" Micah knelt over Amelia in the center of the mall's atrium. "We have to wait for the seizure to pass."

"Oh, hell!" She whirled and took in the blazing inferno that was now Fieldwell's furniture store. Sparks flew from the flames licking the wide archway. Thick coils of smoke billowed into the atrium.

The atrium boasted dozens of potted plants, tufted benches, and lush carpet. The fire was big enough, hot enough, that practically anything would burn. The fire would chew its way toward them in only a matter of minutes.

If the fire didn't get them, the smoke would. Willow's lungs burned. Her breath rasped in her aching throat. Her head hurt and her limbs felt sluggish and slow.

And then there were the rats. A few dozen of them scurried in crazed, haphazard circles, squealing in terror.

Willow paced, as panicked as the rats. At least Finn had Benjie. He would keep her brother safe. But what if he had an asthma attack? She fingered the inhaler in her pocket, cursing herself. She should have thrown it to Finn, should have done something else, something better.

But there was nothing to do about it now. She had to worry about her own survival. It wasn't looking good. She didn't even have a gun, only her hunting knife. She pulled it out of its sheath at her side. "How long?"

"I don't know!" Micah gently turned Amelia on her side. Her whole body had gone taut. She shook uncontrollably, her eyes rolling in their sockets.

Willow rubbed her stinging, leaking eyes. She crouched low to the ground, forcing herself to breathe the hot air. She'd never seen a seizure before. "Is she—is she okay?"

"I don't know." Micah's expression was tense, filled with barely repressed panic.

Amelia was unnaturally stiff, her face blue-tinged, rigid and mask-like. Her tongue lolled out of her mouth.

Willow's heart constricted. The girl looked like she was dying.

Micah gripped Amelia's hand and bent over her, his mouth moving in a silent prayer. He squeezed her fingers and spoke so softly it was hard to make out. "I'm right here," he whispered over and over. "You're not alone."

Willow looked away. Even surrounded by fire and killer rats and chaos, it was an intimate moment, one she wasn't a part of.

A rat scurried at her. She kicked it away. Another one crept stealthily from behind a potted plant, whiskers twitching, beady eyes gleaming. Three more scrabbled down the escalator.

She coughed loudly and cleared her throat. "Uh, Micah? It's time to go."

"I think it's over," he rasped. He gathered Amelia's unconscious body in his arms and cradled her like a baby. "My gun is in my side holster, beneath my jacket."

"Oh, hallelujah." She grabbed it and unlatched the safety. "Let's go!"

Two more rats slithered closer, sniffing only a few yards from her feet. There were several dozen on the escalator now. They were still skittish of the fire, but seemed to think they were safe for the moment. If she had more bullets in her gun, she would blast them into oblivion.

Instead she went left, crouching, her body bent almost double to escape the smoke, following the main corridor. They ran past a bath shop, a makeup counter, a personalized home robot store, a Smart-Flex repair place. They needed a store large enough to have its own separate exit; otherwise, they risked hemming themselves in. The store entrances were all too wide, with only the metal grate doors as a barricade, which the rats would easily squeeze through.

The more distance they placed between themselves and the raging fire, the easier it was to breathe. Willow heaved great gasps of sweet, sweet oxygen.

Unfortunately, the stupid rats could breathe, too. One of them nipped at her heels. She kicked it, but there were a half-dozen more right behind it. For such small, ugly creatures, they were incredibly fast. "We need a freakin' door!"

"There!" Micah pointed three shops ahead and to the left—a narrow hallway with an 'emergency exit' sign above it.

She ran for the exit, making sure to stay just behind Micah. He wasn't as fast with Amelia in his arms. She had the weapons. It was her job to keep them all safe.

They careened into the hallway. Heavy with shadows, it was hard to see, but she could just make out a metal door with a narrow, rectangular window at the far end.

Micah stumbled but righted himself, his glasses half-sliding off his face.

"I'll cover you!" She whirled and shot, taking out a massive rat about to leap at Amelia's dangling feet. She took out two more skittering for Micah's legs.

Another huge, hunched rodent climbed on a bench, ran along it, and sprang at Willow. She hissed as sharp claws dug into her right thigh. She slammed the butt of the gun against the creature's bulging back.

The rat fell off. She sprinted the last dozen yards to the door, which Micah held open. "Go, go, go!"

She hurled herself through the door, spun, and slammed it shut —right on a squealing rat's head. She shuddered at the sickening crunch of its tiny, splintering skull.

For a minute, the only sounds were her ragged panting and the roar of her heartbeat in her ears. Slowly, other sounds came to her. The wind, still shrieking around the corners of the buildings. The freezing rain, hard little pellets splatting her face and pounding the sidewalk. Micah, whispering a prayer of gratitude.

Her throat felt scorched. Her eyes and chest burned. Her legs were weak and trembling. Her stomach wrenched with anxiety for Benjie and Finn. But she stood there, her eyes closed, in the frigid cold, and simply took it all in.

They were beautifully, gloriously alive.

"You did good," Micah croaked. His glasses were a fogged, dripping mess.

She grinned at him. "Can you even see me right now?"

He shrugged. "It would be worse if I took them off. I'd walk into closed doors."

"I'd like to see that sometime. Not today, though. I guess I'll lead then."

"Great. It'll be like the blind leading the blind."

"Hardy har har. Keep working on your poetry skills, 'cause your comedy isn't exactly cutting it."

He glanced down at Amelia, his face growing serious, concern etching the skin around his eyes. "She's still out."

She watched him for a moment, the way he cradled Amelia so carefully, like she was something fragile and precious. She hadn't missed the way he'd looked at her during the seizure either, like he felt every excruciating second of her suffering, as if he were dying right along with her.

Micah was falling in love with Amelia. She was too numb to feel envious or irritated or even pleased. She'd figure out what it all meant later. "She's been through too much to quit now," she said simply. "We all have."

They left the parking lot and made their way down a street lined with naked oak and maple trees, their branches white and bare, gleaming like bones. Shadows thickened all around them as they maneuvered between the hulking shapes of cars, vans, and transports looming out of the darkness.

As they walked, the freezing rain turned to snow.

14

GABRIEL

The rats poured down the hallway toward Gabriel. Adrenaline shot through him. "Follow me out!"

He spun, pried open the doors, and shoved his way through. Celeste and Horne were right behind him, trembling and terrified but moving fast. He slammed the doors closed. Several dozen bristling, hunch-backed rodents smashed against the glass.

He sucked a single cold, oxygen-infused breath into his starving lungs and launched himself at Alvarado. There was no cover in the wide-open parking lot. The nearest vehicle was the van twenty yards away. The only cover he was going to get was human.

The man started to turn, sensing movement, but Gabriel reached him first. He slammed the butt of the gun against the man's skull, hard enough to stun him, not hard enough to knock him out. With one hand, he jammed his knife against the man's throat, with his other, he pointed his gun at Mohawk.

"Drop your gun and kick it away," Gabriel croaked. His throat was seared. He needed air. He couldn't gulp in enough oxygen.

Alvarado obeyed. His voice was laced with hatred. "You're dead, you hear me? You just don't know it yet."

"Not today." Gabriel had to bend his knees and partially squat to keep his head from becoming a target, keeping as much of Alvarado's short, meaty body between himself and the female Pyro's bullets as he could.

The woman with the mohawk swore. She dropped into a crouch and aimed her rifle at him.

"Run!" Gabriel shouted hoarsely. Horne and Celeste edged out from the mall's entrance into the freezing rain. Mohawk's gun swiveled toward them.

"I'm the one who's going to shoot you!" Gabriel unloaded a blast at Mohawk's feet. Chunks of asphalt sprayed her legs. She leapt back, her weapon swinging back to him.

"Come on!" Celeste yelled. Horne froze like a deer in the headlights. She shoved Horne, almost knocking him over, but it got him moving. Celeste and Horne sprinted into the darkness. Safe, at least for the moment.

Gabriel turned his attention to the task at hand. He clenched his jaw. He should kill Mohawk. She had no cover, nowhere to hide.

An image flashed through his mind, sudden and uninvited. Simeon instructing him in an old, graffiti-scarred gym, teaching him how to kill ruthlessly and efficiently. Training him to become a mindless, unthinking soldier, able to kill enemy combatants and innocent collateral alike.

This woman wasn't innocent. She was the enemy. She'd nearly burned them alive. Still, he hesitated.

He thought of Micah. He thought of Nadira. He remembered the square of blue cloth in his pocket, remembered the dirt beneath his nails from burying the girl who'd given her life for his. He'd sworn to seek redemption, to earn her sacrifice.

Was more blood on his hands the way to do it?

"Drop the weapon!" he shouted. He offered her the same deal he'd given to the boy. "Leave now and we'll let you go, unharmed."

"Do what he says, damn it!" Alvarado gasped.

The Pyro shifted, and Gabriel dug the knife deeper into his throat, drawing blood. The blade was slick in his hands. He adjusted his grip, blinking water out of his eyes. "Put the gun down, and we can all walk away."

"Don't!" Alvarado cried.

Gabriel caught the shift in her eyes, the twitch of her finger. She fired a short, controlled burst. The bullets ripped into Alvarado's thick body, tearing through flesh, muscles, organs, shattering bones. Gabriel felt the juddering vibration in his own body.

Alvarado began to slump, his arms and legs useless.

Time seemed to slow. Gabriel felt the throbbing of his own heart. The icy numbness of the rain and the cold. The searing burn in his lungs and throat. The roar of his blood in his ears.

Kill or be killed. Sometimes it was that simple. He pulled the trigger.

A streak of red, crackling energy struck the woman in the chest. Bulletproof vests did nothing to stop the firepower of a plasma pulse.

Her eyes widened in shock. Her rifle clattered to the wet pavement. She clutched at her chest. "You—you—"

But she had nothing more to say, not then or ever. She toppled to the ground, twitched, and lay still. The gaping wound in her chest sizzled in the freezing rain.

Gabriel rubbed the wetness from his face with a trembling hand. His body was ice. His blood was fire. He'd given her a chance. He couldn't feel an ounce of guilt for doing what he had to do to survive and keep his people alive.

He turned to Jericho and Sykes. They were locked in battle, wrestling furiously for Alvarado's dropped pulse gun. Gabriel leveled his own gun, looking for his opening, but it was too risky. He was just as likely to hit Jericho as the Pyro.

Sykes struck a flurry of blows against Jericho. They exchanged feints and dodges and attacks. Sykes was clearly skilled. But so was Jericho. He just needed an opening.

You could just run. He could leave Jericho to his fate and flee, saving his own skin. No one would ever know. Jericho was the one who'd captured him and locked him in handcuffs. The one who swore to turn him in to the Sanctuary to be executed for his crimes.

Without Jericho, Gabriel would be free.

Slowly, Gabriel lowered the gun. His free hand curled into a fist. He stood there for a long, torturous minute, doing battle in his own mind. He owed Jericho nothing. He had everything to gain—his freedom, his life. All he had to do was walk away.

Nadira's scrap of cloth burned in his pocket. There were people he answered to now. One was already dead, but that didn't matter. His life was not his own. It was not his to destroy. It was not his to live as he pleased.

He knew what he needed to do, what he had to do.

The shadows grappled in the dark and the rain. Jericho's shadow was darker than Sykes'. It was the only way he could tell their shifting, blurred shapes apart.

Sykes punched his fist beneath Jericho's ribs, right at the kidneys. Jericho grunted, doubling over. For a moment, their shadows separated.

Gabriel aimed his gun. He adjusted his target and pulled the trigger. A coughing fit seized him. The plasma blast went wide.

But Sykes reacted, ducking and flinging himself to the side.

Jericho took his chance and threw an open palm strike to Sykes's forehead, bouncing his head back and exposing his neck. Quick as lightning, Jericho's left hand darted in and struck the man in his throat.

Sykes staggered, clutching his neck and gagging, eyes bulging.

"Jericho!" Gabriel grabbed the pulse rod and tossed it.

Jericho seized it with one hand and spun back for his adversary. He swung it at the Pyro, who managed to dodge, but just barely. The pulse rod caught his billowing coat, slicing a two-foot rent in the fabric.

Gabriel darted in, gun up, ready to pull the trigger, but Sykes whirled and landed a kick to his ribs. Pain exploded in his side. He recovered, spinning to attack, but Sykes was already on him.

Sykes threw back his arm and aimed a vicious punch at Gabriel's face. He couldn't avoid it. He had a fraction of a second to lower his head. The blow landed on his forehead, the hardest bone in the body.

Gabriel staggered back, stunned, his vision blurring as stars exploded behind his eyes. But the move worked.

Sykes cursed, clutching his bruised, possibly broken right hand to his chest. His gaze flitted from Jericho to Gabriel. They flanked him, Gabriel with the pulse gun aimed at Sykes' head, Jericho's pulse rod humming at his side as they closed in on either side.

Sykes was outmatched, and he knew it. "This is only the beginning. You're already dead. You just don't know it yet, you hear me?"

He turned and ran, fleeing into the shadows.

Gabriel let off a volley of useless shots, none of them hitting his target. It was too dark. The freezing rain obscured his vision. He needed to get closer. "Should I go after him?"

"No." Jericho bent double, holding his ribs, coughing and gasping for breath. He spat blood on the puddled asphalt. "There's been enough killing for one night."

"He'll alert the rest of his people."

"Trust me, they're alerted. They're already looking for us. We're the ones who need to run now."

The rain turned hard and dense. Gabriel held out his hand, watching the tiny balls of ice smack his palm. "Snow is coming."

Jericho rested his forearms on his thighs. He straightened, took steady, deep breaths, and faced Gabriel. "You saved my life. I won't forget that."

Behind them, flames engulfed the department store. The fire surged through the shattered windows, hungrily licking the sides of the building, smoke pouring out. The air cracked like thunder, like the sky splitting open.

Gabriel holstered the pulse gun. "It was the right thing to do."

15

WILLOW

The snow fell harder, a thick, white curtain. It stung Willow's eyes and clung to her eyelashes. The icy wind bit at her exposed face.

Even in the freezing cold, the smoke of the fire burned her throat. They were exposed and helpless, stumbling around in the dark and the snow.

They passed cafes and storefronts and apartment buildings and businesses, all of them blank and featureless. They took a serpentine route, making sure they weren't being followed, though there was no way to be sure, and no way to hide the footprints they left behind in the gathering whiteness.

Soon, a blanket of snow covered everything. Drifts piled against stop signs, abandoned vehicles, electric poles, storefronts. The snow-covered hulks of cars, trucks, and transports reared out of the gauzy moonlight. The night was a dreamscape of snow and shadow.

Every sound was both muffled and amplified. The stillness seemed to swallow them up. They didn't speak. They didn't need to, their minds consumed with fearful, anxious thoughts for the people they loved most.

Was Benjie okay? Was Finn still alive? Had they escaped? She needed to believe they were okay. It was the only way she could focus on staying alive herself.

Once, there was movement several blocks ahead. They took shelter inside a convenience store, hiding for long, torturous minutes, waiting for the threat to move on.

They lost their way several times in the cold and the dark. Finally, the moon peeked through the thick clouds. Micah caught sight of the cylindrical Westin skyscraper through the forest of buildings towering around them. They used it as their guide to find Peachtree Street, and from there, the smaller hotel tucked a block behind it.

Three freezing, exhausting hours later, they made it to their rendezvous point, Peachtree Suites. The hotel atrium was filled with shadows. She glimpsed the glint of crystal chandeliers high above her head, dark hulking furniture, the gleam of wood floors.

Gabriel was waiting for them. He took Amelia from Micah, lifting her easily into his arms. She groaned as she drifted in and out of consciousness.

"What about Benjie and Finn?" Willow asked breathlessly.

"They're here," Gabriel said. "Finn is fine. Benjie needs you."

They followed Gabriel to a suite on the second floor, where the others waited. They'd closed the drapes and used only the glow from a couple of SmartFlexes for light. Finn sat on a brocaded sofa, his shoulders hunched, rocking Benjie.

Benjie was wheezing and coughing violently, his light brown face tinted an unhealthy shade of purplish gray, his eyes wild and terrified.

Concern furrowed Finn's brow. "He's been like this since the fire."

"The smoke triggered his asthma." She didn't bother to kick the snow off her boots as she dashed across the small room and knelt beside them. She yanked the inhaler from her cargo pocket and thrust it to Benjie's mouth.

He sucked in the aerosolized spray, his rigid features softening. She thanked whatever god or angels or lucky stars that she'd kept the inhaler in her pocket instead of the backpack.

She stroked Benjie's splendidly messy hair. No sooner had she brushed it flat with her fingers then it stuck up all over again. She kissed his forehead tenderly.

Benjie lowered the inhaler and took a deep breath. "I lost them," he wheezed, his small face etched with sadness.

"What did you lose, kiddo?"

His mouth contorted as he struggled to hold back tears. "My backpack. All my magic stuff. The cards Daddy got me…Mom told me to keep them forever, but I lost them…"

Except for Micah, they'd all lost their packs, forced to leave them behind in the chaos of the fire. No one missed anything that couldn't be replaced. Except for Benjie. He'd just lost the ratty Star Wars backpack he'd been lugging his magic stuff around in since he was three years old. Since their father died.

Memories flashed through her mind, tender as a bruise when she pressed on them: The night the cop-bot came to their door with a recorded holo solemnly reporting their father's death—a car crash, automatically ruled an accident because the vehicle had been in manual drive mode. Zia screaming. Her mother collapsing to the floor, sobbing. Little Benjie whimpering in confusion, clutching the brand-new Star Wars backpack their father had bought for his birthday the day before, paying with the last of their savings.

It was just a backpack. And yet she felt suddenly bereft, like someone had died. She hadn't saved Zia or their mother. She hadn't even managed to salvage that ratty old backpack, severing their last connection to their old life.

She took a breath, steeling herself. She pressed her forehead against Benjie's, cupped his head with both hands, and gazed into his eyes. "It's going to be okay. I promise you. You did your best. You were brave as hell. If Dad were here, he would understand. So would Mom. They would both be so proud of you today."

Benjie nodded, tears still glimmering in his eyes.

Finn leaned in and grinned conspiratorially. "Sir Benjie, this means we must embark on a quest! A very important quest to restore the sacred magical objects of this land. Do you accept?"

The smallest smile quivered at the edges of Benjie's lips. "I accept the quest, Mister Finn," he said gravely. He unfurled his fingers, revealing the carved bird Raven had given him. "I still have this."

"A lucky charm!" Finn boomed in delight. "A good omen, my boy!"

Benjie's smile widened. He'd just escaped a blazing fire and a gang of murderous thugs, but heartened by Finn's imagination and enthusiasm. He was okay again.

She sank back on her heels. Deep gratitude filled her. "Thank you, Finn," she rasped and cleared her throat. It was more than the lingering effects of the smoke making her eyes water. "If something happened to him..."

Finn gave her a lopsided grin, revealing the adorable gap in his front teeth. He grabbed her hand and squeezed. "I was worried about you."

Her stomach did a weird flip-flop. Her cheeks heated. She pulled her hand away. "You don't have to worry about me."

He shrugged his huge shoulders. "I know you can take care of yourself. But I worried anyway."

"Yeah. Okay, thanks." She scrubbed at her face, secretly cursing herself. She was terrible at this kind of thing, whatever *this* was.

Emotions or feelings or whatever. She much preferred shooting rats and punching Silas. That, at least, she understood.

She forced herself to get a grip and looked around the room again. Amelia laid on the bed in the master bedroom, still out of it. Micah sat with her, refusing to leave, Gabriel hovering anxiously over them both. Silas sulked in the corner with his arms crossed, his expression hard as stone. Jericho paced the opulent living room in tense circles.

They were safe—coughing, cold and exhausted, but alive. She took in everyone's scared, dirty, weary faces. They were the most beautiful faces she'd ever seen. Finn, Benjie, Jericho, Amelia. Gabriel and Micah.

The group was incomplete. Something—someone—was missing.

"Where's Celeste?" she asked. "And Horne?"

"They're not here yet," Jericho said in a strained voice.

Anxiety twinged in her gut. Had they gotten caught in the fire? Bitten by the rats? Captured by the Pyros? Trapped or lost out in the freezing cold? There were too many possibilities—none of them good.

"They've been missing for far too long." Gabriel rubbed his throat with a wince. They were all still feeling the effects of smoke inhalation. "We need to look for them."

"We must find a safe place for the rest of us first, then we will," Jericho said.

"They could be in trouble, or hurt," Micah said.

"I volunteer." Gabriel rose to his feet, his shoulders squared, his hands flexing into fists at his sides. "I'll go right now."

"We're not risking it," Jericho said firmly. His dark eyes flashed, his jaw squared. "Especially now when we've lost most of our weapons. Gabriel and I managed to steal two of the Pyros' guns. Micah has his handgun, and Silas his rifle. But that's it. We have no additional ammo. We're outmanned and outgunned."

She knew it was bad. She didn't realize how bad. Willow exchanged worried glances with Finn. They were lucky to have survived unscathed this far. They'd barely escaped the Pyros and the fire. What were they going to do now?

"I'll go without a gun," Gabriel said.

Silas sneered. "You'll just get yourself killed."

What do you care?" Gabriel snapped back, bristling. "We wouldn't even be in this situation if not for you."

Silas's mouth tilted in a savage smile. "You have something you need to get off your chest? Wanna take a potshot at me?"

"Enough! Both of you." Jericho coughed hard, bending double for a moment before straightening. When he regained his composure, he shook his head. "We'll go first thing in the morning, and not a second before."

Celeste and Horne weren't her favorite people. That was no secret. But they were part of the group. And maybe Celeste wasn't as awful as she used to be. Horne was irritating as hell, but there were worse people in the world. "Gabriel's right. We should look now."

Jericho ran his hand over his head and sighed. "Believe me, I hate this as much as you do. But it's too dangerous."

Willow hated feeling sorry for an elite: first Amelia; now Celeste and Horne. But they must be terrified out there, alone and weaponless, maybe lost or hurt or both. She didn't wish that fate on anybody. "But the Pyros are gone for now. We chased them off—"

"We can't go traipsing around in the dark when we're already exhausted. From now on, we can't risk being seen. We must be invisible."

Willow just stared at him. Dread crept up her throat. She didn't ask the question. She already knew the answer.

Silas said it anyway, his expression flat, his eyes hard. "We're being hunted."

16

GABRIEL

"There's someone out there." Gabriel crouched behind the service desk in the hotel lobby. Morning light trickled through the windows, revealing stuffy, antique decor slightly worn around the edges: burnished wood floors, crystal chandeliers, a bank of last generation SmartFlex charging stations, and heavy leather sofas surrounding a massive stone fireplace.

"What do you see?" Jericho asked from beside him.

Silas scowled. "Just shoot if it's a Pyro."

Gabriel peered around the side of the counter with the scope of the semi-automatic he'd taken from Mohawk yesterday. Jericho carried both the pulse rod and the gun.

Amelia had regained consciousness late last night, but her mind was still foggy. She'd had a difficult time walking or talking for several hours, though she seemed to be coming out of it now.

They'd all spent the night in the same hotel suite. No one wanted to be alone. Gabriel had remained awake, standing watch. The lingering scorched sensation in his throat was a harsh reminder that they couldn't let their guard down for a moment.

Gabriel squinted through the scope. A lone figure trudged toward the hotel from the south. He was dressed in black cargo pants and a dark jacket. He limped slightly. A red blotch stained the front of the jacket—blood. The head was bowed, the masked face in shadow.

Gabriel tweaked the zoom on the scope, narrowing in on the figure's face. But the person stepped into the street between an SUV and a minivan.

Gabriel lost his bearings, spinning wildly and seeing only blurred close-ups. He pulled back, reset the scope, and zoomed in again.

It was Tyler Horne. There was a scrape across his temple and blood crusted along the side of his sculpted features and square jaw. But it was definitely Horne.

"What can you see?" Micah asked.

"It's our favorite person."

Silas groaned. "Is the girl with him, at least?"

"The girl has a name," Willow snapped.

Gabriel shook his head. "Alone. No sign of Celeste."

He scanned the street, the sidewalks, storefronts, and the surrounding buildings through the scope, searching for movement, for any sign of a tail, of surveillance, or that their position had been exposed. But there was no movement. Nothing.

"Get him inside before he gives us away," Jericho said, his voice strained.

A minute later, Horne was sagging against the concierge desk, bloodied and bruised but still in one piece.

"What happened?" Gabriel asked. "Where's Celeste?"

"Nice to see you, too." Horne lifted back his hood and ran shaking fingers through his matted blonde hair. "After barely surviving a night of horror, you'd think a more pleasant greeting would be in store."

"We're happy you're alive," Jericho said evenly.

"Speak for yourself," Silas growled.

Gabriel grunted. "Get on with it. What happened to Celeste?"

"I'm clearly wounded. And utterly exhausted. Let me attend to my needs first—"

Gabriel stepped closer, until he was less than a foot from Horne. His patience had run out. He gritted his teeth and forced himself to remain calm. "Why isn't she with you?"

"I'm certainly not her keeper." Horne gave a haughty sniff. "I had no responsibility for her. She made it perfectly clear on numerous occasions she wanted nothing to do with me."

Gabriel wanted to seize Horne by the collar and shake him. His hands curled into fists. He restrained himself—barely. "You both ran out the south entrance just ahead of me. I provided cover so you could escape. You were together."

Horne's eyes flickered warily from Gabriel to Jericho to Silas. He wrung his hands, clasping them together like a prayer. He cleared his throat uneasily. "I'm sorry. She didn't make it."

"No," Willow said, taking a step back. "No."

It hit him like a swift kick to the balls. Celeste was an elite, but she'd managed to survive and live alongside them all these months, in spite of her whining and complaining. She was part of their group, for better or worse.

The thought of losing someone else after Nadira was too much. He would not accept it. "Tell me exactly what happened."

Horne shifted nervously. "There was nothing I could do. I swear. We ran as far as we could, but we got disoriented in the darkness and the rain. There were rats, too many of them. We got cornered in an alley. There was a dumpster with the lid closed. I told her to climb on top of it. I didn't even have a weapon. I jumped in front of her, kicking and punching as many as I could. She fell and..." His voice trailed off. His face contorted and he swiped at his eyes.

"There was nothing I could do. Nothing. I barely escaped with my life."

Gabriel inhaled sharply. "Where is she?"

"I...I wanted to carry her, but...she's infected, now. It was too dangerous."

Gabriel spun and stalked across the room. A hot spark of anger flared through him. He couldn't stand to be near that slimy, self-serving asshole for a second more. There was something in his face, something guarded, some shadow Gabriel couldn't pin down. But he didn't like it.

"You did what you could," Micah said gently. "What's done is done. You were lucky to make it back."

Gabriel met Silas's gaze for a moment. Silas said nothing. He slouched against the counter, his fists thrust deep in his pockets. His face was an expressionless mask, his eyes hard as stones.

Gabriel aimed a savage kick at the stone fireplace, doing nothing but stubbing his toe. But the splinter of pain centered him. It felt like he'd personally lost her. Like he hadn't done enough to protect them all. That he'd failed his promise to Nadira. That he'd failed himself.

He pushed his hand in his pocket and felt the soft square of cloth. He turned back to Jericho. "I'll get her."

"What?" Horne said.

Amelia said nothing, her face tight. Willow and Finn stared at him like he'd grown a second head. But what they thought didn't matter. "She deserves to be buried. We can't leave her out there to rot."

"Her body is infected," Horne sputtered.

"It's too dangerous," Jericho said.

"You'll get yourself killed," Horne said. "And for what? She's already dead."

Everything Horne and Jericho said was true. His own mind

whispered all the reasons this was a terrible idea. Why should he risk himself for an elite, for someone who didn't even like him?

But it didn't matter. None of that mattered. Nadira would have done it, if she were here. In a world of violence and chaos, they needed to mourn their own. Leaving her body out there for the rats...it was wrong. He needed to find her. It was part of his penance. Gabriel felt the rightness of it in his bones. His posture stiffened. "Let me do this."

Jericho hesitated.

"She was one of us," Willow said.

"She's right," Micah said softly. "Let him go."

Gabriel glanced at his brother, relieved that he understood. He clenched his jaw, the muscle in his cheek pulsing. "Give me twenty-four hours. Forty-eight, tops."

Jericho finally nodded. He swiped his SmartFlex and studied the map of the city. "We can't stay here, it's too dangerous. We have to move, and we have to do it quietly and carefully, slipping from building to building if we have to."

He pointed to three different dots. "Within the next twenty-four to forty-eight hours, I expect us to reach one of these three points. Silas scouted the High Museum of Art and this office building, here. It appears to be clear. I've saved the GPS coordinates. Take my SmartFlex. The charge is low, but hopefully it will last you. I'll use Amelia's."

Gabriel nodded, every muscle in his body tightening. Jericho handed him the cuff, and he slipped it over his right wrist.

"We can't wait for you." Jericho's eyes were black and hard as obsidian. "I can't endanger the group for one person. Getting Amelia to the Sanctuary is our most critical mission, even more than saving Elise from the Headhunters, more than saving any one of us."

"I wouldn't expect anything less." He didn't want anyone endangering themselves for him. His life wasn't worth it. As long as Amelia, Micah, and the others were safe, that was all that mattered.

He would find Celeste's body, bury her, and find his people again while avoiding aggressive rats, infected humans, and the Pyros, all on a deadline. He knew he was capable. He could do it.

He turned to Horne. "Tell me everything you remember about where you were."

17

AMELIA

When she awoke, Amelia couldn't remember where or who she was. She was floating in a liquid gray haze, drifting in and out of consciousness. Over the next few hours, she remembered her mother and father but didn't recognize the faces peering down at her.

They were strangers. Her own mind was a stranger to her. Everything was distant and unfocused.

Memories rose through the mist. She tried to grasp them—the bright spotlights blinding her eyes as she performed at one of her father's galas; the way her mother brushed her hair, one long stroke at a time; Silas chasing her through a grand house of grand rooms filled with grand furniture that still felt empty; her shaking hands as she chopped off her own hair, the way the tendrils swirled like silk ribbons on her lap.

Some memories turned solid in her hands; others fell through her fingers, slippery and insubstantial as ghosts.

By the next day, she remembered Micah and Gabriel and Benjie and the *Grand Voyager* and Sweet Creek Farm. She remembered she loved dark chocolate and classical music and that ocean blue was her favorite color.

And then Kane came back. And Simeon and her father and Gabriel. The Hydra virus. The Headhunters. Nadira's death and her mother's capture.

Her muscles were shivery and weak. Her brain felt bruised. Her mouth tasted of copper, no matter what she ate.

But she was alive. She held onto that as tightly as she could.

She drifted off again, and this time, Kane invaded her dreams. She awoke gasping, drenched in sweat even in the bitter cold, her heart a frenzy inside her chest. She lay shaking, blinking back the awful images of his thick, meaty fingers reaching for her, clawing her neck, choking off her breath, that bone-crushing fear clamping over her throat.

It wasn't real. He wasn't real. He was a ghost, a demon from the past, a stubborn memory that wouldn't fade. Slowly, the day and time and place came back to her in bits and pieces.

She was wrapped in a heated blanket on the floor of the High Museum of Art. A museum once visited by millions of people, people all dead now. People with no more memories to make, no memories to lose.

The light wood floors echoed with Benjie's muffled laughter as he dashed between life-sized marble sculptures from Greek myths. The high white walls held famous paintings, photographs, and holo prints, two- and three-dimensional artwork hung in antique gilt frames.

Looters had slashed much of the art on the first and second floors, knocking over statues, pissing in corners, and doing what-ever damage they could. But they must have gotten bored or tired, because little had been touched up here.

She stared at the painting on the wall across from her—Claude Monet's *Autumn on the Seine, Argenteuil.* Her father had a Monet in his collection. Not because he'd particularly loved art, but because he could. Because he liked to own beautiful things. He liked to control them. She looked away.

In the two hours since they'd taken shelter at the museum, Willow had brought her food, Benjie showed her magic tricks with an old quarter Micah had found for him, and Finn cracked his usual goofy jokes, trying to get her to laugh.

Jericho checked her forehead and fussed over her, his perpetual frown always on his face. She remembered his frowns, his sternness, and the concern that lay beneath his tough veneer.

Silas was around, but he spoke little, prowling the halls of the museum like a frustrated ally cat instead. She knew this, too. How hard and cold he was, always keeping things inside, lashing out at everything and everyone.

Then there was Micah, always hovering nearby, but never over-whelming or irritating. He was simply there. He was the one who carried her through the cold and snow for hours as they made their slow, painstaking way through downtown. She'd been groggy through much of it, which was a blessing. She hated the thought of someone cradling her like a vulnerable, needy child.

When she was awake, he sat beside her, reading from a book of poetry or a novel, but always reading. He leaned against a magne-tized, floating bench decorated with antique Coca-Cola bottle caps, a ratty paperback in his hands.

She pushed herself into a sitting position against the wall and groaned. Her head still ached. Her whole body ached. Her muscles felt weak and watery. Kane's vicious, viper eyes were still in her head. She needed a distraction. "What are you reading?"

"My favorite. J.R.R. Tolkien's *Lord of the Rings*." He smiled shyly at her, tucked a bookmark to neatly mark his place, and set down the book. Only Micah would care about bookmarks in the apoca-lypse. "Welcome back. How are you feeling?"

"Better," she said, half-lying. "Except for the ball of fuzz between my ears."

"Your memories aren't back yet?"

"Most of them. I think." She tugged the leather thong from around her neck so she could hold the diamond charm bracelet. The cold metal was comforting. It had been a gift from her father for her thirteenth birthday.

A memory flickered: a bunch of important senators and business tycoons smiling down at her, her father boasting about the quality-sourced diamonds, her brother kicking her beneath the table and rolling his eyes.

She couldn't remember her mother. Hadn't she been there? She closed her eyes, focusing with all her limited brain-power. Her mother was in her memories, but it was like she'd been blurred out. Amelia couldn't make out any distinguishing features, couldn't recall her smile. "I can't remember my mother's face."

Micah gave her hand a squeeze and quickly let go. "Maybe once we rescue her and you see her face, then everything will come back."

"Maybe." What if she'd lost some memories forever? What if she'd lost some elemental part of her?

With every seizure, part of herself wouldn't come back. What if next time she forgot how to walk or talk or how to play the violin? What if the next time she woke up, she was no longer *herself*? To lose yourself piece by piece was the most terrifying thing in the world.

And how long until the next one came? Six weeks? Six months? Every seizure was potentially devastating. How long until she was permanently brain-damaged? A paralyzed vegetable? Dead? "I feel like I'm grieving for something that hasn't happened yet."

"Don't give up hope," Micah said. "The doctors at the Sanctuary will help you at the same time they find the cure." He picked up his book and held it out to her. "Rage, rage against the dying of the light."

She'd heard it before. She'd liked it then, but now she held it in her mind like a lifeline. "What's it from?"

"It's a Dylan Thomas poem. It's about the beauty and tenacity of the human spirit, about fighting against the inevitability of death. We know it will take us, but we're going to fight until our dying breath anyway. 'Do not go gentle into that good night.'"

"It's lovely." She suddenly felt very self-conscious. Embarrassment flushed through her. And shame. Micah had seen her at her worst, helpless and ugly and disgusting. "Thank you for...being there. When it happened."

He jabbed his glasses up the bridge of his nose with his finger. His dark wavy hair was a little unkempt, as always. His face reddened slightly. "It was nothing."

But it felt like more than nothing to Amelia. It felt like everything. "I'm sorry you had to see that."

"Vulnerability isn't a weakness," Micah said quietly as if he could read her mind. "It isn't something to be ashamed of."

She flushed, grateful for his words even if she couldn't believe them yet. The suffocating shame her father had drilled into her over the years—she was defective, and her defect was ugly, revolting—was hard to shake. She pushed the point of the violin charm against the pad of her pointer finger until it hurt.

She glanced at Micah, about to say something else, but she caught a fleeting shadow flickering across his face. His expression was tense. She could tell he was chewing on the inside of his cheeks, his brow furrowed. He looked like he was taking the weight of the world on his own shoulders.

She resisted the urge to grab his hand. "You're worried about Gabriel."

"I shouldn't be, but I can't help it."

"He's your brother."

He stared down at the book in his hands, frowning. "He's doing a good thing, I think."

"He's been doing a lot of good things lately," Amelia said softly. She didn't know how to reconcile the Gabriel who'd betrayed her, who'd given her up to the likes of Kane, who'd stood by and allowed it to happen, who'd bristled with unrestrained rage—with this new remorseful, penitent Gabriel, who'd nearly killed himself to rescue her from Cerberus, who'd thrown himself in front of the rats, who'd valiantly taken on the Pyros so they could escape.

And now he'd put himself at risk to find Celeste's body, one of the elites he'd so despised. It didn't make sense. And yet. "Does that make up for..."

"Everything?" Micah smiled grimly. "I haven't decided yet."

Benjie dashed up to them, his wild hair sticking up all over his head. "Lo Lo says it's bedtime, but she won't sing to me because she's on guard duty. She says she's a terrible singer anyway and to ask you."

He clasped his hands together, his big brown eyes pleading. His voice was still wheezy from the smoke inhalation, but he seemed to have his energy back. "Pretty please, Miss Amelia?"

"I'm not much better," Amelia said, though she remembered those nights with Benjie in abandoned offices and houses and hotels, quarantined from the rest of the group while they waited for the Hydra virus to show itself.

Benjie quirked his eyebrows and leaned in to whisper conspiratorially, "You're better than Lo Lo. Way better. But no telling her I said so."

Micah laughed. "I have to check in with Jericho on plans for tomorrow anyway. See you later."

"He'll be fine," Amelia called to Micah. "If anything, he's a survivor."

Micah adjusted his glasses with his thumb. "Yeah, I suppose he is."

Amelia patted the sleeping bag beside her. Benjie dove in, nestling against her side. "Where's everybody?"

"Guarding stuff or exploring stuff. I already saw every single exhibit." He wrinkled his nose. "There's lots of naked statues and paintings and stuff."

"What do you think about that?"

"Totally gross."

Amelia smiled and tilted her head back against the wall. She hummed the classics, Peter and the Wolf and Brahms' Lullaby, the familiar melodies more comforting than she could say.

She hadn't finished the third song when Benjie sniffled. Tears streaked his small face. "What's wrong?"

He sat up and wiped his eyes. "I'm sorry, I know I shouldn't be crying, Miss Amelia."

"Who said you couldn't cry?"

He sniffed.

Amelia touched his shoulder. "You can tell me."

"Lo Lo always tells me to be brave and strong. I try as good as I can, I swear."

"But?" she prodded gently.

His face collapsed. "I miss Mommy."

Amelia's stomach twisted in iron knots. The poor kid. This was hard for all of them. She couldn't imagine how awful it was for an eight-year-old. "You know what? I miss my mother. And I know Willow misses your mom, too."

She gathered his small body into her arms. He nuzzled into her like a puppy and wrapped his thin arms around her neck. His heartbeat thudded against her chest. She still wasn't entirely used to physical touch. Her family was reserved, to say the least. But Benjie made it easier with his exuberant hugs, his sweetness, his unconditional trust.

She gently stroked his back. "Willow doesn't need you to be strong for her, Benjie. She's a big girl. She can be strong for herself. And I'll let you in on a little secret. Crying doesn't mean you aren't strong. Tears aren't weak. Emotions aren't weak. They're part of what makes us who we are. We can be happy and brave and strong, but we can also be sad and worried and scared. So don't wipe your tears away, okay?"

He nodded. "What about my snots?"

"You can totally wipe your snot. Just not on your shirtsleeve."

"Aww, nuts." But he was grinning.

"There's toilet paper in the bathroom. Remember, just a couple of squares. And then you come back and snuggle and cry with me as much as you want."

The shadows lengthened around them as Amelia hummed classical music long into the night. She practiced the movements on an imaginary violin in her hands, her fingers moving with a memory that lived deep in her bones.

When the tears came, she didn't stop them.

18

WILLOW

There was something lurking in the shadows of the pharmacy. Willow could feel it. The hairs on the back of her neck prickled. She turned, gun clasped in both hands, and faced the shattered door. She made her way inside, careful not to make a sound.

They'd spent the last two days on high alert, staying as hidden as possible, traveling through alleys and side streets. They'd trudged in single file through the crusty snow, doing their best to step in each other's footprints so they appeared to be one or two people instead of the group the Pyros were hunting.

Micah had carried Amelia, who was still incredibly weak, slowing them all down. Gabriel wasn't back yet. Silas and Willow had acted as runners, branching off into false trails and doubling back on themselves. It wasn't near enough, but it was all they could do.

Snow drifted down in lazy spirals from the dreary gray sky, but they needed a few more hours of heavy snowfall to completely hide their tracks.

They'd gone several blocks out of their way to avoid a half-dozen infected people wandering around in the cold, blood smeared around their eye sockets, mouths, and ears. One was a teenage girl with short dark hair that made Willow's chest constrict. She'd looked so much like Zia.

Only a few blocks later, they'd had to backtrack to avoid two dozen dead laid out side by side in front of a burning, ancient-looking stone church sandwiched between two diamond-glass skyscrapers. The bodies were covered with a writhing, wriggling carpet of black fur. She glimpsed pink-scaled tails and sharp yellow teeth as the rodents chewed on rotting flesh. She'd nearly vomited the meager contents of her stomach.

"We're going slower than a turtle stuck in molasses," Finn had muttered, shivering as he untucked his hands from beneath his armpits to gnaw on a Twizzlers he'd scavenged.

Willow was exhausted. All that work and effort, and they'd barely made it a few miles. Finally, around mid-afternoon, Jericho gave them the go-ahead. She and Silas scouted ahead to find a shelter for the night.

Less than a half hour later, the first drone had appeared fifteen feet above the street, cruising silently between two buildings. She and Silas hid inside a liquor store, ducking behind the bar. The mirrored counters were smashed. Most of the bottles had been stolen, but a few were shattered across the floor. The scent of alcohol burned her nostrils. She crouched, heart beating in her throat, as several pairs of feet tramped past. The Pyros were still hunting them.

They waited ten minutes before daring to move again. Before they'd left, Silas had grasped the neck of a bottle of bourbon that had rolled beneath the bar. He started to open it, already tilting the bottle toward his mouth. Willow seized his arm. "Oh, no, you don't."

He'd hurled a few petulant insults at her, but they both knew it was half-assed.

Now, she stared into the looted pharmacy, letting her eyes adjust to the darkness. She scanned the shadowy rows of mostly empty shelves, ripped prescription boxes and tipped bottles, pried open and long emptied.

She gestured to Silas, a few yards behind her, and slipped inside, gun level, careful not to step on the glass shards littered across the floor. She inched around a corner. Was she just being paranoid? Had she just imagined the sensation that she wasn't alone—

A woman with a tangle of matted dark curls was bent on her knees, reaching beneath a shelf for something, her backpack and rifle on the floor beside her.

Willow's blood quickened. She licked her dry, parched lips. "Don't move."

The woman let out a hiss, but she obeyed, her body going rigid. "I'm no threat. You don't have to hurt me."

"We'll decide that," Silas said, coming up behind her.

Willow shot him a warning glance. Silas glared back at her, but he lowered his rifle slightly. They both took a step back, making sure they were outside of the ten-foot infection radius. The woman wasn't coughing and didn't appear feverish, but you could never be too careful. "Where's the rest of your group?"

"I'm alone."

"You expect us to believe that?" Silas asked.

"Can I sit up?" The woman asked. "I'll answer your questions, but I'm very uncomfortable."

The woman spoke with a faint Middle Eastern accent. Willow thought of Nadira with a savage pang in her chest. She gestured with her gun, even though the woman couldn't see from her position. "Sit up, face me, your hands in the air."

The woman obeyed. She looked about mid-forties, but the strain of the last few months could have aged her a decade. Beneath the smudged dirt and grime, her skin was honey-brown. Her mask was tight against her mouth and nose. She clutched a bottle of pills in her right hand. Antibiotics.

They'd lost most of their meds in the fire, though Micah had a few supplies in his pack. But not enough. "We'll take those," Silas said.

The woman's face blanched. "Please. My daughter's sick. She needs these. I never would have ventured into the city unless I was desperate."

"If she's sick, she's already as good as dead." Willow kept her voice hard, made her face impassive. The woman looked scared, but it was fear that made a person the most dangerous. If the woman sensed weakness, she might attempt an attack.

"It's not the Hydra virus. She has sepsis. She fell and cut her leg. A visit to a clinic would have taken care of it in the old world. But now? It's infected badly. Look—you can take anything else. Take my pack. My gun. I've got three days' worth of food. Two water filters. Vitamins. A fire starter."

"How old is your daughter?" Willow asked.

Silas gave her a withering stare. "It doesn't matter."

"Seven," the woman stammered. "Her name is Lily. She loves unicorns."

"Give us the meds," Silas said.

"Her little girl loves unicorns," Willow said. She imagined Benjie. She couldn't help it.

"She's playing you." Silas's mouth puckered in a sullen scowl. He knew he'd already lost the battle. "She can see you're a gullible sucker from a mile away."

Willow kept her gun up, but she eased her finger off the trigger. Maybe she was gullible, but she didn't think so. The woman didn't seem like a hardened criminal. She looked like a mother, with the same strained worry around her eyes as Willow's mom used to have. "We'll trade you. You give us info, we let you keep the antibiotics."

"Thank you," the woman said, relieved.

"Willow—" Silas growled.

She ignored him. She was the one who found the woman. She got to decide how this went down, not him. "We're headed north. Any advice?"

The woman stuffed the antibiotics inside her pack and pulled herself to her feet. She glanced at Silas warily. "One survivor to another, you're going the wrong way."

Willow licked her lips. "We just have to get through the city and—"

"I wouldn't be here myself if there were any better options. This is Pyro territory."

"We've had the pleasure of their acquaintance," Silas said stiffly.

"What happened here?" Willow asked. "How did the Pyro gang gain control of the whole city?"

The woman's gaze flitted to the sliver of sky between two soaring buildings and back to Willow. "Atlanta's been a dangerous place for a long time. That was no secret. Poverty and zero jobs mixed with anger and helplessness make for a toxic mess. I lived outside midtown with my daughters. There was nowhere else for us to go. But then that Hydra bioweapon wreaked havoc on the world. The infection spread like wildfire. My oldest daughter, she—she didn't make it. By the time the vlogs and newsfeeds were reporting death tolls, half the city was already gone. The cops, the soldiers, the government officials—they all died or bailed within a couple of weeks.

"Then all hell broke loose. The survivors joined up with other survivors, some of them already members of established militias and gangs. You joined up or you were a target. Three major factions warred for control of Atlanta—The Right Hand of God, the Cobras, and the Pyros.

"There were sporadic battles in those first weeks, but most people were still shell-shocked. The smart ones were scavenging food, water, and weapons. Then all of a sudden, the Pyros were on the warpath. They were burning bodies, burning apartments and condos. They tramped down streets armed with pulse guns and grenades and RPGs. Atlanta was a war zone for a week. We hid in our apartment building, too terrified to move. Then it was over. The Pyros won. They killed off their competition. But they're crazy. And they're brutal. Their leader—Tobias Moruga—he's bad people."

Willow swallowed the lump in her throat. "Thank you for the warning."

The woman bent and grabbed her rifle. She looked up at something beyond their heads and stiffened. "Drone."

All three of them ducked, crouching behind the shelves. Willow peered around the corner as the sleek black shape drifted by, snow swirling in eddies beneath its whirring rotors.

After they were sure it was out of sight, the woman stood again. "I have to get back to my daughter. Thank you."

Willow nodded. The woman hurried toward the exit in the back of the pharmacy, seeming to dissolve into the shadows.

They made their way back out to the sidewalk. The sky had darkened ominously. In the distance, several fires flared. The red X's encased in circles were everywhere. She repressed a shudder. "We're in incredible danger."

"Congratulations," he quipped. "You have a remarkable grasp of the obvious."

"Oh, shut up already." Suddenly all she wanted to do was get back to Finn and Benjie. She needed to wrap Benjie in her arms and never let go. "There's an office building up there, to the right. No fire damage. No Pyros' mark. Let's clear it and we can get the rest of the group."

"We needed those antibiotics," Silas said to her back. "We don't have enough. Giving them to her was a mistake."

She saw her mom's eyes again. Worried, exhausted, stressed, but always full of love. "No," she said, "it wasn't."

19

MICAH

"There's another fire." Micah pointed above a squat ten-story parking complex several blocks to the east. Billowing smoke stained the darkening sky, rising from somewhere behind it. If that fire came from the Pyros, they needed to know.

He and Jericho were securing the perimeter of the nondescript office building they'd sought shelter in for the night, the third night without Gabriel.

Beside him, Jericho wheeled and stared up, shielding his eyes. Towering corporate buildings blocked their view. "We can't see a damn thing from down here."

Dusk was falling quickly, the world fading into pale shadows. Micah adjusted his glasses and peered up at the skyscrapers surrounding them, turning in a slow circle. Something flickered at the edge of his vision. "There's a light up there."

A single square window was lit in the black steel and glass corporate high rise across from the museum.

"Damn it," Jericho said. "We have to get rid of that light before it gets dark or it will lead the Pyros to us like a beacon."

"Everyone's exhausted. We've already walked all day. Amelia's still recovering. We can't just move—"

"I know." Jericho shouldered his rifle. "Come on. And look alive."

Micah gestured to Willow, who was standing guard inside the office entrance, Silas's semi-automatic tucked into her shoulder. He signaled their intention to check out the building. She nodded and flashed him a thumbs-up.

They wove silently between the snow-covered husks of cars, buses, and transports. Something skittered over the road, kicked loose by his boots. Several spent tear gas canisters lay half-hidden in a heap of snow drifted against the curb. More signs of a turf war. The Pyros had obviously won.

Micah swallowed. The hairs of his neck prickled. Anyone could be watching them from any of the hundreds of thousands of darkened windows glinting above them.

He moved as quickly as he could behind Jericho, stepping carefully inside his prints as they made their way to the corporate tower. The doors were already broken. They slipped inside, crouching, weapons up.

They cleared the lobby—mirrored walls, huge chrome spheres hanging from the ceiling, strange statues made from wire and welded steel. A few bloated bodies slumped against the far corner. Two possums and a racoon skittered deeper into the shadows.

Micah covered his nose against the stench as they hurried into the stairwell. The metal door clicked silently behind them. The beams from their scopes gave them just enough light.

"What floor?" Jericho asked.

"Twenty-fifth," Micah huffed, already exhausted from the day's long trek. "But you know that."

"Just checking to make sure you're paying attention."

Micah's legs trembled by the time they reached the twenty-fifth floor. He gritted his teeth and pushed away the pain. Jericho signaled and went in first, Micah right behind him.

They moved slowly, but the vast, open space was relatively easy to clear. There were no cubicles, just self-contained banks of computer towers without desks or chairs. This business venture had been virtually managed by AIs. Very few humans had worked here.

Jericho pointed to an enclosed glass office. They crept toward it. Bland white floors and walls. A holoscreen, integrated computer desk, and blank wallscreens where the family vids would play on a loop. Against the floor-to-ceiling window was a rumpled sleeping bag, crumpled balls of trash and empty food tins, and a solar lantern.

Rust-colored spatters stained the floor next to the sleeping bag. Dried blood. Jericho picked up a spent shell casing, studied it, and tossed it back on the floor.

Micah switched off the lantern. From this vantage point, they could see everything below them more clearly. The building they'd holed up in was squat and gray and several decades past its prime, its paint peeling, the roof sagging slightly. But there were no dead bodies to draw the rats or spread infection.

Amelia was down there. She was on her feet now, though still weak. He'd sat beside her for hours while she lay unconscious, listening to the ragged rise and fall of her breathing, begging God to let her be okay. The seizure had terrified him. He'd thought she was going to die. The next one might kill her, or the one after that.

She'd had a nightmare last night, thrashing and moaning in restless sleep. He'd half-reached for her, wanting to take her hand, to touch her, to offer reassurance, comfort, anything. He'd thought better of it, his hand dropping helplessly to his side. He couldn't risk their friendship. She meant too much to him.

Jericho nudged his arm and pointed, drawing him back to the

present. He had a job to do. He peered through the zoom on his scope and checked out the surrounding buildings. Many of them had red graffiti scrawled on the exterior walls, the circle with the X inside it that Amelia and Willow had warned him about.

"Over there, north and west." Barely visible through the buildings, he could make out side streets where it appeared a bulldozer had forced its way through, vehicles crumpled and smashed on either side of a narrow pathway in the center of the road, wide enough for a single vehicle to pass through.

He froze. His gaze had snagged on something. There were piles of burnt corpses. At least a half-dozen of them, scattered over the surrounding blocks. If he didn't already know what they were, his mind would have refused to identify them. He recognized charred bones and scraps of blackened clothing. The piles of bones and ash were mounded high, at least the height of a man.

He gagged, fighting down the acid burning his throat.

"I see it," Jericho said softly. "We're inside Pyro territory now."

Micah's heart constricted. "Gabriel."

He'd try to play off his concern with Amelia, but the truth was, every hour that passed tightened the band around his chest. It had been forty-two hours since Gabriel left. What if he didn't come back?

He could barely speak to his brother. Yet the thought of something happening to him made him feel like he was teetering on the lip of a black hole, about to fall. Like the ground was opening up beneath him and he was falling with nothing solid to grab onto.

He bit the inside of his cheek. Could he ever forgive Gabriel? Could they ever go back to what they'd had before? He didn't know the answers. He only knew that he'd prayed for his brother's safe return every single hour since he'd left.

If Gabriel died, his own heart would split into pieces.

"Gabriel is tough," Jericho said. "You both are."

Micah glanced at him in surprise. That was the last thing he expected to hear from Jericho. "What?"

"When I first saw you, huddled behind that slot machine about to piss your pants on the *Grand Voyager*, I thought you were a sniveling coward. Then I thought you were one of those book-smart, feel-everything morons who thought they knew better than everybody else but never lived a day in the real world."

Micah wasn't sure how he was supposed to respond. "Thank you, I guess?"

Jericho smiled wryly. "Like I said, I was wrong. You've got a moral compass, kid, and you stick to it. That takes guts. A world like this, it takes good people, churns them up and spits them out, turns them into monsters."

Micah thought of Harmony, a normal person desperate enough to do something despicable to save someone she loved. Gabriel had been willing to kill for a cause, even if it meant taking innocent lives. People killed for much less all the time. They killed for food, for safety, for self-preservation, for power, for revenge.

"He who fights with monsters should be careful lest he becomes a monster," Micah said, quoting a line by Friedrich Nietzsche he recalled from history class. He'd memorized it because it sounded so poetic, so essential, so *true*.

"It's what we'll become," Jericho said. "Monsters. Every single one of us."

"No," Micah said. He didn't believe that. He couldn't. "Not if we're careful. Not if we continually fight to choose the good. There's always a choice."

"I hope you're right."

"We all have choices. We all get chances. It's what we do with them that matters."

Jericho turned to face him. A shadow passed across his tense features. "And the choice Silas made?"

"Harsh times call for harsh choices, sometimes. I get that. But we still have a choice. We may have to kill to protect ourselves, but we shouldn't do it until we have to, until we've tried everything else."

"I taught Silas how to kill," Jericho said in a strained voice. His jaw worked, the muscle in his cheek twitching. "I never regretted it…until he killed that kid."

Micah looked down at the city. In the distance, fires illuminated gleaming steal and diamond-glass towers. Twisting elegantly among the monoliths, the AirRail glittered like a diamond snake.

From up here, there was a dangerous beauty to it all. A design, a purpose. Down on the street, it all looked like chaos. Everything felt like chaos now. Was there a reason for all of this? A purpose? Something beautiful that might rise from the ashes? Micah hoped so. He believed so. He closed his eyes for a moment and said another prayer for his brother's safety.

"There are consequences either way," he said slowly. "You act, and someone innocent dies. You don't act, and you endanger someone you love. For me, I've got to live inside my own soul. There is a cost for everything. Some things cost too much."

Jericho stared out the window, his jaw working. "What does that mean?"

"If I had to kill an innocent person or steal the last bit of food someone else needed to survive in order for me to live, I wouldn't do it."

"You would rather die?"

"I would rather die with honor than live as a coward. If the cost is my soul, my humanity, then it's too high. I refuse to pay it." The words felt right as he said them. He believed it down to the marrow of his bones. Death wasn't the worst thing. He refused to let anyone take his soul from him. If he died, he would die by his own terms.

Jericho raised his eyebrows.

Micah thought of his mother on her deathbed, squeezing his

hand in her frail, trembling one. *Be good. Be brave.* "Survival isn't the most important thing. It can't be. Otherwise, this world could be run by cut-throat savages and murderers, and that would be a win for humanity. Why? Because humans are still alive.

"But it's not a win. It's a tragedy. Because those humans are no better than animals. They're worse. For humanity to truly survive, we have to preserve what keeps us human."

"And what is that?"

Micah leaned against the glass. "Whatever sets us above even the most intelligent animals. Our ability to love, to be just, to be merciful, to forgive, to dream. To believe in something greater and better than ourselves. To hope."

Jericho flashed him a wry smile. "Maybe you missed your calling as a preacher."

Micah blushed and adjusted his glasses. "I'm just trying to be the best person I can, in spite of the circumstances. If everybody did the same thing, we would turn out okay."

Outside, dusk descended over everything. Treacherous shadows lurked in the alleys. The stars were invisible, the moon barely a murky glow.

"Growing up in Nigeria during the revolution, you were hard or you died, simple as that," Jericho said quietly. "I served as private security in the Chicago and Tampa riots. I saw what people did to each other during the water crisis uprising in Arizona. You learn to live your life one way. It's difficult to see there are different paths, let alone better ones."

He'd never heard Jericho string so many words together at once in the months they'd been living together, day in and day out. He was tough as a mountain, stern and demanding, unafraid, unflinching. He'd never voiced his own doubts. Until this moment, Micah had been sure he didn't have any. But like everything, most people were more than they seemed.

Jericho fell silent for a long moment. "I let Silas down. I taught him how to kill. Maybe … maybe the better lesson is how not to."

Micah smiled. "Be careful. I think you're in danger of growing a conscience."

Jericho shook his head ruefully. "You know what they say. An old dog can learn new tricks."

"I don't think that's how the saying goes."

"No? Well, I never understood American slang anyway." Jericho ran his hand over his head. "You'll be a good leader, someday, Micah."

"What do you mean? We have you." But still, he flushed, deeply flattered. Jericho was a man who commanded respect. To have that respect returned, even a little, was an honor.

Jericho clapped him on the back. Micah almost stumbled from the strength of the blow. "You've got too much dirt in your ears. I said someday."

They made their way back down the twenty-five flights of stairs. A racoon startled them in the stairwell, hissing, its eyes shining in their light beams. But it wasn't infected, and they carried on without further incident.

They'd barely returned when Willow signaled from her post at the front doors. "They're back!"

"Gabriel?" Micah asked, his pulse quickening. Was his brother safe? Was he okay? Then Willow's words sank in. What did she mean, *they*?

Micah hurried after Jericho to the lobby, where Willow, Amelia, Horne, and Finn were already gathered.

Micah's mouth fell open, dumbstruck.

Gabriel had returned. But he wasn't alone.

20

GABRIEL

Gabriel wrapped his arm around the girl, steadying her as they stumbled through the entrance. Her clothes were bloodied and disheveled. Her face was smudged with dirt and ash, her coppery curls a matted, frizzy mess. Blood dripped down her leg, smeared boot-prints streaking the floor behind them.

Celeste was alive.

Willow leapt to her feet, gaping. "We thought you were dead!"

Celeste trembled from blood loss and exhaustion, but her eyes were clear. "I'm not."

He placed his hand on her back to keep her from falling. He was exhausted himself, his eyes gritty, his body almost numb from the hours in the freezing cold and snow. He'd given Celeste his coat. She'd needed it more.

Gabriel blinked, his eyes adjusting to the dimness. The sky was darkening outside the windows. The lobby was filled with shadows. Only the light of the moon reflected off the snow provided a soft glow.

Jericho's gaze sharpened in suspicion as he turned to Horne. "You told us she was dead."

Horne's face drained of color. His features contorted in a barely disguised grimace. "Celeste, I was sure you—I never would've—it must be a miracle—"

"Do not speak!" Celeste straightened, all six feet of her. Gabriel grabbed her arm to hold her up. Her eyes blazed with fury. "You did this!"

Horne took a step back, then another. He lifted his hands, palms out in a placating gesture. "We must celebrate this joyous occasion. You came back from the dead and—"

"I didn't come back from the dead," Celeste forced between gritted teeth. "You *left* me for dead."

The room fell silent. No one spoke. No one breathed.

Micah looked from Celeste to Horne and back again. His gaze flicked to Gabriel, questioning, searching for confirmation. Gabriel gave a small shake of his head, barely restraining his own rage. This was Celeste's story to tell. He wouldn't do or say anything until she'd said her piece.

"What do you mean?" Micah asked finally. "Horne left you behind?"

"Worse." Celeste leaned down to her bloody leg and unwound the makeshift bandage Gabriel had managed to make out of torn strips of a linen tablecloth.

Micah gasped. Amelia made a wounded animal sound in the back of her throat. Willow looked even more furious.

A deep, ugly gash marred Celeste's leg from the underside of her kneecap to her thigh. Blood welled in the cut as Gabriel carefully rewound the bandage. It wouldn't stop the blood loss for long.

Celeste pointed a shaking finger at Horne. "That man tried to murder me to save his own worthless skin."

Horne shook his head frantically, his perfectly styled blonde hair falling into his panicked eyes. Shadows flitted across his face. "No! No, I would never...there's been a mistake. A misunderstanding—"

"Does that look like a misunderstanding to you?" Silas snarled, pointing at Celeste's leg. A small puddle of blood formed on the floor beneath her, almost black in the dim light.

Micah turned to Benjie. "Go get the bandages and the antiseptic spray in my pack."

Benjie stared wide-eyed at Celeste. "But—"

"Go!" Willow said, her voice deadly calm.

He scooted off his stool and dashed for the stairs, the beam of his small flashlight bouncing off the walls. A minute later, he was back. Micah and Amelia cleaned and bound Celeste's wound as best they could.

Gabriel forced his gaze from her leg. Anger ran through him like an electrical current. He caught Silas's eye and dipped his chin, angling his head at Horne.

Silas knew what he wanted. He drew his gun, thumbed off the safety, and stepped silently behind Horne. Just in case.

Once she'd swallowed several aspirin, Jericho spoke in a low, cold voice, his eyes hard as obsidian. "Tell me exactly what happened."

Celeste squared her shoulders. Gone was the whiny, manipulative sweetness. Gone was the helpless, pampered elite. She was fierce, her entire body vibrating with rage. "We were running in the rain. We got lost, unsure how to get back at night. We decided to hole up until morning. We tried a pizza place that wasn't boarded up, but it was infested with rats."

She paused, sucking in a harsh breath at the memory. "We tried to go out the back—there was an alley—but there were too many of those filthy rats. Horne tripped, and I stopped to help him. I risked my life to *help* him. I reached out and grabbed his hand, pulling him to his feet. When I tried to let go, he gripped me harder, pulled out his knife, and slashed my leg. I twisted away at the last second, so it wasn't as deep as he'd intended. But it was enough.

"The rats smelled my blood and came after me instead of him. He escaped through the alley and left me for dead."

"I always knew you were a worthless bastard." Silas jammed the muzzle of his gun against Horne's head. "Shall I pull the trigger?"

"Now wait just a minute!" Horne cried. He glanced at Jericho imploringly. "That's not how it happened—"

Willow looked ready to punch Horne in the face. "Shut up for once!"

Jericho held up his hand. "How did you escape?"

"The rats were chasing me, biting at my ankles, swarming up my shins." She shot Willow a grateful look. "My thick boots protected me. But those suckers' teeth are sharp. They half-chewed through them in a matter of seconds."

Everyone's gaze drifted to Celeste's torn and tattered boots, the leather gouged with dozens of tiny bites. Gabriel's stomach dropped, though he'd already seen them. They were more than half-chewed through. Celeste was lucky. Very, very lucky.

"I was bleeding everywhere, but I hardly felt it. Not then. I climbed on the counter and stabbed a few of the hairy bastards with a kitchen knife. There was a tall, heavy-duty metal shelf next to the fridge. I noticed the ceiling had drop-tiles, so I climbed up the shelf, pushed aside one of the tiles, and climbed into the ceiling. I huddled there all night, just trying not to faint. All I could think about was that I couldn't die after what Horne did to me. I refused."

Her eyes glittered in the dim light, her teeth bared. "Sometime during the night, a pack of dogs came sniffing around the dumpsters. The back door was open and the rats, they—they attacked the dogs, swarming over them like...it was awful. The dogs could've gotten away if they'd just run, but they stayed to fight...after that, the rats scurried off to find more interesting prey, I guess. I didn't know what to do. I was afraid to come down and brave it outside, hobbling on a wounded, bleeding leg.

"I wouldn't make it. I knew that. But I wasn't going to just die there, either. I'd just worked myself up to making an attempt anyway, rats and Pyros be damned. Then I heard a noise. I thought it was one of the crazy assholes who'd attacked us." She glanced at Gabriel in chagrin.

Gabriel grimaced at the memory. "She dropped out of the ceiling, shrieking like some kamikaze warrior. She about eviscerated me with her knife."

Horne had told as much of the truth as possible, as all skilled liars do. Gabriel had searched the city for the pizza place Horne had described, careful to stay in the shadows, to travel from building to building where he could to avoid leaving tracks, switching and doubling back on himself when he had to go outside, doing whatever he could to move silently and invisibly.

He'd observed two more groups of Pyros piling and burning bodies and tagging buildings with that ominous X encased in a circle. Some buildings they left alone other than the graffiti, others they set ablaze. They rode in armored trucks through narrow paths they'd made in the side streets, shouting and laughing, every one of them carrying high-powered pulse guns.

He'd stayed as far away from them as he could. He'd taken out dozens of rats, but no hordes. In small numbers, he made short work of them with the pulse rod. He'd fended off three stray dogs, two infected, one not.

The uninfected stray was starving, its ribs showing through its matted brown fur. Gabriel opened several tins of prefab beef and scattered the meat on the snowy ground. The dog pounced on the food, devouring it within seconds.

He'd left that one alive, feeling a strange affinity with this fellow creature struggling to survive out here in the savage city, alone and hunted by enemies, but not defeated.

He'd found the carcasses of four more dogs by the dumpster in the alley as dusk fell, a bone-chilling cold descending with it. His breath steamed from the edges of his face mask. Blood was on the ground, blood in splatters and streaks and hundreds of tiny claw-prints.

He'd moved into the restaurant's heavily shadowed industrial kitchen, dread seizing his gut, his jaw clenched, gripping the pulse rod in his fist.

He was so startled when Celeste pounced on him, dropping from the ceiling like some crazed, demon-creature of the night, he'd nearly killed her. He left that part out of the story.

She was trembling, terrified, and half out of her mind, but she'd been willing to fight to keep herself alive. Gabriel found himself revising his opinion of her during the hours they'd stumbled through the city in the darkness, trudging through the snow, shaking from the cold and pain, desperate to stay hidden from the deadly things hunting them.

"You're both lucky to be alive," Jericho said.

"Celeste survived, no thanks to Horne," Gabriel growled, his fury returning in full force. "The only question now is what to do with him."

Willow fisted her hands on her hips. "Didn't he want Silas banished, turned out into the freezing cold to fend for himself?"

"It was an accident, I assure you," Horne squeaked. His face was pale as bone, his expression stricken. "If you will just—"

"Shut the hell up!" Gabriel lost his temper. He strode forward and seized Horne by his scrawny neck, lifting him clear off the floor. Horne flailed, punching at him desperately. The whites of his eyes glimmered in the shadows.

Gabriel didn't even feel the blows. Righteous anger pulsed through him. "You should die for this!"

"Gabriel!" Micah shouted. He jerked at his arms, pulling him back.

Something moved out of the corner of his eye. A streak of light in the darkness outside.

Glass shattered. Something exploded. Smoke filled the air.

Gabriel spun, dropping Horne like a sack of potatoes. He yanked out his gun, searching frantically for the threat.

But it was too late.

The first bullet whizzed by his ear. The second found its mark.

Gabriel watched in horror as Finn lurched. His huge body fell in jerky slow motion, tumbling to the floor with a crash.

21

WILLOW

Willow couldn't see a thing. She could barely breathe. Her heart beat a frantic rhythm against her ribcage. Her wrists burned from the electric shackles roughly binding her hands. The fabric of the black hood covering her face sucked against her nostrils and opened mouth with every gasping breath.

She stumbled awkwardly, prodded forward like an animal with something sharp against her back. She didn't know where she was or where she was going. She had only a dim awareness of open space, then claustrophobia as she was crammed into a cramped space. The sensation of movement jolted through her, her body jostling against the others. They were in the back of some kind of van or truck.

Her attempts at whispered communication were cut short after a few sharp blows against her shoulders. Based on the moans she heard, the others received the same treatment.

Someone's shoulder bumped against hers. On her other side, she felt knees, someone's thigh pressed against her own. But she didn't know who it was. Benjie whimpered, but she couldn't go to him, couldn't comfort him or tell him to be strong.

She could barely comfort herself. Where was Finn? Was he with them? Was he alive? Was he okay? The smoke had obscured their vision, something like tear gas burning their eyes and lungs, incapacitating them. Seconds after Finn crashed to the floor like a felled tree, a dozen armed men had swarmed them, binding their wrists and shoving hoods over their faces.

The Pyros must have tracked Gabriel and Celeste through the snow. Everyone had been so focused on Celeste, they'd let their guard down, noticing nothing as the Pyros closed in like hyenas to a kill.

"This is all a terrible misunderstanding!" Horne shouted. "You can't do this to me—"

"Shut the hell up," a deep voice snarled.

She was jerked out of the vehicle. She staggered over uneven ground as someone pushed and shoved her through a large, echoing space. She stumbled up several sets of stairs. She fell once, bruising her knees and nearly pitching face-first to the floor, but she managed to regain her balance.

Panic galloped through her. Fear and dread clawed up her throat, but also a low, buzzing anger. They'd come too far to die like this, captured and killed by common street thugs. She yanked against her shackles. The electric cuffs sent a painful shock shooting up her arms.

"On your knees!" Someone shouted, shoving her down.

The black hood was lifted from her face.

She blinked rapidly, sucking in deep breaths. Everything snapped into focus.

She craned her neck, searching frantically for Benjie and Finn. They were all kneeling in a line. Everyone was there. Micah on one side of her, Benjie next to him. Amelia knelt stiffly on Willow's other side. Then Jericho, then Finn.

His huge shoulders were slumped, his brown skin ashen. Over his right chest and arm, blood stained his shirt. How badly was he hurt? She couldn't tell. But he was upright. His eyes were open. He was alive. She could have cried in relief.

The others were battered and bruised—Benjie had a large yellowish lump on his forehead, making her want to punch someone's teeth out—but they were otherwise unhurt. For the time being.

Her gaze swept the room, or rather, the theater. They were kneeling on a large stage in an enormous auditorium. There had to be close to five thousand seats ringing the stage on several levels.

The auditorium was magnificent, a sumptuous re-imagining of a Middle Eastern mosque blended with an ancient castle. She craned her neck to stare up at the soaring turreted ceiling, painted a stunning cobalt blue and shimmering with thousands of twinkling holo stars. Sweeping archways were ornamented with ornate, gold leaf carvings. Elaborate lanterns like elongated globes hung from the ceiling, spilling circles of soft, golden light.

She blinked against the glare of a bank of spotlight directed onto the stage. The Pyros had electricity. They weren't afraid to use it, didn't care who might see it. And why would they? They ruled the city. Who did they have to fear?

A large, furred shape loomed out of the corner of her vision. She gasped, startled.

A lion leapt from the orchestra pit and paced the perimeter of the stage. He was enormous, with a tawny mane and amber eyes that gazed at her from a great, regal head. A second lion lay beside one of the guards, long tail twitching.

They were mods. It was in their eyes—they watched her blankly, with little interest and zero hunger. Yet they both wore shock collars around their shaggy necks. A mod shouldn't need a shock collar.

But she didn't have time to worry about modded lions. Someone cleared his throat.

A half-dozen people stood in front of her. They were dressed in tactical gear and armed to the teeth with guns and knives. They all had the flaming skull tattoos on their necks. Four more guards watched them from a metal catwalk high above the stage.

"Well, well, well. Look what we have here." The familiar lilting, sing-song voice sent a shiver of dread through every cell in her body. Sykes, the man with the black trench coat, stood glaring at them, his arms crossed, his right hand wrapped in bandages, a wicked-looking pulse gun gripped in his left. "We caught the little piggies after all. Every. Single. One."

"That's enough, Sykes." Another man stepped forward, flanked by two enforcers. He was as tall as Finn but scarily gaunt, his cheeks hollowed like a skull, his lips thin and bloodless, his black eyes dark wells that sucked in all the available light.

"My name is Tobias Voya Moruga." He turned his sharp gaze on them, eyes darting from face to face. His body hummed with some invisible current, his feet constantly shuffling, his hands flexing and unflexing.

He held a silver lighter in his long, thin fingers. As he walked the line of hostages, he flicked it on and off, on and off. "Which one of you assholes killed my wounded, defenseless son?"

Willow sucked in her breath. Fear plunged into her belly like an icepick. For half a second, she'd allowed herself to believe that this was just a mistake, a misunderstanding, that they'd still be able to walk away from this. But somehow these people knew who they were, what they'd done.

"Oh, hell," she whispered.

One of Moruga's enforcers thrust the butt of her gun beneath Willow's chin and forced her head up. "You have something to say?"

The Pyro was young, maybe only a few years older than Willow. She was Indian, with rich, velvet-brown skin. Her hair was shaved to her skull on either side, with a knot of purple braids on top that tumbled thick and ropy down her back.

She was slim but muscular and dressed in black, tight-fitting clothing, a knife strapped to her thigh and another longer knife sheath at her hip, along with a gun holster. She clenched a cigar between her teeth. A tendril of sweet-smelling white smoke drifted toward the cathedral ceiling. "Cat got your tongue, is that it?"

"No," Willow said, willing the tremble out of her voice. She wouldn't give these people anything. She wouldn't give them the satisfaction of her fear.

"So that's how it's going to be." Moruga tutted. He bounced on his heels, grinning fiendishly. "How unfortunate. How can we better encourage your cooperation?"

"Let me gut one," Sykes snapped. "That should get them talking."

Moruga held up a hand. "Not quite yet. Any ideas, Cleo?"

The girl smiled at Willow, the skin on the left side of her face crinkling. She turned her head, fully revealing the burn that blossomed from below her left eye across her cheek and jawline to the side of her neck—a shiny, jumbled topography of scar tissue.

Willow bit back a gasp.

Cleo's smile widened. Her teeth looked like they were filed into fangs. But, no, that was just her terrified, overactive imagination. "See something interesting?"

She wanted to curse at her, claw her eyes out, and then strangle her for what they'd done to Finn, for the terror that raced up her spine and iced her insides. She licked her lips and glanced at Micah, who knelt next to her. He gave the smallest shake of his head. *Don't antagonize them,* his look warned. *Be smart.*

She gritted her teeth. He was right. They had to be smart. She had to be smart and in control. For Benjie. For Finn. For all of them. "No, nothing. I'm sorry. Please just let us go. We're good people. We won't hurt anyone."

Cleo's eyes glinted fiercely. "Oh, is this the part where you think because I'm a girl that there's some tiny little soft spot deep inside me that maybe you can reach, some pearl of empathy or pinprick of compassion?"

She had no idea how to answer. There were traps and tripwires tangled everywhere in that question. "Uh. Well, I—"

"Do you think that I should show you mercy, is that it? Girl to girl?"

Willow's gaze darted frantically from Cleo to Sykes to Moruga, who fidgeted with the lighter as he watched, a sinister smile curving his lips. Like Cleo was putting on a show for his pleasure, and he was enjoying every second of it.

It was all scripted. They didn't give a steaming bucketload of crap what she said, but she spoke the words anyway, a desperate futility settling over her. "Yes...we would be very grateful."

Cleo cocked her brows, her features approximating a look of concerned sympathy. One arched higher than the other due to the burn scar. But it was her empty eyes that gave her away.

"We just want safe passage through the city," Willow said.

She took a puff of her cigar and blew it out slowly, straight into Willow's face. "Really? Why?"

Willow coughed and leaned back, turning her face to the side. "We aren't looking for trouble."

"You may not have been looking, but you found plenty."

"We don't have all night," Sykes said in his disturbingly musical voice. He massaged his bandaged hand and stared daggers at Gabriel. "We're wasting time talking when we could be killing."

Cleo's expression turned cold, savage. Without warning, she slammed the butt of the gun into Willow's stomach.

Spasms of pain shot through her body. Her eyes streamed. Blinding whiteness burst inside her head. Everything went blurry and dim, like she was underwater.

"Don't hurt her!" Finn cried.

Willow watched through blurry eyes as Cleo sauntered down the line. She stopped in front of Finn, raised the gun, and smashed it across the side of his head. He fell sideways with a groan.

Willow cried out. He was already wounded. How much more could he take? Acid burned her throat, roiled in her stomach. She fought not to puke all over the stage.

"I can do this all day," Cleo said. "Who's next?"

Willow managed to raise her head, fighting down the pain and dizziness. If psycho girl was gonna go after someone, let it be her. Not Finn. Not Benjie. "Leave us alone, you crazy bitch."

Cleo tapped ash from her cigar as she strode across the stage back to Willow. She bent close, only inches from Willow's face. "This one has a smart mouth. You need to know When. To. Stop. Talking."

She seized a hunk of Willow's hair with one hand and slowly brought the burning cigar end to within an inch of her right eye. Her already blurred vision filled with a burning circle of ash and smoke. She tried to jerk her head back, but Cleo's grip was like iron.

"You want to know what it feels like to burn?" Cleo hissed. "Curiosity killed the cat. What's it gonna do to you?"

"Don't hurt her, please," Benjie whimpered.

"You don't have to do this!" Panic filled Micah's voice.

"I'm sure we can have a civilized discussion—" Horne started.

"Shut up!" Moruga said. "I'm enjoying this."

Heat from the cigar singed her eyeball, her eyelashes. Panic fluttered in her chest. She wanted nothing more than to close her eyes, to block it all out, but she couldn't. She wouldn't. She wouldn't let Benjie see her cower. "Go to hell," she spat.

Moruga smiled in mild amusement, as if he were humoring a small child. "Oh, I think we're already there, sweetheart."

A white-hot riot of anger, panic, and hatred exploded in her chest. So much for diplomacy. Willow reared back and spit in Cleo's face. "That's for hitting Finn."

Cleo gave a hard laugh. She wiped the spittle from her cheek with the back of her hand. "You're gonna regret that."

She traced the cigar down the side of Willow's cheek, so close she could feel the heat. Ash sprinkled her shoulder. She stiffened. The tension stretched unbearably. *Just do it already.*

Cleo yanked Willow's head to the right, exposing her throat, and thrust the lit end of the cigar against the side of her neck.

Pain seared her flesh. She bit her tongue to keep from crying out. She couldn't help it. A low moan escaped her lips. Blackness flickered at the edges of her vision. She refused to pass out.

Cleo released her head and stood up, taking a slow drag from the cigar.

Willow glared at her, hot traitorous tears streaming down her cheeks, her teeth clenched against the pain. It felt like Cleo had burned a hole through her skin, scorching through muscles, tendons, and veins, searing the very center of her.

"Undo these handcuffs and fight me," she growled. "Let's see how strong and brave you really are. Only a coward strikes people who can't defend themselves."

Cleo's eyes flashed, but she said nothing.

"Tobias," Sykes said in a low voice. His left arm hung loosely at his side, his gun tapping impatiently against his thigh. "I can take care of this. Let me—"

"Anyone else wish to speak before we continue?" Moruga said,

almost giddy. His gaunt body shivered like he was filled with some
internal tension, a spring about to be released.

On the other side of Micah, Horne straightened. His lip was
split, a yellowish bruise pooling beneath his left eye. "I wish
to speak."

"Ahh, you again," Moruga said, coming to stand in front of him,
his thin hands twitching at his sides.

Her thoughts came slow and groggy. The pain made everything
disconnected and confusing. What did he mean by *you again*?

"Release this man," Moruga ordered.

Cleo unshackled Horne's cuffs and jerked him to his feet. Horne
huffed and rubbed his wrists. "I have never been treated in so
undignified a manner in my life."

One of the lions yawned. Moruga flicked his lighter on and off,
on and off. His lip twitched. "My apologies. Once the hoods were
on, we didn't know who was who."

Dread and confusion roiled in Willow's gut, a sickening sensation that made her nearly gag. A fresh wave of dizziness washed
over her. What was happening? What was Horne doing?

"Is this all of them?" Moruga asked.

"Yes, of course." Horne bobbed his head, his blonde hair flopping
into his eyes. "It's just as I told you. I've kept my end of the bargain."

Silas let out a string of curses.

Willow jerked her head up. A blaze of anger burned the fog
away. "What did you do, you asshole?"

Horne's gaze flicked to hers then darted away. "You would do
the same in my shoes, I'm sure."

He pulled something out of his pocket and handed it to Moruga.
It glowed with a faint, pulsing blue light. A tracking beacon.

Her mind raced, putting all the pieces together. It was Horne
who led the Pyros to the Fieldwell's furniture store. And it was

Horne again who used the beacon to reveal their hideout in the office building.

Finn's gunshot wound was Horne's fault. Their capture was Horne's fault.

But how had he gotten the beacon in the first place? The realization struck her, lodging in her brain like an ice pick. "That night you were lost—after you left Celeste for dead. The Pyros found you. You betrayed us."

"I cut a deal." He gave a scornful sniff, lifting his chin. His eyes flashed with righteous indignation. "Every single one of you is willing to do whatever it takes to survive—you fight, you even kill. You have no right to judge me for doing the same thing."

"It's not even close to the same thing!" Willow shouted. Horne was a selfish, arrogant bastard. Everyone knew it. But even she hadn't thought he'd stoop this low. That someone she slept near, shared meals with, fought beside, and *protected* could hide such savagery beneath his smarmy veneer.

Silas swore. "I'll kill you! You're dead, do you hear me?"

"You'll never get away with this," Gabriel growled.

Horne's face tightened. He turned his back on them and waved his hand airily to Moruga. "Like I said, I've kept my end of the bargain. These are the people you want. They're the ones who murdered your son."

22

AMELIA

Amelia stared at Horne with a cold, crystallized fury. They should have known he was slippery and dangerous, the one who would betray them the second his skin was on the line.

There was something rotten inside him, some invisible poison. Over time it had eaten its way through to the outside, spreading into every part of him. She should have seen it. She could have stopped this from happening.

"Tell me everything." Moruga tapped his lighter against his chin, bouncing on his heels and grinning fiendishly. He was enjoying this. It was all a game to him. An act. She blinked against the hot glare of the stage lights.

Horne pointed at Jericho. "He has a private security, special ops background." He moved down the line, bypassing Finn, Benjie, Celeste.

Amelia gritted her teeth when he hesitated before Silas, expecting Horne to name her brother the killer. But he didn't. Instead, he stopped in front of Gabriel. "This one is a New Patriot."

Moruga raised his thin eyebrows. "A New Patriot?"

"A terrorist. An enemy of the state. A card-carrying member of the revolutionary group that released the bioweapon—"

"Yes, I'm aware," Moruga said impatiently.

Sykes pointed his gun at Gabriel, his expression seething. "You people destroyed the world."

"I did no such thing," Gabriel said between clenched teeth, the muscle in his jaw bunching.

"We held him captive as a prisoner," Horne said, "until Jericho got soft and released him."

"Shut up, you filthy traitor!" Silas shouted.

"Shhh," Amelia hissed. She kept her gaze on Moruga, dread filling every cell of her body.

Moruga seemed bored. His sharp gaze swept the auditorium, his fingers twitching. He was filled with a tight, bristling energy, a darkness begging to be let out. His men feared him. They stiffened when he neared them, their eyes darting to the floor. Everyone but Cleo.

She was different. There was a proud jut of her jaw, a ferocity in her eyes. The damaged skin on the right side of her face didn't make her look ugly. It made her look dangerous. When she looked at Moruga, she gazed at him straight in his ghoulish face, without fear or hesitation.

She'd enjoyed burning Willow, fed off her terror. She enjoyed meting out pain, just like Moruga. They both liked to burn, to destroy. They reminded Amelia of her father. He, too, had fed on fear.

Moruga sighed, his gaze flickering out over the seats. The lavish trappings of the theater were garish, the stained glass windows, ornately carved box seats, and opulent tapestries grotesque in the face of the horror playing out on the stage. Moruga knew it. That was part of the pleasure, part of the game for him. "Anything else?"

"You'll be interested in Amelia Black," Horne continued hurriedly, trying to regain Moruga's attention. "She was infected, but she survived. She has the cure in her blood. She'll be very valuable to the Sanctuary."

Moruga squatted in front of her. He cocked his head, examining her like a specimen with those black, depthless eyes. Eyes like eels from the underwater caverns of the deepest, darkest sea. Predatory eyes. Like Kane's. "Is that so?"

Gut-wrenching terror clamped down on her, sucking out her breath, her thoughts, everything but the fear. She felt herself tipping into the blackness, into the void. She clawed her way back, her mind focusing on a single word. *No.*

She lifted her chin in defiance. She was afraid, she couldn't help that, but she wouldn't cower for him. She wouldn't let him—or anyone—break her.

After a moment, Moruga seemed to lose interest in her. He unfolded his long, thin limbs like some grotesque praying mantis and stood, turning away from her.

"You could sell her for a high price," Horne said, his voice high-pitched, almost squeaking. "I have experience negotiating as the CEO of—"

"Shut up," Sykes snapped, cutting him off. "It's time to get down to business."

In an instant, the devilish smile dropped from Moruga's face. Now he just looked like a devil. "Do you know what we do here?"

"You're burning Atlanta," Celeste said in a quivering voice.

"We're burning the *infection* out of Atlanta. It's difficult work. Do you know how many millions of people died here? In their cars, in their homes, in their places of work and pleasure houses? Who's going to get rid of those bodies? Who's going to make this great city livable again?" He gestured behind him at the silent guards. "We are.

If the rest of the world wants to label us Pyros, so be it. A little fear never hurt anyone."

Sykes laughed. The disconcertingly melodious sound echoed in the cavernous theater. He kept stroking his bandaged hand and staring murderously at Gabriel and Jericho, his pale eyes cold and lethal.

"Of course, certain members among us do enjoy fire." Moruga flicked his lighter on, stared for a moment at the fire. Twin flames reflected in his black eyes. "Fire is so...cleansing. Only fire can rid the world of the infection. If half the world must burn with it, then so be it."

"You killed people," Amelia said.

His eyes flashed dangerously. "Only those who deserved it. The gangs, the infected, the refuse. We're clearing the way by any means necessary."

"Clearing the way for what?"

He made a grand, sweeping gesture with both hands, as if he were performing for a full audience. "For society to rebuild itself. The Sanctuary has plans for all of this." He spun and scowled at the guard standing next to a now sleeping lion. "Wake him up!"

The guard was a Chinese guy in his late twenties, slim but wiry, with a sharply angled face. Below the flaming skull on his neck, a shimmering green snake tattoo wound from his collarbone, slithered around his Adam's apple, and disappeared into his hairline.

He slipped his right hand into his pocket and jerked the lion's silver chain with his other hand. The lion leapt to its feet, shook its mane, and roared.

The sound blasted Amelia's eardrums. She felt the vibration all the way through her bones. A strangled cry escaped her lips. She clenched her teeth.

It was just a mod. Mods weren't violent. They were genetically engineered to be docile and tame. But this lion wasn't tame. It looked like it could swallow her whole.

The lion growled, revealing long, sharp teeth. It lunged at Amelia.

Her heart shuddered inside her chest. Her mind shouted at her to run, but she couldn't move. Every instinct honed over thousands of years of human survival screamed that she was the prey, that a predator was seconds from mauling her to death in the most horrific, gruesome way imaginable.

The guard yanked the lion's thin, silver chain. The beast jerked to a stop less than five feet from Amelia's trembling form. It roared again, shook its magnificent mane, and settled back on its haunches with a low growl.

Amelia inhaled sharply, her chest heaving. There wasn't enough oxygen in the auditorium, in the entire theater, in the world. That thing had nearly killed her. A single, lazy swipe of its clawed paw would have done the job well enough. Another shudder ripped through her body.

"Impressive, isn't he?" Moruga's eyes darkened. A pained expression crossed his face. For the first time, he went completely still. "My son named him Apollo. My son, Hector. He was thirteen. Did you know that? I sent him with Harrison, my most trusted soldier, to tag his first buildings. He never returned. Imagine my heartbreak. Imagine the grief I feel." His jaw worked, his tongue sliding over his dry lips. "Imagine my *rage*."

She bit her tongue, the taste of fear sharp and metallic as blood. This man wouldn't hesitate to kill Silas. He wouldn't hesitate to kill any of them. She had to do something, had to at least try. "It was an accident."

Moruga whirled on her. "There are no accidents. Not when bullets are involved."

She swallowed. "It was a terrible mistake. Please—"

"Enough," Cleo said. "You're boring me. Worse, you're boring him."

Moruga held out his hand, his skeletal fingers splayed. Cleo placed her gun in his palm and winked at Amelia.

Amelia's heart punched into her throat. Tension crackled the air. No one dared to move. No one dared to speak.

Moruga considered the gun, turning it over in his hands. He flicked the safety on, then off, just like the lighter. His eyes burned like twin, smoldering coals. "There's just one more thing I need to know. One pertinent little detail. Who actually pulled the trigger? Which one of you is the killer?"

Before anyone could speak, Jericho raised his head. His shoulders were straight, his back stiff. His dark eyes blazed bold and fearless. "I did. I killed your son."

"No!" Silas shouted.

Amelia had no time to react, to think, to protest.

Moruga's gaunt, hollowed-out face was like a living skull. "Thank you for your honesty."

Tobias Voya Moruga shot Jericho in the head.

23

MICAH

J ericho toppled forward. His body struck the floor with a
horrific thud.

Micah stared, helpless and horrified.

Amelia screamed.

"No!" A black hole tunneled through the center of him. Jericho
couldn't be dead. This wasn't how it was supposed to happen. In a
second. In a heartbeat. Before he'd even registered what was
happening, it was already done.

Jericho's face was turned toward Micah. A single bead of blood
trickled down his forehead. His eyes were open, unseeing. His
mouth was opened in a startled wet O.

Jericho. The man who'd rescued him on the *Grand Voyager*. The
man whose strength and skills and quick thinking had saved them
all. He was tough and grim, hard and unrelenting. He was also fair
and selfless, risking himself again and again to protect the group.
Jericho was the only reason they were still alive.

Now he was dead.

Something broke open inside Micah. Grief crested over him in waves. He could barely hold it back. He yanked against the electric cuffs, desperate to get free, to *do* something, even though it was already too late. A painful zap of electricity shot up his arms. The cuffs didn't give a millimeter.

"We have our own justice here," Moruga said. "For your parts in my son's murder, I sentence you all to die."

Micah barely heard him over the roaring in his ears.

Jericho was dead. Soon, they would be, too. He was helpless. He bit the inside of his cheeks so hard that coppery blood flooded his mouth.

Silas was swearing, Finn and Celeste begging for their lives, Benjie whimpering. Beside him, Amelia wept quietly, silent tears streaming down her cheeks.

Micah was the one who believed, who trusted in faith and God and the goodness of others. But in this moment, his faith abandoned him. He prayed, his lips moving feverishly, but his prayers struck the opulent, cobalt blue ceiling. They fell back, unable to penetrate past the thousands of twinkling holo stars, as trapped in this place as they were.

Sykes pressed the muzzle of his gun against Gabriel's forehead. Gabriel stiffened, unflinching. "We can take care of this right now."

Micah stopped breathing.

"Do not sully my theater," Moruga barked, whirling on Sykes. "Take them out back. Line them up and shoot them."

"Happy to," Sykes said, his pale eyes glittering with malice. "These pigs deserve a good slaughter."

Cleo puffed a circle of white smoke. "Tobias, wait."

He turned toward her, attentive to her every word. His lips peeled back from his teeth in a ghoulish smile. Micah stared at him, dread scrabbling up his spine. They were already facing certain death, but warning signals exploded in his brain like fireworks.

Things were about to get worse.

"These people murdered Hector," Cleo said silkily. "Not just anyone. Your son." She placed her hand on his arm and lowered her voice. Micah was close enough to hear every word. "What does the king of the Pyros, the prince of fire do to his enemies?"

Moruga traced the burn on her face, his fingers trailing from her lumpy forehead to her scarred cheeks to the damaged tissue of her jaw. His black eyes flashed with a fiendish delight. "You, my dear, are brilliant."

She gave an impassive shrug and tapped ash from her cigar. "The punishment must fit the crime."

"Gather the wood for a fire," Moruga commanded Sykes with a flick of his wrist. His whole body was taut, thrumming with that dark, deadly energy. "And get them out of my sight. Tomorrow, they burn."

The memory of blazing flames, scalding heat, and choking smoke seared his mind. This couldn't be happening. This couldn't be real.

Micah gagged. Vomit and spittle dripped off his chin.

"What about the girl?" Cleo asked darkly, pointing at Amelia.

Moruga rubbed his jaw with his skeletal hand. "If what they say about her is true ... we'll keep her alive. But throw her in with the rest for now."

Horne smoothed his clothes and hair, regaining his composure. He cleared his throat loudly. "I'm happy to facilitate negotiations with the Sanctuary." His pleasant, jocular tone sounded grotesque in the same room as Jericho's crumpled body, the friends he'd just betrayed sentenced to burn at the stake.

"And him?" Cleo's lips curled in open disdain as she hooked her thumb at Horne.

Moruga took out a crisp white handkerchief, polished the gun that had killed Jericho, and handed it back to Cleo. His attention roved restlessly over the auditorium, not even pausing on Horne as he determined the man's fate. "I don't care."

He bounced on his heels, that dangerous, jittery energy vibrating off him, and strode down the short staircase at the far right side of the stage. Sykes and another guard flanked him as he sauntered up the aisle past thousands of plush seats to the auditorium exit.

Cleo turned to the hostages. She flashed that lethal smile, like she wished she could kill them all herself, with her own bare hands. "Li Jun, please place this man in cuffs and throw him in with the others to await their fate."

Horne blanched. "We had a deal!"

The Chinese guard grabbed Horne's arms. Horne tried unsuccessfully to yank his hands free as the guard slapped electronic cuffs on him.

"Now, wait just a minute!" he cried in desperation. "I kept our end of the deal! I did everything you asked!"

The lion ambled up to Horne and sniffed hungrily at his stomach. It growled deep in its chest. Horne froze. A dark stain appeared over his crotch and leaked down his pant legs.

Maybe Micah should feel vindicated that at least Horne would get his due, but he didn't. He just felt sick. Sick with dread and fear and a bone-deep grief.

His mother always said God had a plan for everyone, a purpose for everything. Where was the purpose in this?

Cleo stroked the lion's head, that predatory smile twisting her lips. She blew white smoke into Horne's face. "What use do we have with a faithless traitor?" she asked sweetly. "If your friends can't trust you, why should we?"

"You can't do this!" Horne screamed.

Cleo ignored him. She signaled the guards, who dropped hoods over the hostages' heads. One of the guards shoved a hood roughly over Micah's face.

He was plunged into darkness. Strong hands grabbed him and hauled him to his feet.

"Please don't do this to us! You don't want to do this," he cried through the thick fabric, hating the helpless pleading in his voice but pleading anyway.

He felt a presence hovering in front of him and smelled the sickly sweet scent of cigar smoke. Cleo leaned in close. When she spoke, her breath stirred the hood against his ear. "Enjoy the last day of your life."

∽

"Let me kill him!" Silas snarled. "I'll rip out his guts with my bare hands!"

Micah seized his arm and held him back with all of his strength. Silas was lean but incredibly strong. His eyes were wild, his face contorted in savage rage.

Micah stood between Silas—between everyone—and Horne, who cowered in the corner, his hands clutching his head, weeping like the pathetic coward he was.

They were crammed into a single twenty-by-twenty room. The walls were white. The floor and ceiling were white. There was no furniture, no beds, no nothing. Just blinding whiteness everywhere.

A rectangle-shaped crack outlined a door on the far wall. A tiny, barely visible camera attached to the ceiling watched them silently. A drain in the opposite corner from the door served as a bathroom. There was no privacy. Micah was too numb and shell-shocked to care.

He had no idea where they were. They'd been led through cold and darkness and snow, bound and hooded, shuffling single file for probably five minutes, prodded with guns and tasers until they were

168

forced up several sets of stairs, through a long, echoing corridor, and into this room.

Even if they knew where they were, it wouldn't matter. There was no escape. No way out. And no one to come and rescue them.

"Let me at him!" Silas cried. "Get off me!"

He threw a punch at Micah. In his frenzied state, his arm flailed aimlessly. Micah easily ducked the blow.

"Stop this, Silas." Amelia stood a few feet away. She was trembling, her arms wrapped around herself, her pale face streaked with tears. "Just stop!"

Micah glanced at Gabriel for help. But his brother looked ready to join in. He paced the narrow space like a caged tiger, his fists balled at his sides, his face dark with fury, his jaw muscles pulsing.

"Maybe you should just let Silas do it," Celeste said wearily. She leaned against the wall next to the door, her wounded leg stretched out in front of her. The bandage over her thigh was stained red. Her features were pinched, her face ashen, a heavy line between her brows. "What more does he have to do to deserve death?"

"Why the hell are you protecting him?" Willow asked.

"He does deserve it." If anyone deserved death, it was Horne. Jericho was dead because of him. They were all facing their own death because of his betrayal. He was a cringing, worthless coward. A murderer.

And yet. His gaze flickered to Benjie, who curled next to Finn, staring at them with stunned, unblinking eyes. Finn slumped against the wall, clutching his bloody shoulder, a stricken expression shadowing his face.

Benjie had witnessed enough violence today. They all had.

He bit the inside of his cheek. The sharp pain cleared his head. He forced himself to think, to calm down. He couldn't let them do something they would regret. *Be good. Be brave.*

There was self-defense. And there was revenge. The difference between the two was murder. "But not here," he said. "Not like this."

"Fine!" Willow growled in frustration, but she grabbed Silas's other arm and helped Micah shove him back against the wall. "Silas! That's enough!"

Silas blinked as if coming out of a fugue. He stared at Willow, stunned to stillness.

"Listen to Micah," she said more softly. "Please."

The hardness in his face collapsed. "They killed him," he whispered. Suddenly he looked much younger than he was, young and vulnerable and heart-broken. "They killed Jericho."

"I know," Willow said, her own face contorting. She shook her head, her hair falling away from her neck to reveal the angry red welt of the cigar burn. "I know."

Micah's heart wrenched. Waves of helplessness crashed over him. What could he do? He couldn't do a thing to fix any of it. After everything they'd struggled and fought and suffered for, was it really going to end like this? With betrayal and hatred and death?

Silas jerked from their grasp. He spun with a vicious growl and punched the wall. He slammed his fists again and again, growling and grunting and hissing in pain. His knuckles split. Blood spattered everywhere.

"Silas! Stop!" Micah went to grab him again.

Willow seized his arm. "He needs to do this," she said tightly.

"But—"

"Let him do it," Amelia said, though she winced with every impact Silas's fists made against the wall.

Finally, Micah nodded. He didn't understand it, but Amelia and Willow seemed to. They both knew Silas better than he did. That was enough for him.

He backed away from Silas, who pummeled the wall like he

could destroy it, like he could obliterate his grief and fear and panic if he could only punch hard enough.

In the far corner, Tyler Horne straightened. He rubbed the wetness from his face and smoothed his hair, raking it back into place. He cleared his throat. "I appreciate this, Micah. I'm sure once I get this misunderstanding straightened out, I'll speak to Tobias on your behalf and—"

"Shut up!" Willow screamed, whirling on him. "Shut up! Shut up!"

"I didn't do it for you." Micah's voice shook. "You betrayed us."

"It wasn't personal," Horne whined.

"Jericho is dead because of you," Amelia said. "We're going to die because of *you*."

Horne narrowed his eyes, suddenly indignant. "None of this would be happening if you'd banished Silas like I told you to. But none of you listened to me. You never do."

"Enough!" Gabriel roared. He was shaking, his jaw tight, his dark eyes blazing. He strode past Micah, seized Horne, and lifted him off his feet.

Horne dangled, kicking ineffectively at Gabriel's shins, his hands scrabbling desperately at Gabriel's bulging arms. "Help me!"

"Gabriel—" Micah warned.

"I've got this." Gabriel glanced back at him, their eyes meeting. "Trust me."

He was angry, but his rage was restrained. He was controlled. And he was waiting for Micah's permission. He wanted Micah's approval. He wouldn't kill Horne; Micah could see it in his eyes.

Micah wasn't a killer, but he wasn't a saint, either. His own righteous anger burned bright and hard in his chest. A little just punishment wouldn't be the worst thing. Slowly, he nodded.

Gabriel dropped Horne. He sagged against the wall, batting ineffectively at his wrinkled jacket, the collar torn, unchastened and irate. "You savage monster, I always knew it was a mistake to free you—"

Gabriel punched him in the face, smashing in his nose with his fist. It was a single blow. But it was enough.

Horne's head snapped back against the wall. His eyes rolled back in his head. He crumpled to the floor without a sound, unconscious. Blood streamed from his crooked nose and leaked into his lax, half-opened mouth.

Gabriel turned away in disgust, rubbing his bruised knuckles.

"Finally," Celeste muttered.

"That asshole deserves so much worse," Willow said.

"He does," Micah said, his resolve coming back to him. "And he'll get it. But not from us. We're not murderers. And we're not going to let scum like him turn us into something we're not."

"You're right," Gabriel said, surprising him.

Even Willow nodded. "He's lucky we're not like him, the slimy—"

"Lo Lo," Benjie said, his voice quavering. "What's wrong with Mister Finn?"

Willow rushed to Finn and Benjie. She knelt and hugged her brother. She pressed her forehead against his for a long moment. Then she turned to Finn. "How badly is he hurt?"

"*He* can hear you, you know," Finn mumbled. "*He* is right here."

"Finn, you big oaf," Willow said. "How badly are you hurt?"

"Never...better."

She rolled her eyes. "Why did I even ask?"

Micah crouched next to them with a twinge of guilt. They should have attended to Finn right away, but Silas's attack on Horne had demanded their immediate attention. "Let's check you out."

Together, he and Willow carefully lifted Finn's jacket, sweater, and T-shirt. Finn sucked in his breath. His skin was ashen. "There are easier ways to get me naked, you know."

"Hush," Willow muttered, her face flushing.

"Next time…" Finn said shakily, still managing to wink, "just ask me."

"Stop moving," Micah said.

The bullet had bitten into Finn's upper shoulder. The wound was a small, puckered hole. Blood leaked down his arm, but less than he expected.

His own back and shoulder suddenly ached with phantom pain. The memory pulsed through him: the hoverboard park in the ritzy neighborhood, the cruel smirk of the bully who'd shoved him from the top of a concrete ramp, the agonizing pain as his right shoulder blade was shredded to the bone. He'd been twelve. Gabriel had cradled him in his arms, carrying him the twenty-eight blocks home.

He glanced at Gabriel, who still paced, grimacing and rubbing his bruised knuckles. Gabriel had protected him back then. He was still protecting them now.

"Ow!" Finn cringed beneath his hands, bringing him back to the here and now. Micah pulled Finn gently forward and checked his back. "There's no exit wound. The bullet's still inside you. But maybe that's a good thing, for now. There's not a lot of blood. It missed major arteries."

Finn groaned. "Are you a doctor, then?"

"Yes, he is," Willow said. "Now shut up."

Amelia hovered over his shoulder. Her face was pale as the pristine white walls surrounding them. "Should we try to get the bullet out?"

"We'd only do more damage." Micah tore strips from the cleanest sections of Finn's discarded shirt and handed them to Willow. "We need to keep pressure on it. We're going to try to wrap it, okay? We need to keep pressure on it. This might hurt."

"Please not Willow," Finn mumbled. "She's not gentle like a... teddy bear...or a cuddly blanket."

Micah rocked back on his heels, frowning in concern. "He's going into shock."

"Nah, he always talks like that." Willow wound the cloth around Finn's shoulder. "Stop acting like a baby, you big overgrown troll."

"Thank you."

Willow grunted as she gently pulled down Finn's shirt. "That wasn't a compliment."

"Would it offend you...if I take it as one?"

"You should save your energy and rest," Micah cut in. "You'll need it later." He took off his own jacket and draped it over Finn's chest. They needed to keep him warm. What Finn really needed was antibiotics, a hospital, and a robotic surgeon, but there was nothing Micah could do about that.

Silas stopped punching the wall. He turned and faced them, his hands hanging limply at his sides. Blood dripped from his fingertips and splattered on the white floor. "He's going to die anyway. We're all going to die, anyway."

Willow glared at him. "Not helpful!"

Benjie started to cry. "Is that true, Mister Micah?"

"No," Micah lied. "Finn's going to be fine."

"It's the darkest...before dawn, right, Sir Benjie?" Finn managed to smile at Benjie, even as he gritted his teeth against the pain. "We're knights...trapped in the dungeon of the dragon's lair. It looks hopeless...but we'll find a way out...if we're clever and brave."

"Okay," Benjie said, his face brightening a little.

Wincing, Finn leaned gingerly against the wall. He tilted his head back and closed his eyes, his face going slack. "Besides...we've been in worse situations."

"Really? When?" Willow muttered.

"I'll have to...get back to you on that."

Some part of Micah wanted to laugh, crazily, defiantly, madly. Another part of him longed to break down and sob. He thought of Virginia Woolf's words: *The beauty of the world...has two edges, one of laughter, one of anguish, cutting the heart asunder.* It was true. He felt like he was split down the center of himself. This life was harsh and tragic, but it was also beautiful, and he loved it. In spite of everything, he loved it.

He didn't want to die. He didn't want any of them to die. But even if they did, even if these dark, painful hours were the last he spent on this earth, it would be worth it. They made it worth it—his friends, these people he cared about, loved.

Gabriel placed his hand on Micah's shoulder. It was the first time they'd touched since before the *Grand Voyager*.

Micah didn't flinch or push him away. He didn't know how he should or shouldn't feel. His whole body was a tornado of fear and grief, panic and dread. But this was his brother. This was Gabriel.

"I'm right here," Gabriel said simply.

Tears stung his eyes. "I know."

"Don't give up on us yet, brother."

He felt hollowed out. Was this it? Was this the end for all of them?

But it wasn't in him to give up. It wasn't in him not to believe, not to love, not to hope. "I won't."

24

AMELIA

Hours passed. It felt like days. Amelia did not sleep. She couldn't. She couldn't stop shivering. She wrapped her arms around herself to keep warm, to keep still, to keep her brain from shattering into a thousand pieces.

The fluorescent bulbs integrated into the ceiling never turned off. The glaring light burned into her eyes. Hour by hour, the others finally fell into exhausted, restless sleep. All except for Amelia, Gabriel, and Silas.

She tugged her charm bracelet out of her shirt and closed her fingers around its familiar shape. "Hey," she said softly. "Are you awake?"

Silas grunted. He had finally stopped punching the wall, settling down enough to collapse beside Amelia. His tense body radiated grief, pain, and rage. His hands were bruised and bloodied, the flesh over his knuckles raw and shredded. Blood smeared his cheek.

He stared blankly at nothing, his hands lying limp on his lap. She didn't know how to reach him. He felt like a stranger.

"Can you talk?"

"You're talking now."

"I'm sorry, Silas. I'm sorry for Jericho. I know how much he meant to you." Jericho was dead. There was no turning back time to do something differently, to somehow alter fate. He'd been a fixture in her life for six years. She'd always felt safe with him.

But it was Silas who grieved for him most deeply. She knew that. Jericho had never been rude or dismissive; he'd always been respectful, had always protected her. But he'd never taken an interest in her like he did with Silas, taking her brother under his wing and teaching him everything he knew about guns and combat and war. Jericho had loved Silas in a way that their real father never had.

"What are you sorry for? You didn't kill him."

"It's what people say, Silas. I'm trying…I'm trying to help you."

"Well, you can stop trying. I don't need your help."

She loved him dearly, but he was so hard, always bristling with contempt and rage. Most of the time, she just let him be. But now the gulf between them stretched vast as a canyon. "Why are you fighting me so hard?"

"Don't you get it?" His voice was raw and gritty, like it was being dragged from somewhere deep inside him. "I'm the reason he's dead. I may as well have pulled the trigger myself."

She felt like a hand had reached inside her chest and ripped her heart out. "Oh, Silas—"

"I know what I did," he snarled. "I know this is all because of me, that we're going to die—that you're going to die—because of me."

She longed to touch his face, to pull him into her arms and comfort him, to take his pain and grief and self-loathing away. But he would never let her. "I don't blame you for this, Silas. You made a decision in the heat of the moment. I didn't agree with it, but you didn't intend to shoot an unarmed kid."

Silas made a sound like a wounded animal.

"You didn't kill in cold blood. These people did. These people are to blame for this."

He didn't answer. She didn't expect him to. He flexed and unflexed his fists in his lap. His hands were trembling.

She pressed the violin into her palm until it indented the skin. She couldn't leave him like this, suffering like this. "You aren't alone. There are people who care about you, who love you. I love you."

He said nothing.

"Jericho loved you, too."

Her words were met with silence.

She tried to think of something to say, to keep him talking. He couldn't keep everything bottled up inside. It would destroy him. She had to find a way to reach him. "I'm glad you had Jericho. I know Father wasn't exactly loving. Especially to you."

Silas scrubbed his face with the back of his hand, leaving a fresh streak of blood across his cheek and the bridge of his nose. "He was a world-class asshole."

That old, familiar pain burrowed inside her. If she had to lose memories, why couldn't she lose those? All those years of never measuring up, always striving for perfection and failing. The deep, soul-wrenching shame she'd felt every time Declan Black stared through her with disdain in his eyes.

Their father had trapped them both in a gilded cage of shame, anger, and fear. It didn't matter how hard they tried or how perfect they were, it had never been enough. "I'm not sure if he ever loved us."

Silas's voice was filled with bitterness. "To hell with him."

Across the room, Finn groaned as he shifted position, his face sharp from pain. Willow and Finn slumped against the wall, Finn half-sideways, his head on Willow's shoulder, Benjie curled into a fetal ball on their laps, Finn's coat draped over him.

Horne cowered in the corner, facing the wall, unconscious or asleep. Micah and Celeste had spread their jackets beneath their heads and stretched out next to Gabriel, who sat facing the door, his hands balled into fists on his knees. His face was drawn, the muscle over his jaw twitching. His eyes smoldered with fury, but when he met her gaze, they softened.

Her stomach lurched. She looked away.

She stared down at the permanent indentations on the pads of her fingers. She couldn't think about him right now, what she did or didn't feel. None of it mattered anyway if they all died tomorrow. "We're not going to die here. We're going to get out. Somehow, we're going to rescue Mother. We'll get her back and then—"

Silas snorted. "And then what? Even if we survive, even if she's somehow still alive, you think everything will be rainbows and unicorns? It won't make a bit of difference. Not for me."

She glanced at him, confused. "What?"

His lips twisted in a sneer. "You were always the favorite."

The realization came slowly, like a stone sinking in cold, dark water. "You're not talking about Father."

His silence said everything.

Even as she spoke, she knew. A cold, dull dread stole over her. "You mean Mother."

Her mind scrolled back through the years, through hundreds—thousands—of memories, some still foggy and unclear. But she knew.

All the times they were both in the room, but her mother spoke only to her. The way her mother's gaze would sort of slide over him, like he was an ornamental piece of furniture or a service bot. All the times her mother would brush back her hair or press her shoulder gently, but never touching Silas. She couldn't recall a single hug or handshake or...anything.

The words were razors in her throat. She forced them out. "You think...she doesn't love you."

He clenched his fists. Blood oozed from the cuts in his knuckles. "She never did."

It was true. She knew it was. What made them so different? Why did her mother love her and not Silas? It made no sense—

And then she understood. Amelia was not Declan Black's biological child. Silas was. Amelia was pale and blonde and reserved. She had none of her father's dark, bristling energy, none of his disdain or contempt or innate cruelty.

But Silas did. Silas was so like his father. He shared the same lean, wolfish face and sharp gray eyes as Declan Black. He was cold, proud, contemptuous, and petty.

Her mother did not love her son. She did not love Silas because Silas belonged to Declan Black. The man she'd chosen to marry solely to save Amelia. The man who humiliated and debased her with his cruelty, his tyrannical control, his verbal and emotional abuse.

Her mother hated him. And because she hated the father, she also hated the son. "Oh, Silas."

"It doesn't matter," Silas hissed between clenched teeth. "Love is a weakness."

"No, it isn't." She was his sister. She should have been there for him. Instead, she'd let him protect her. Sacrifice for her. Shoulder their father's wrath for her. And she'd given him so little in return.

She should have forced through his defenses, loved him wholly and completely and watched out for him the way he'd protected her. She'd thought she had, but she could see now that she hadn't. Not enough. Not like she should have. "Love is everything that matters. The only thing that matters."

He grunted, his expression stony.

But she still saw the pain reflecting in his eyes. She knew him better than anyone. "Please, talk to me."

"I just did." He turned his face, retreating into hostile, bristling silence.

Amelia grabbed her brother's hand.

He flinched as if she'd branded him. He tried to jerk away.

She'd always let go before. He'd spent his life pushing others away. She, of all people, should have pushed back. Should have seen what was right in front of her. That she at least had a mother who loved her.

She had a mother who would do anything for her. And Amelia would do anything for her mother. Silas only had Jericho, but it wasn't the same. It couldn't be the same. Now Jericho was dead, and Silas had no one.

Not no one. He had Amelia. He had his sister.

"I love you," she said softly. "No matter what." Maybe it was too little too late. She could never make up for the years they'd lost or the pain and loneliness he'd suffered.

They were facing death. Facing the end. As the last hours ticked down, she would do what she should have done all those years ago.

She gripped his hand, slick and bloody and pulling away as hard as he could. She didn't let go.

She held on.

25

GABRIEL

Gabriel's red and gritty eyes burned. His muscles ached from the hours of tension and panic. He had no idea how long it had been since they'd been thrown in this room without food or water. Several hours, at least.

He couldn't remember the last time he'd slept, but the others needed it more than he did. So he stayed awake, watching and thinking. The seconds, minutes, and hours ticked by, leading inexorably toward morning, toward their execution by fire.

He did not fear his own death. After the *Grand Voyager*, he'd longed for release from his overwhelming shame and self-loathing —from the haunting nightmares of the girl in the bright yellow bathrobe, her tiny body crumpled in death, her vacant eyes eternally accusing him of his own culpability.

Nadira had given him a reason to live, a purpose. He'd done what he could to earn his redemption, to pay penance for the things he'd done. But it wasn't enough. Maybe nothing could ever be enough.

He didn't fear death. Not his. The terror that choked his throat was for the others in this room, the people he cared about more than anything. The people he loved.

Micah and Amelia first and always, but he cared for Benjie and Finn and Willow, too. Even Celeste had grown on him.

And Jericho, too. But now Jericho was gone. If someone was going to save them, it would have to be Gabriel.

Even now, when things seemed so hopeless, he refused to give up. Micah hadn't. Nadira wouldn't, if she were here. He slipped his hand inside his pocket and fingered the blue cloth, soft as velvet now from his constant touch.

Micah had faith. He believed there was a purpose for everything, just like their mother had, always rubbing her Catholic beads. If there was a purpose in Nadira's sacrifice, maybe it was so Gabriel could save them now.

If only he could figure out how.

There was a sound outside the door. Several new cracks appeared in the smooth white door. Two vertical black lines and two longer, horizontal ones. There was an electronic hiss and part of the door retracted, revealing an open rectangle approximately one foot long by two feet wide.

Cleo, the vicious Indian girl with the shaved head and purple braids, stood on the other side of the door. One of the other Pyros, the guard Cleo had called Li Jun, waited just behind her.

Cleo pointed a rifle through the opening in the door. Her white teeth flashed threateningly. "Good morning, bitches."

Gabriel leapt to his feet. Amelia and Micah clambered to their feet more slowly, wiping the grogginess from their weary, grief-stricken faces. The others remained on the floor.

She hammered back the slide and aimed her gun at Gabriel's chest. "Hector was a good kid. Nothing like his father. Such a shame you had to go and murder him."

Gabriel didn't flinch. He didn't move. He stood closest to the door. He could keep her attention and take the brunt of her wrath. If she was going to shoot someone, he'd make sure it was him.

Maybe it would be a blessing to die quickly by bullet rather than slowly, tortuously, burning in agony for who knows how long. But he couldn't bring himself to stand by and watch someone else he cared about die. "What do you want?"

"Maybe I won't wait until tomorrow. Maybe I'll just shoot you all now."

"It'll be faster," Silas muttered from where he sprawled on the floor.

She cocked her eyebrows at him. "What happened to your hands? Did the wall attack you?"

He glowered at her. "First chance I get, I'm going to carve your heart out with a rusted spoon."

Cleo sneered. "And I'm gonna cut off your balls and hang them from your ears."

Silas gazed up at her, nonplussed. "Sounds unpleasant. I dare you to try."

Cleo only rolled her eyes. "Now that introductions are out of the way..." The gun muzzle tracked around the room, coming to a stop on Willow. "Maybe I'll be generous and just kill one of you. You spit on me."

Willow surged to her feet. "You burned me!"

"You deserved it."

Willow tried to shove past Gabriel. "Choke on a cactus, you stupid—"

"Play nice," he hissed. He pushed her back, keeping her behind him. "Leave her alone. Kill me instead."

He balled his hands into fists, ready to spring into action. The second her attention strayed, or the guards were distracted. Maybe he could fit his arm through that opening and reach the lock on the other side. He could wrestle the gun from her and turn this all around ...

Cleo studied him. Her sharp gaze traveled slowly around the room. She swiveled the gun and pointed it at Amelia. "Or maybe... I'll kill her."

Amelia sucked in a startled breath.

Gabriel's heart surged in his chest. No one was hurting Amelia on his watch. He'd give his own life for hers in a heartbeat. He stepped in front of the gun, blocking Cleo's view. "I said take me instead."

"You have a death wish?" she asked, irritated. "You don't interest me. Get out of the way."

"She's the future. She's the only chance at hope that we have."

Her lip curled in a sly smile. "Is that the only reason you'd give your life for hers?"

He raised his chin, his jaw clenched. "She's a good person. I'm not."

Cleo's gaze flickered around the room again, her dark eyes taking in everything in the span of a few heartbeats. "And you...have feelings for her."

He hesitated for only a fraction of a second. He didn't look at Amelia or his brother, but he felt their eyes on him, boring into him. "That's not a secret."

"We're wasting time," Li Jun said behind her.

With Cleo's gun pointed at his face, he'd forgotten the guard was even there.

Cleo sighed. "And I was so enjoying myself." Her eyes narrowed. "I am going to open this door, and if any of you try anything stupid, so help me, I will shoot you in the face."

"Also," Li Jun added, "Apollo is with me. Unless you fancy having your head ripped off by a lion, I'd listen to her."

Gabriel and Micah exchanged shocked glances. Why would she

open the door? Was it some kind of trick? An easier way to kill them?

This girl enjoyed the pain of others. Maybe she just wanted a front row seat to watch them die, either through a rain of bullets or the savage jaws of an attacking lion.

Indecision gripped him. Should he jump at her as soon as the door swung open? Risk it all to take her down and hope a few of his people could make it out, even if some of them died?

"Gabriel," Micah said, warning him. *Stay calm. Keep your wits. Don't be reckless.*

Gabriel used to be reckless. Was he any more? Reckless could get you killed. It could also save your ass.

The entire door retracted into the right side of the wall. Li Jun and the lion stood on his left, a hover cart loaded with a large canvas bag next to them. Cleo stood directly in front of him in the brightly lit corridor. She was dressed in the same dark, tight-fitting clothing, Jericho's pulse rod clipped to her belt next to a large hunting knife.

He ignored the pang at the thought of Jericho. There was no time for that now.

He sprang at Cleo. With his left arm, he seized the gun, thrusting it to the side and up, so if she pulled the trigger the bullets would fly harmlessly over everyone's heads. With his right hand, he jerked the hunting knife from the sheath at her waist and thrust it against her throat.

"Got you," he said, inches from her face.

She flashed that enigmatic smile, the right side of her face crinkling, her teeth bared like fangs. "You're good. But not good enough."

He felt the press of cold steel against his upper thigh, the razor-sharp blade of the knife strapped to her outer leg a moment ago now jammed against his femoral artery. "You cut me; I cut you. Who dies first?"

"It doesn't matter," he said, "as long as they escape."

"How very noble. Unlike your partner in crime, who squealed on you the second we captured him. I didn't even get to torture him, which was a real shame. Now, put your big knife down like a good boy and we can talk."

"What makes you think we have anything to talk about?" He jerked the blade harder against her neck, forcing her chin up.

She swallowed, but her dark eyes revealed no fear. "If you refuse, my guard releases that king of beasts over there."

Gabriel spared a quick glance at the cat. The thing was massive. Its collar shimmered like blue lightning through its tawny mane. It shook its great head and growled, a loud rumble that trembled the floor beneath his feet.

The lion strained against its thin silver chain, hungering to get inside the white room, hungering to devour Amelia and Micah and Benjie and the others.

Li Jun tugged on the chain. "Sit."

Unbelievably, the lion sat. It stared into the room with ravenous golden eyes, ready and waiting.

"He's well trained, but starving," Li Jun said almost apologetically. "Moruga hasn't fed him since Hector died."

"So you see," Cleo continued calmly, "mine is bigger. Let's all put our dicks back inside our pants and try this again."

"Go to hell," Silas spat, scrambling to his feet beside Amelia.

Cleo sighed. "This is why I hate men. If you would shut your pieholes and listen for a damn second, you might learn something."

"Put the knife down, Gabriel," Micah said. There was no question in his voice, no quavering hesitation. He spoke with quiet authority, and Gabriel obeyed. He had no choice, really. She had him.

He dropped the knife.

He realized suddenly that he didn't *want* to die. Not anymore. He was willing, but he wanted to live, if given the choice. Nadira had died for that choice. He didn't have much faith in the God his mother had believed in, but he sent up a desperate prayer anyway. He had so much left to do.

Cleo shifted, her blade sliding from his femoral artery to his crotch.

He stiffened, his mouth going dry. Was this all just a game? Was she simply torturing them? Would she gut him like a pig now? Or worse?

She cocked her eyebrows, daring him to move. He didn't move.

She took a step back and laughed. She slid her blade into her thigh sheath and rubbed her throat. "Just yanking your chain, asshole."

Gabriel let out a long breath, refusing to let her see how she'd shaken him.

"What the hell do you want?" Willow scowled, her hands fisted on her hips. Finn was beside her, a towering hulk even with one hand gripping his wounded shoulder, his expression contorted with pain. Benjie hid behind them both.

"What I want—" Cleo picked up her rifle and slung it over her shoulder, "—is a mansion with a floating Jacuzzi and five man-slaves to rub my feet with oil every hour of every day. Not because I like men, but because they would hate it, and that would make it awesome."

They all just stared at her.

She rubbed a smudge of dirt from her damaged cheek with the back of her hand. "I want to save your undeserving asses. But if you don't stop standing there gawping like idiots, I guarantee I'll change my mind."

26

WILLOW

Willow stared at Cleo, stunned. She was sure she hadn't heard correctly. Her neck still burned; her stomach felt like it had been turned inside out, her ribs aching. She must be hallucinating.

"Why should we trust you, scar-face?" Silas said, sneering. "You're just screwing with us."

Cleo grinned savagely. "If I was screwing with you, silver-dicked rich boy, you'd know it."

Silas let out a bitter laugh.

Cleo's grin widened. "Unfortunately, I am not screwing with you today. Maybe tomorrow."

"We're here to rescue you," Li Jun said.

Willow touched the scalded skin on her neck gingerly, wincing. This girl was a sociopath. The Pyros were depraved killers. This had to be some kind of vicious trick. "Why? Why in the world would you help us, when a few hours ago you were delighted to maim and torture?"

Cleo whirled on Willow. "You really are as dense as you look, aren't you? You should be thanking me."

Willow sputtered, momentarily unable to form a coherent thought.

"What are you talking about?" Micah asked her.

"Sykes wanted to put a bullet in your head then and there." Cleo cocked her head, her long purple braids tumbling over her right shoulder. "Or were you not paying attention to that part? I'm the only reason you're all alive."

Li Jun glanced at his SmartFlex. "We need to go."

"We're not going anywhere until you give us some answers," Willow snapped, finally finding her voice. "None of this makes sense."

Cleo sighed impatiently. She drew out her words like she was speaking to small children, or idiots. "I'm not actually a Pyro. I'm a New Patriot. I'm working for General Reaver, the leader of the surviving remnant of the Atlanta chapter, now Georgia and the whole southeast."

"A New Patriot," Gabriel repeated, startled, his eyes widening.

Cleo's gaze snapped to him. "Is there an echo in here? That's what I said."

"Wait a minute, a *New Patriot*?" Rage ignited inside her chest. This was some horrible, twisted nightmare mingling the past with the present. Just when she thought things couldn't get worse. "You're a terrorist! You people attacked the *Grand Voyager*. You killed my family! You created the Hydra virus—"

"I'm going to stop your little rant right there," Cleo interrupted in an infuriatingly calm voice. "One. What happened on the *Grand Voyager* did not go according to plan. Two. Our chapter was not involved in that particular mission. Three. The New Patriots had nothing to do with the Hydra virus. I would think your resident New Patriot would've cleared that up by now."

"Well, of course he *said* that, but—"

"It's true," Amelia said quietly.

Everyone stared at her, gaping.

"How could you possibly know that?" Willow asked incredulously.

"I'll explain later, I promise. The New Patriots are what they are. But they did not create the Hydra virus. They were trying to stop it."

"But—" Willow sputtered.

Micah touched her shoulder. He leaned in close. "We'll tell you everything, but right now we have to get out of here. I don't like this either, but we don't have a lot of options."

Willow gritted her teeth and nodded. Micah was right. If it took betting on a demon to get them out of hell, then she'd bet on the demon.

"If you're a New Patriot, what are you doing with the Pyros?" Amelia asked.

"They were easy to infiltrate. Moruga has a thing for fire. My face was made for him." Cleo gestured airily at her scars. "Yuan, our science geek who also knows his way around a gun, came with me. The Pyros do contract work for the government inside the Sanctuary. We've been undercover for three months now. Feels like a year, honestly. But what better way for us to get intel than to hide in plain sight?"

"We won't be hiding anymore," Li Jun said.

"We're breaking cover for you people," Cleo said. Her gaze narrowed at Amelia. "For the cure."

Willow looked at Benjie. She was *Ate*. It was her job to keep him alive, no matter the cost, no matter the risk. It was like jumping from the frying pan into the fire. But there was no choice. They either took a chance and put their lives in the hands of the enemy, or they stayed here and died.

Cleo circled them, prowling like the predator she was, taking everything in. Her eyes narrowed as she assessed them. "A motley bunch. Rather pathetic."

Silas bared his teeth. "Not so pathetic I can't break your neck with one arm tied behind my back."

Willow felt a sort of perverse pride. Silas was an ass, but he was their ass. She'd take Silas over this chick any day.

"There's no going back after this," Cleo said. "You'd better be worth it."

Willow grimaced. "We are."

She grabbed Benjie's hand, helped him to his feet, and strode out of their prison. They were in a long, wide corridor bracketed with dozens of doors. The walls were not as blinding but still white, the floors muted gray tiles.

She blinked against the fluorescent lights, still not used to electricity after all this time. Everything looked very sterile, like a hospital or lab.

"What is this place?" she asked.

"Rodell Industries' research and development lab," Cleo said briskly. "It shares a skybridge with the Hyatt Renaissance, aka Pyro headquarters, and is kitty-corner to the Fox Theater, which Moruga loves for some reason. That room he kept you in was used for some kind of selected sensory deprivation experiment. It's Moruga's favorite jail cell."

Willow stopped dead in her tracks. Cleo wasn't the only predator in the room. One of the enormous lions sat only a few feet away, its tail twitching. It was as tall as Benjie and looked so bizarrely out of place that it was surreal, almost comical. Until it yawned, showing off every single one of its long, pointed teeth.

Benjie's fingers tightened on hers. "Can I pet him, Lo Lo?"

"No way. That thing will swallow you in one gulp."

"Actually, lions tear and chew their food into smaller chunks before swallowing," Li Jun said as he bent over a large, lumpy canvas bag on the hover cart beside him. Though they usually kill their prey quickly by crushing the windpipe with their powerful jaws—"

Willow blanched. "We've got the picture, thanks."

Finn and Micah inched past Apollo, both their faces ashen. Silas looked like he was about to vomit. Amelia's face was as white as the walls around them. Only Celeste seemed more curious than scared, probably due to blood loss.

Yuan winked at Benjie. "Actually, Apollo's harmless."

Cleo scowled. "Are we giving away all our secrets now?"

Willow stared at them warily. "What do you mean?"

Yuan pointed at Apollo's shock collar, which had faded to a dull blue. "The lions are mods, but Moruga fitted them with electrified collars. The shock makes them angry. They'll bellow and growl and roar and look fierce, but they won't attack. Moruga uses them to frighten and intimidate."

"It works," Micah said.

Celeste hobbled past Willow and went right up to the lion.

"What are you doing?" Willow asked, alarmed.

Celeste reached out her hand, palm flat, toward Apollo. "I always loved cats."

"That's no cat," Willow said.

Celeste ignored her. "My Mom had a modded cheetah named Psyche."

Willow rolled her eyes, but she watched, half-fascinated, half-horrified, as the lion allowed Celeste to rub the top of its head between its enormous ears. A rumbling sound erupted from deep in its throat. It chuffed softly.

Cleo arched her brows. "At least one of you isn't a scaredy-assed baby."

"*I'm* not a baby." Before she could stop him, Benjie darted forward and buried his hands in Apollo's mane.

Willow's first instinct was to scream at him, to drag him back to safety, to throw herself at the mercy of the lion's jaws—whatever she had to do to protect her brother.

Finn grabbed her arm, swaying unsteadily. "He's okay. The kitty won't hurt him."

Willow hissed out a breath. "Kitty?"

But the lion only sat there, apparently harmless, placidly purring like a house cat. Although she'd read somewhere that lions couldn't purr. Which just made the whole situation even more bizarre.

Her instincts remained on high alert. This might still be a trick. Cleo could not be trusted. But what choice did they have? The only alternative was burning at the stake like the Salem witches in the 1700s. Those people had been innocent, too.

"Two patrol drones headed our way," Li Jun said tensely as he looked down at his SmartFlex, where a glowing 3D blueprint of the building projected over his arm, rotating slowly. It was some kind of biometric sensor map. Two blinking red dots moved toward them from the east.

Cleo swore and looked at her own sleek black cuff. "The drones aren't supposed to reach this floor for another ten minutes."

"The net is back online?" Willow asked, hope surging through her.

"No," Li Jun said. "The Pyros hacked into a local, closed network."

She was more disappointed than she wanted to admit.

Two more red dots appeared from the west, blinking rapidly. "What the hell?" Cleo hissed. "These aren't on the schedule."

"We've got four human guards at the south entrance, six at the west," Li Jun said. "It's time to go."

Cleo pulled out two auto-injector syringes and handed them to Gabriel, who stood closest to her. He looked like he wanted to strangle her about as much as Willow did.

"What are those?" Willow asked suspiciously.

"Adrenaline stims. We have a doctor at the compound, but these will keep your wounded on their feet for twenty-four hours."

"And what if we don't get to your little hideout by then?" Willow asked.

Cleo's expression didn't change. "Then it won't matter because we'll all be dead."

Gabriel injected Celeste and Finn. Finn sighed in relief. "Much better."

Li Jun pulled a handful of masks and gloves from the canvas bag and handed them out. Willow tugged hers on, put on Benjie's, then stood on tiptoe to help Finn with his.

Dark purple circles rimmed his eyes. His skin was gray. He didn't look good. The adrenaline needed to kick in soon, or he'd be in trouble. More trouble than they were already in.

Horne staggered to his feet, clutching his nose. His left eye was purple-black and swollen, his nose misshapen and an ugly yellowish-green. It was clearly broken. Gabriel had a powerful right hook. "What about me? I'm in extreme pain. I'll pass out without something to alleviate my suffering."

Willow hooked a thumb in Horne's direction. "Please tell me we can leave him behind."

Yuan frowned. "He'll tell Moruga everything as soon as they find him."

"True." Cleo raised the gun. "So we kill him, then."

"Please!" Horne cried, sniffling pathetically, raising both arms as he begged for his life. "I made a mistake! I was wrong. I was terrified and out of my right mind. Please—"

"No!" Micah said. "He's unarmed. That would be—it's wrong. Besides, we've got a kid with us."

Cleo made an irritated noise. "If I knew I was gonna get stuck with the morality police, I wouldn't have bothered."

Willow would have agreed with Cleo if not for Benjie. She shoved her hair behind her ears. "Fine. Let's go, numbnuts."

"T-thank you," Horne stammered. "You have no idea how appreciative—"

"Unless you want to be cold-cocked again," Willow said, "I'd advise you to shut the hell up. Do not speak. Do not make a single sound suggestive of internal thought."

Mercifully, Horne fell silent.

"Less talking, more ass-moving." Cleo gestured toward a steel door at the end of the long corridor. "That way."

Willow and the others followed Cleo. She and Micah stayed close to Gabriel. Silas took up the rear. Finn grabbed Benjie with his uninjured hand.

Celeste took a few steps and stumbled. She put her hand on the wall to steady herself. "I'm fine."

She clearly wasn't. "Oh, hell. Come on." Willow rolled her eyes but offered her arm. Celeste rested her forearm on her shoulder, using her like a crutch.

"Don't say a word," Willow growled.

Celeste pursed her lips. "Wouldn't dream of it."

Horne hobbled along behind them, holding his broken nose and moaning. No one offered to help him.

"What about weapons?" Silas asked, his hostility slightly subdued now that they were actually getting out of this hellhole. Maybe.

Cleo signaled to Li Jun. As they walked, he pulled several knives, guns, and ammo packs from the canvas bag. "I have access to the armory, but the guards wouldn't let me take more than our allotted four rifles in addition to mine and Li Jun's. The pulse guns were already checked out. Who can fight?"

Gabriel, Silas, and Micah raised their hand. Willow raised her free arm.

Cleo shot her a dubious look. "You? Aren't you, like, ten?"

Willow gritted her teeth, the wound on her neck pulsing. "Look, you little—"

"She can handle herself," Silas said. His face was impassive, but he watched Cleo's every movement with razor sharpness. He hated her, too. Another thing they had in common.

Willow gave him a grateful look as she bit back her anger. She held out her hand for a weapon. Li Jun gave her a small handgun. Gabriel, Silas, and Micah received semi-automatic rifles with two extra magazines.

Yuan handed them each a small, round object the size of the head of a thumbtack. "These are comms. Stick them inside your ears. I've already set up a secure channel. The Pyros could hack it fairly easily, but by the time they think of it, we should be long gone."

Willow put in the comm and slipped the gun into her holster. She planned to use it on Cleo the first chance she got. They needed her to get out of the building. But once they were clear ... all bets were off. "Just how are we getting out of here?"

"The only way we can. We're going under."

Beside her, Finn stiffened. "Under like under the city? Through the sewers?"

It took a moment for Finn's words to sink in. A tremor went through her. "As in, the home of millions of rats on a good day? I thought you were trying to rescue us, not get us eaten alive by little mutant monsters."

"Plans changed," Cleo said. "Plan A was to sneak out the south entrance while Rodgers took his twice-nightly twenty-minute dump. Plan B was to stun or kill a few of the guards if we needed to, but there's too many for us to surprise. Moruga sent extra security. He's a half-crazed pyromaniac, but he's not stupid." She glanced at Amelia. "He knows how valuable you are. He probably suspects one of his own people might try to steal you and sell you to the Sanctuary themselves to pocket the profit. We have no choice. We're moving to plan C."

Willow's stomach sank. "How are we going to make it through the sewers? Have you seen how fast those rats move?"

"Rats are very intelligent creatures," Li Jun said cheerfully. "Some say they're as smart as dogs. Their social hierarchy is close to ours. Their eyesight isn't great, but once they learn a navigation route, they never forget. They can communicate through sound frequencies humans can't hear. Some of the reasons they make both excellent pets and research subjects—"

"In other words, we're dead meat," Willow said. Celeste's bony elbow dug into her shoulder. She gritted her teeth as they passed a few dozen doors on either side of the corridor, all closed.

"We're gonna scare them away." Cleo's tone was matter-of-fact, without a hint of anxiety or concern. She either truly didn't get the danger they were about to leap into, or she really was a sociopath.

Willow voted for sociopath. "The only thing those freak rodents are scared of is fire."

Cleo paused at the top of the stairwell. She pulled a long object out of the canvas bag on the hover cart and hefted it with a wicked smile. "Which is why we brought flamethrowers."

27

AMELIA

Amelia and the others raced down the first set of stairs without encountering any obstacles. In her right hand, she gripped the flamethrower Li Jun had given her, a sleek white weapon with twin top-mounted canisters, a propane tank in front, napalm behind it.

They'd left Apollo on the seventh floor, sitting at the top of the stairs, its tail twitching, placidly waiting for someone to fetch him. Since the other Pyros knew he wasn't dangerous, the lion no longer served a purpose.

"And he eats like an elephant," Li Jun said. "Try scavenging food for six of them."

At the landing of the third floor, Cleo and Li Jun paused to check their SmartFlex building schematics. "Four guards just hit the second floor."

"Should we go back up?" Amelia adjusted her grip on the flamethrower. Cleo had brought four of them—one for herself, Li Jun, Amelia, and Willow. She had no real idea how to use it. Would it be enough once they'd reached the sewers? Could they really hold off the infected rats? But there was no time to second-guess their plan.

"The drones are too close," Cleo said. "They're one floor up and checking the second to last door. They'll scan this stairwell within thirty seconds."

"The third floor it is." Gabriel moved ahead of them and opened the steel-reinforced door. Everyone rushed through as quickly and silently as possible.

Just as Gabriel closed the stairwell door behind them, a sound came from the second floor. The bang of a heavy door closing.

"Hostiles on the second floor," Gabriel whispered. "It won't take them long to clear it, then they'll head up to us."

'What now?" Amelia tried not to panic, tried to control her rapid breathing. That old familiar fear swelled inside her, coating her insides. The fear that made her useless and weak.

"Give me a second," Cleo snapped.

Amelia and Willow exchanged nervous glances. Celeste leaned heavily on Willow's shoulder, her features rigid with pain. She felt every second of passing time like a bomb ticking. "We don't have all day," Willow said.

Cleo turned in a slow circle and finally pointed. "There's another stairwell at the opposite end of the building, but it doesn't take us where we need to go. It accesses the main level reception area, but not the basement."

"We can cross the skybridge to get to the Hyatt," Li Jun said. "The lobby elevators go to a basement storage area with sewer access."

Cleo swore again. "Too many drones. A single alert ping and they'll shoot to kill."

Yuan shook his head. "Those drones only monitor the hotel's perimeter. They're programmed to protect the *outside*, not the inside. Plus, Moruga has dozens of guards at street level, but there's only two on each end of the skybridge."

"And we can reach the skybridge from the third floor." Cleo studied the schematics with a fierce frown. "It's the best we can do."

She glanced up at Gabriel, her gaze hard and calculating. "You're a New Patriot. You know your way around a combat zone, yeah?"

Gabriel tightened his grip on his weapon. "Of course."

She jerked her chin at Li Jun. "He's merely adequate. I need someone to take point with me."

"I'm not offended at all," Li Jun said, sounding more exasperated than angry.

"I'm a better shot than he is," Silas said indignantly from behind them.

Cleo shook her head. "I don't trust any of you. At least I know what I'm getting with him."

Gabriel glanced at Amelia, his eyes dark and unreadable. "You okay?"

Her heart beat with frenzied wings inside her chest. Her body buzzed, her fingers tingling, hands shaking. It was like she was back on the ship again, trapped in the Oceanarium, trapped with nowhere to run.

Gabriel was looking at her the way he had back on the *Grand Voyager*, like he was drowning and only she could save him, like he was falling and only she could catch him. "Amelia."

"Yes," she managed, her throat thickening.

"I'll stay with Amelia," Micah said.

A look passed between the brothers. Gabriel nodded tightly, the muscle in his jaw bulging. He was protective of her. They both were. In this moment, surrounded by enemies, with panic and gut-wrenching fear threatening to undo her, she was grateful for it.

"I'm fine, too," Finn mumbled. "Thanks for asking."

"We can do this," she said as much to herself as Gabriel. She couldn't let the fear win, couldn't let it control her like it had all those years she'd cowered before her father's cruelty and contempt. She was stronger than that now. She took a breath, steeling herself. "We're not made of glass."

Gabriel nodded curtly.

"Stop picking your asses and move," Cleo called over her shoulder.

They sprinted down the corridor. Her legs felt like lead, but she forced them to move. "Why can't we go out a back door?"

"Too many guards, and they'll track us easily in the snow," Cleo said. "We need the sewers to get us to the subway tunnels, which will get us far enough away from headquarters that we can slip back to the surface without being seen—or tracked. Then we use the AirTrain track to get to our rendezvous point."

They hesitated outside the cafeteria double doors. Gabriel and Cleo cleared it, then gestured for the others to follow. Micah held the door open for them. Willow helped Celeste hobble through, then Amelia followed.

The cafeteria was enormous, with high, wood-beamed ceilings and white-washed walls. The dozens of tables and chairs were made of transparent polymers, so that at first glance the room appeared sparse and empty.

A sudden sound stilled her breath.

"Little piggy, little piggy, come out, come out, wherever you are!" Sykes's eerie voice filled the cavernous room. It echoed off the walls, the ceiling, the polished floor. It seemed to come from all directions at once.

Gabriel, Micah, Silas, and Cleo dropped into crouches. They spun in different directions, guns up, sighting for movement.

Amelia twisted, frantically searching for the source of the voice.

There was nothing to see. White walls. Whiter floor. Several white doors opened to a kitchen and more corridors led deeper inside the building. There was no one there. And there was nowhere to hide.

"Where is he?"

"He must have jacked his comms into the sound system," Cleo said.

"He's not on the map." Li Jun studied the biometric sensor map projecting from the SmartFlex, his voice rising. "He deactivated his tracker. He knows it's us."

"Relax," Cleo said tightly. "He knows it's someone on the inside, he doesn't know who."

"Now they've all dropped their trackers," Li Jun said in growing horror. "We don't have any way of knowing where they are or how close—"

"Don't make me blow your house down," Sykes boomed over the sound system.

Amelia's blood went cold. It was like Kane all over again. Kane taunting her, stalking her. Kane's hands snaking around her throat, squeezing, squeezing until she couldn't breathe, until blackness swirled at the edges of her vision. Kane's crazed, viper eyes and leering, vicious grin looming over her—

"Amelia," Willow reached back, squeezing her arm.

Amelia blinked back to the present, shaken and dazed.

"You've survived worse than this," Willow hissed. "Get it together."

She nodded, hesitantly at first, then harder. Willow was right. Her own fear was her greatest threat, her greatest weakness. Her fear made her forget. She was a survivor. She'd outlasted Kane. Simeon. The sinking of the *Grand Voyager*. The Hydra virus. Sweet Creek Farm. Cerberus. The fire. And now, she would survive the Pyros.

She was the girl who lived.

She didn't have a free hand to touch her charm bracelet, but she felt its comfort around her neck anyway. She pushed her fear deep down and concentrated on the present, channeling all of her focus on getting out of this place alive.

Cleo raised her finger to her lips. She pointed across the cafeteria, toward a door standing ajar. From the cafeteria windows, Amelia could see the transparent skybridge arcing over the six-lane road three stories below. It was still dark outside, but the Hyatt Renaissance across the street was lit up like a Christmas tree.

Cleo gave the signal, and they hurried across the cafeteria, Willow and Celeste beside her, Micah directly ahead. They wove between the round tables, careful not to knock over the chairs.

Amelia tripped on a chair leg. She lurched, her limbs flailing.

She pitched forward, sure she was going to fall, that the noise would draw the enemy, that it would all be over—

Celeste snaked out her hand and seized Amelia's arm, jerking her back. The flamethrower hovered above a chair's hard plastic seat, threatening to fall. With a muffled curse, Celeste managed to pull her to her feet.

She sucked in her breath. That was far too close. She shot Celeste a grateful, relieved glance. Willow rolled her eyes and tugged Celeste along.

Everyone paused, waiting for Cleo. Amelia hardly breathed as she focused on the glowing, rotating map over Cleo's right arm. The red light of the drone blinked just outside the cafeteria.

"Get down!" Gabriel hissed.

Amelia ducked. She, Willow, and Celeste huddled against the wall to the left of the door. Celeste winced as she bent her wounded leg, but she didn't make a sound.

If the drone spotted them, it would send an alert to every other drone on its network as well as the guards' comms. Even if Gabriel or Cleo shot it down before it could injure anyone, it wouldn't be fast enough to stop the signal.

Above them, the lion roared. Even three floors away, the powerful sound vibrated inside her chest. Someone had found Apollo, which meant they'd found the empty jail cell.

They were running out of time.

28

GABRIEL

Gabriel wiped his sweating palms on his pant legs.

After an eternity, the drone finally moved away from the cafeteria toward the third-floor stairwell, drawn by Apollo's roar. He let out a relieved breath.

Cleo gave the signal, and they exited the cafeteria through the double doors. A sharp right-turn led to a wide alcove and the skybridge access point. Cleo hugged the wall, Gabriel right beside her. It would be better to sneak up on the guards and attack silently and swiftly with knives, but the element of surprise was not an option. The guards were already on alert. The suppressed rifle Cleo had given him would have to do.

She peeked around the corner and raised two fingers for two guards. *One, two*, she mouthed.

Three. Gabriel spun around the corner, caught a blur of movement, and aimed and fired as the guard lifted his gun. The guard staggered and fell back, his limp body sliding down the glass window behind him. He didn't move.

Cleo took out the second guard with two sharp pops to the chest.

"Aren't they wearing armored vests?" he asked as they rushed onto the skybridge.

Cleo tapped her magazine, grinning like the cat with a canary still stuffed in its mouth. "I made sure I stole the armor-piercing rounds."

The skybridge was a transparent tunnel forty yards long. They were exposed. Out in the open. Vulnerable. Gabriel's heart rate jumped as they sprinted over West Peachtree, the road below strewn with the husks of thousands of cars.

He risked a glance down. On several side streets, cars and transports were crushed to either side, spilling onto the sidewalks. A bulldozer must have rammed a path through them, allowing the Pyros to travel by vehicle through their territory.

"More lions!" Benjie said. "Look, Mister Finn!"

"I see them, Sir Benjie." Finn placed a hand on Benjie's shoulder. "Thank goodness they're friendly kitties like Apollo."

"Too bad their owners aren't so friendly," Silas said.

The Hyatt Renaissance was a magnificent white steel spiral arcing one hundred and thirty-two stories above them. The hotel was a feat of modern ingenuity, one of the last great skyscrapers built in Atlanta over a decade ago—before the developers and investors abandoned it for less disease-plagued, war-torn pastures.

Concrete barriers and barbed wire fences rimmed the perimeter of the hotel. A dozen guards patrolled the area, several of them with enormous lions at their sides. At least two dozen large, armored drones zoomed back and forth, their gun turrets swiveling menacingly.

"The drones won't detect us," Gabriel said. Hopefully the Pyros didn't have some advanced tech he didn't know about.

"They're not designed to scan above, only below." Cleo scrubbed sweat from her forehead with the back of her arm.

She pointed to the northwest corner of the plaza, where six groups of hostiles had formed, two dozen Pyros in each group, all armed to the teeth. A tall, gaunt figure took point. Moruga. They slowly fanned out, heading in all directions.

The Pyros were hunting them. He knew it would happen. Still, the sight of so many enemy combatants in one place chilled him to the core.

"They're expecting us to run away," Cleo said, "not run straight into the hornet's nest."

He clenched his jaw. He hated having to trust this girl he didn't know. A Pyro or a New Patriot—either way, she was slippery as hell. He hated not knowing the plan, the layout, every emergency exit, every contingency. He hated his own helplessness. "This is a massive risk."

"It's a gutsy risk," Cleo countered. "And one they won't expect. With any luck, we won't have to engage the guards outside at all."

They exited the skybridge and cleared the alcove. There were no guards waiting for them. The walls and floor were white marble swirled with gray. A plush, blood-red carpet ran along the length of the corridor. Gabriel gestured for the others to follow. "I don't believe in luck."

She scowled, the scarred side of her face shiny and wrinkled. "Me neither."

And yet, at least for the moment, it seemed luck was on their side. They didn't run into any interference as they made their way down the corridor, passing numerous wooden doors leading to massive conference rooms, to the stairs.

Her finger to her lips, Cleo gingerly touched a frosted glass door labeled 'lobby.' The door slid open with the faintest hiss, soft as an expelled breath.

The lobby ceiling stretched a full thirty stories above them. Each hotel suite opened onto a five-foot-wide walkway lined with a three-foot brass railing. Instead of baluster posts, the railing was constructed of solid brass panels embossed with artistic, swirling shapes. The railing was broken up every few dozen yards by thick marble pillars that held up the balcony above it. The walkway began on the left side of the enormous circular lobby and spiraled gently upward like a single apple peel.

The lobby itself glimmered with polished floors, sleekly curved loungers the same garnet-red as the carpet, and a grand, three-story fountain at the center of the atrium. Three glass revolving doors marked the entrance, opposite the concierge and check-in desks. Six elevators with brass-overlaid doors were located perpendicular to the entrance.

"You sure they're working?" Gabriel asked in a strained whisper. "An elevator takes an awful lot of electricity."

Cleo nodded. "They use it to transport scavenged goods they bring in through the parking garage."

He glanced at the guards patrolling outside the glass revolving doors. A dozen or so remained. Every guard faced the street, expecting any threat to come from the outside.

Several large, armored drones glided past. "What about them?"

"They're programmed for exterior protective measures only," Li Jun whispered. "Deadly machines, but dumb as a box of rocks. These are fifth gen. They were discussing adding AI features to the next—"

"Li Jun," Willow hissed. "Please stop talking."

Gabriel felt the first jolt of hope. Maybe they would actually make it. "I'll stay and provide cover. You lead them to the elevators."

"I'll stay, too," Micah said.

He turned to his brother. "Are you sure?"

Micah didn't bother to respond. He crouched behind the closest marble pillar, hiding as much of his body as possible. He adjusted his rifle butt against his shoulder and rested the muzzle on the top rail.

"If we crawl, the railing will block us from sight," Willow said.

Silas dropped to the floor first. "We're not serving cake and tea here, people. Move."

"Can you crawl?" Gabriel asked Finn.

"I can do anything right now," Finn said with a grimace. "Tomorrow's another story."

"We're fine," said Celeste, though she winced as Willow lowered her to the floor.

"We're going to do this." Gabriel's throat thickened with sudden emotion. He pushed it away. This wasn't the time. "We're going to get out of here. All of us."

Amelia met his gaze, her ice blue eyes striking all the way to the core of him. He saw fear, but also an unfaltering, unflinching resolve. "We'll see you on the other side."

The others dropped to their hands and knees. They crept quietly down the gently descending walkway, Cleo and Li Jun leading them, Benjie between Willow and Finn, Amelia helping Celeste, and Silas and Horne taking up the rear.

Gabriel took cover behind the closest pillar. His pulse thudded against his throat. His blood rushed in his ears. He winced at every muffled sound, the bump of a shoulder against the railing, the scrape of a boot scuffing the floor.

The group reached the lobby. There were forty-five wide-open yards between them and the elevators. So much empty space to cross with so little cover.

"How's it look?" Cleo said into his comm. The sound was loud and clear in his right ear.

"It's clear. You're a go."

Cleo and Li Jun stepped into the lobby, crouching and scanning either side before they crept forward. There was nowhere to hide. Nowhere to run if it all went sideways.

He glanced at the guards outside again. One of them coughed into his mask. Another scratched his butt. Their posture was stiff but not on edge. They hadn't noticed anything yet.

His eye snagged on movement. A giant, metallic red mirror hung on the wall behind the concierge desk at the rear of the lobby. Through the mirror, he glimpsed a sleek black desk with a computer interface and several rolling office chairs. A shadow fluttered in the reflection.

He peered through his scope, adjusted it, and looked again. Three dark figures bristling with weapons crept around the concierge desk.

His heart stopped. Everything else faded away. He aimed his rifle, his gaze narrowing, ready to obliterate the bastards from the face of the earth.

The angle wasn't right. Though he could see them in the mirror, they were protected by the massive marble desk. He could shoot through wood, but not dense, two-foot-thick stone.

He bit back a curse, enraged by his own helplessness. He caught Micah's attention and pointed silently. Micah's eyes widened in horror.

Amelia was down there. Willow and Benjie and Finn. Everyone and everything left in this ruined world that either of them cared about.

The group had made it to the fountain, but they were crouching on the opposite side, hiding from any guard who might glance through the glass doors. They were completely exposed to the enemies hunting them from behind.

"Hostiles to your six!" he said into his comm. "I'll cover you. Run!"

As soon as he fired, it would alert the guards outside. It couldn't be helped now. He tucked the stock to his shoulder, pressed his cheek down, and slammed out a flurry of shots at the concierge desk. The Pyros ducked, seeking cover.

His group fled, racing for the bank of elevators. They were thirty feet away when one of the hostiles behind the desk shot at them. The bullet struck the metal doors of the elevator, bounced off, and nailed a holo port, splintering the casing and sending it skittering across the floor.

The elevator doors opened with a ding. A thick, burly Pyro strode out, a pulse gun in each hand.

They were trapped.

"Oh, hell," Willow whispered in his ear.

Gabriel didn't think. He just moved. He darted from the safety of the column and dropped into position. He was exposing himself above the railing, but he had to make the shot. He fired a short, controlled burst.

The burly Pyro crumpled, a single bead of blood dripping down his forehead.

The air exploded in gunfire.

One of the hostiles leapt out from behind the concierge desk. He brought his sub-machine gun around with a precise sweep, emptying the clip, gouging chunks of marble from the walls and shattering a floor-to-ceiling window, striking one of his own men outside.

Before the sweep could reach his actual targets, Micah brought him down, shooting him in the chest.

A second man turned and returned fire at Micah and Gabriel, a spray of bullets whizzing past and puncturing the wall behind them. They flung themselves behind the marble pillars.

Cleo swore loudly. "Run!"

The group ran. They crouched, covering their heads as bullets tore through the air above them.

Gabriel darted out and unleashed a storm of bullets on the hostile still shooting up at them. The man tried to dive for cover, but it was too late. Micah nailed him with a second volley. He went down and didn't move.

Gabriel aimed at the concierge desk. A burst of slugs smashed into the mirror, red metallic glass raining down on the remaining hostile's head.

The hostile headed for the edge of the desk, giving Gabriel his opening. He fired in quick, three-shot bursts. The Pyro slumped across the computer console.

"Gabriel!" Micah cried. The guards had surged inside, already shooting.

"We've got it," Silas said into his comm. He and Willow retreated. They took positions behind the marble fountain, shooting at the guards while the rest fled for the elevators.

Willow shot two in the head, dropping them where they stood. Silas took out another one just as his rifle swiveled toward the elevators.

Gabriel spun and hid behind the pillar, his back pressed against the cold stone. He unclipped his second—and last—magazine from his belt, jammed it in, and slammed out a dozen shots. Spent cartridges dropped to the plush carpet.

The high ground gave him an enormous advantage. But would it be enough? Five guards flooded through the revolving doors. Gabriel picked off four of them in a barrage of bullets.

The fifth one got off a shot, his pulse gun aimed at Silas. The marble head of the fountain's mermaid statue exploded in a crackle of blue, sizzling energy.

Silas ducked, swearing profusely. He shook off the shards and dust, unhurt. "Damn, that thing has power."

Micah leveled his rifle and shot the fifth guard in the shoulder. The man staggered but didn't go down. He lifted his weapon, aiming shakily for the third-floor balcony. The pulsed plasma ripped into the railing several feet away, tearing it from its moorings and gashing a jagged hole in the ramp floor.

Micah pulled the trigger again. This time, the man went down and didn't get up.

Amelia made it to the elevator, Cleo right behind her. Cleo swiped her SmartFlex over the brass-plated ID-scanner. The doors slid open. Two bullets struck the wall above the elevators. The screen displaying the floor numbers hissed and went black.

Not Amelia. He couldn't let them hurt Amelia.

Gabriel spun and leaned out over the railing, heedless of his own safety.

"Gabriel!" Micah hissed.

Gabriel ignored him. He shot two more guards. A third one saw him and opened fire with his pulse gun. The ball of blue flame tore a massive chunk out of the marble pillar inches to his right. The pillar cracked and groaned.

He fired back, but his rifle only clicked. He was out of ammo.

"Get down!" Silas shouted. Gabriel hit the deck, his hands over his head as a second burst smashed into the wall behind him, blasting a several-foot crater clear into the suite.

Swirling white dust choked his throat. His heart pounded so loud in his ears, he could barely hear. There was another controlled blast of gunfire.

"Silas got him," Willow said into his comm. "We're going while we have the chance. Get down here!"

"Don't wait for us!" he said.

Micah dropped his gun, his hands shaking. His face was pale, his wavy hair damp against his forehead, his upper lip beaded with sweat. His glasses slid-halfway down his nose. "I'm out, too."

For a long moment, neither of them moved. They simply stared at each other, breathing heavily, grateful to be alive. Finally, Gabriel risked a peek over the railing. The elevator doors were closed. Everyone, including Silas and Willow, had made it inside. "You did good. We all did."

The lobby was strewn with bodies, spent bullets, broken glass, and chunks of marble, granite, and crumbled drywall. Several drones buzzed angrily outside the stuck revolving doors which were jammed with fallen guards. Their gun turrets swiveled menacingly, but the drones didn't attempt entry.

A bit of luck, but he would take it. They'd all be dead otherwise.

"We've got to get out of here before they send reinforcements," Gabriel whispered urgently.

Micah nodded and jammed his glasses up the bridge of his nose with his thumb. "Right behind you."

A sound came from below them. Gabriel froze.

"Help me!" someone cried.

Gabriel put his finger to his lips and risked another look over the railing. Horne knelt almost directly below them in the ruined lobby. He faced their direction, but he wasn't looking at them.

He was slumped on his knees, his hands uplifted beseechingly as he stared at the man in front of him, aghast. The man stood with his back to Gabriel and Micah. He wore a ripped black trench coat. Sykes.

Horne must have remained behind the fountain, too shell-shocked to flee, the others forced to leave him behind. Now, he blubbered and hiccuped, begging for mercy, snot bubbling from his flared nostrils, tears wetting his face. He didn't even notice the two Pyros striding up behind him. He was caught like a fish on a hook.

"Here piggy, piggy," Sykes said with a cruel, melodious laugh. He held a long, electrified blade with a serrated curve at the end in his left, unhurt hand. "Look what you've done to our home. I knew we should have just lined you up and shot you. But now we can improvise, can't we? I've been waiting to gut you since the day I first laid eyes on you, you filthy elitist scum."

Sykes was going to kill Horne. And it was going to be excruciatingly painful.

Beside him, Micah stiffened. Gabriel could almost see the thoughts churning in his brother's brain. His brother, the compassionate, merciful one.

"Micah—" Gabriel whispered. "We've already lost people. Nadira. Jericho. We should be smart. We need to think of the rest of the group—"

Micah turned to him, his eyes blazing. "I *know*. But it's who I am. It's who we are. It has to be. You go. Save yourself. Don't try to talk me out of it—"

"Micah."

"What?" he hissed.

"I'm coming with you."

Micah narrowed his eyes. "What?"

He grimaced, resigned to his fate. "Tyler Horne is trash. He isn't worth saving and never will be. But you're stubborn as an ass. I know you, and I know you're going, with or without me. Besides, I have to kill Sykes. He'll hunt us into the sewers if I don't."

He took a breath, cramming everything he wanted to say into a few desperate sentences in a few desperate seconds. All the things he could never say but felt in the very marrow of his bones burned through him. *You're my brother, my foundation and my compass. I love you and I would die without you.* "I can never be like you, no matter how much I might want to be. But I won't let you sacrifice your life for him. We do this together."

Micah stared at him, a dozen emotions passing across his face—shock, relief, gratefulness, respect. He grabbed Gabriel's hand. "Say the words."

Gabriel smiled grimly. "Just us."

Micah said, "Always."

29

WILLOW

The sewers were as dark and dank and awful as Willow had imagined. The concrete tunnel walls were rough and looked a thousand years old.

Finn clutched his shoulder and took in his surroundings. What little blood remained drained from his face. "This must be where fun goes to die."

She flicked on the small flashlight attached to the top of the flamethrower. Silas flipped on the light on his rifle scope. Cleo had finagled night vision goggles for both herself and Li Jun but no one else. Willow gritted her teeth. It figured.

"We should wait for Gabriel and Micah," Amelia said, her voice trembling in the dark. Their comms didn't work down here. They'd lost contact ten minutes ago.

"No way, sweetheart." Cleo said *sweetheart* like it was something foul. "They're covering us so we can get away. That's what we intend to do. Now move your skinny ass."

They made their way carefully along the tunnel, sloshing through six inches of oily, stagnant water. Amelia helped Celeste now, so that Willow's hands were free to use the flamethrower if—when—they came across more killer rats.

Willow shuddered. She kept seeing shadowy shapes in the water, imagining furred, bulging bodies slithering toward her. She half-expected to step on something squishy and disgusting.

The air was stale and stank of rotten eggs. Every sound was amplified, every splashing footstep, every panicked breath. Water drip, drip, dripped from the walls and ceiling.

"How long are we trapped in this hellhole?" Silas asked, grimacing.

"Approximately two miles," Li Jun said from the rear. "We'll come out behind Atlantic Station mall. From there, it's less than six hundred meters to the AirRail station. We'll take that to our rendezvous point, where our people will be waiting for us."

"Easy peasy," Benjie said, his words belying his terrified expression. He was pale and shivery, his eyes enormous in the dim light.

Willow squeezed his hand. "You got it."

"We're knights on a quest to rescue a princess, Sir Benjie," Finn whispered. "If we're clever and brave, we'll defeat the nasty dragon lord and win the hand of the lady."

"Who's the princess?" Benjie whispered back.

Finn wrinkled his brow and flashed Willow a crooked grin, only half-wincing. "Can you imagine your sister as a helpless princess all trussed up in pink ribbons and tassels?"

Benjie giggled.

Willow appreciated Finn's efforts. He was distracting Benjie, making them heroes in a fantastical story to inspire Benjie's bravery. She hefted her flamethrower, forcing lightness into her voice for her brother's sake. "Some princesses prefer guns. And kicking ass and taking names."

"Ribbons and tassels are cool, too," Celeste said from behind them.

Benjie grinned, some of the tension draining from his small face. "Whatever floats your boat, right, Mister Finn?"

"Exactly, Sir Benjie," Finn said.

They kept walking. Every ping, splash, and thud sent adrenaline jolting through her body. The hairs on her neck and arms stood on end like they were electrified.

A sound came from behind them. A faint, soft scraping. She twisted, peering into the darkness, expecting hostile enemies or rats or some monstrous form rearing up out of hell to devour them. But there was nothing.

Her heart hammered against her ribs. She wiped her damp palms on her pants. With every passing minute, her trepidation mounted. The Pyros were hunting them, filthy mutant rodents were stalking them. And here they were blundering uselessly in this dark warren of tunnels, forced to trust a sociopath with their lives.

The tunnel walls closed in on her. She felt every pound of the tons of concrete and rock and earth bearing down on her head.

"Are you okay?" Finn asked quietly.

Her chest tightened. It was hard to breathe. "I don't like closed-in spaces," she muttered. "Especially not underground."

"So, you despise heights, but the depths aren't working for you either?"

She took several ragged breaths. The darkness was oppressive and smothering. "Finn Ellington-Fletcher, are you making fun of me right now?"

"If I said yes, would you hate me?"

"A little."

"A little I can live with."

She craned her neck to search behind them, scanning her light along the scarred walls. No furred bodies. No gleaming eyes. "Are you trying to drive me insane?"

He shrugged, then winced, drawing in a sharp breath. "Everyone needs a hobby."

She turned the light on him. He was walking normally, his pallor still an unhealthy shade, though the bleeding seemed to have slowed. "I should be the one asking if you're okay."

"I feel about as useless as tits on a boar," he said wryly.

"That's an apt description if I ever heard one."

"You know I always try my best."

She tried to smile, but it came out like a grimace. She pushed down the anxiety roiling in her gut. Finn would be okay. His arm would be fine. They were all going to get out of this hellhole. She would make sure of it.

Benjie stumbled. Willow gripped his hand. "Be strong, kiddo. Just a little further."

He shivered. "I'm scared. I want Mom."

"I'm going to get you out of here," Willow said, ignoring the pang in her belly. She shot Finn a sidelong look. "This princess can save herself and you, too. I promise."

Cleo pointed to a solid wall. "The subway tunnel is this way."

"I don't see any doors," Celeste said.

"Did you get us lost?" Silas sneered. "Why am I not surprised?"

Cleo only laughed. She pulled something small, round, and metallic from her pocket and pushed it against the wall. "I'd step back if I were you."

There was a low rumbling sound. The ground shivered beneath Willow's feet. The wall itself vibrated, quaking with tiny tremors. A three-foot radius of concrete broke apart, crumbling into a thousand small, jagged chunks. A hole in the wall appeared, surrounded by rubble and swirling white dust.

"How'd you do that?" Silas asked, trying to hide his surprise. "It barely made a sound."

"Techy stuff from the Sanctuary. They've given all kinds of

wicked gear to the Pyros." She ushered them through the hole in the sewer wall into a larger tunnel.

Amelia and Celeste hobbled through the narrow, jagged opening, then Finn and Benjie, followed by Silas and Li Jun. Willow entered last, sweeping her light behind her, checking for movement.

Their lights bobbed over the walls, revealing old rusting tracks and pipes of all sizes running along the low concrete ceiling.

"This section of MARTA was abandoned, what, ten years ago?" Li Jun said. "Too expensive to maintain and everyone used the AirRail anyway."

The concrete floor was damp but not wet. Their soaking boots squelched with every step. The darkness rippled all around them, thick and heavy.

They came to a fork in the tunnel. Cleo chose a path and slapped a blinking tagger on the wall for Gabriel and Micah to follow. Hopefully it would be just Micah and Gabriel chasing after them, not a horde of vengeful Pyros.

Deep shadows flickered outside their diminishing circles of light, the cold, impenetrable blackness beyond hiding any number of monsters, real and imaginary. A looming sense of doom filled the dank air around Willow, like sharp-fanged, leather-winged creatures hovering just out of sight.

It felt like a tomb.

Another sound came from behind her. A whispery skittering. A scuffling, shuffling noise.

She spun, flamethrower up, searching wildly. There was nothing. Only rounded concrete walls, more pipes, grates, tunnels, and darkness. Always the darkness, crouched like a living thing just outside the light.

She kept walking, her feet thudding against concrete, the hairs on the back of her neck standing on end. They were being watched. She could feel it.

After several minutes, they came to a series of three circular openings, three tunnels branching in opposite directions. Cleo hesitated.

"Are you sure you know where you're going?" Finn asked. "Because it feels like we're wandering around like lost farts in a perfume factory."

Cleo shot him a murderous look. She took the center tunnel, first slapping another tagger against the wall. They walked on in silence, the tension mounting like the turning of a screw.

The longer they spent in here, the heavier the tons of concrete pressed against her chest. And the more time the miniature monsters had to find them. She tasted acid in the back of her throat. Her breaths came shallow and ragged.

Zia wouldn't have been shaking and terrified like Willow. She'd loved heights and thrills and faced whatever life threw at her with joyful exuberance. She pushed the thoughts out of her mind. Zia couldn't help her now.

A quarter of an hour later, they passed another tunnel on the left, the opening a gaping black maw. Deep inside it, dark shadows seemed to shift and solidify.

She strained to hear over their echoing steps, the slow drip of water, and the blood pounding in her ears. Her heart leapt into her throat. "Do you hear that?"

"What?" Benjie asked, his voice quavering.

Willow raised her finger for silence.

The sound came again. This time it was unmistakable. The scratching of tiny claws.

She aimed her light into the tunnel, her hands shaking.

Eye-shine. Hundreds of pairs of beady, flashing eyes. A thousand furry, squirming bodies. A horde of rats flooded the tunnel like a raging river.

They were coming.

Benjie screamed. Willow screamed with him.

One rat scrabbled ahead of the others. Before she could react, it launched itself at her and clawed up her leg. She lifted her hand to block it and shove it away.

But the thing latched on, clinging to her fingers, tiny claws digging into the thick material of her gloves. She shook her arm frantically. It wouldn't let go.

Her muscles threatened to lock in terror. One bite. One nibble. One set of jaws sinking into flesh anywhere on her body, and it would all be over.

Yuan knocked the rat away with the butt of his flamethrower.

"Die, you little bastards!" Silas spun and faced the sea of rats, spraying them with bullets. Dozens of rodents burst on impact, blood spattering everywhere. The light from his flailing weapon spun crazily over the concrete walls.

"I'll cover you!" Li Jun yelled to Cleo. He lifted his flamethrower. "Take them and go!"

"Hurry up!" Cleo cried over her shoulder.

Celeste stumbled. Amelia wrapped her arm around her waist and propped her up. "Come on!"

"Get out of here!" Silas shouted as he shot a dozen more rounds into the writhing sea of rats. The others fled, rapidly disappearing into the darkness of the tunnel ahead.

Finn seized Benjie with one hand and swung him over his unhurt shoulder. Blood oozed through his bandage, but he didn't even flinch. "I've got him."

Panic thrummed through Willow, vibrating in her bones. She fought it back. "Are you sure? What about your—"

"Never been better. Hurry up!"

She hesitated, torn between fleeing with the people she loved and staying to help Li Jun fight off the swarms of infected rodents.

She couldn't do it. She couldn't leave someone else behind, not when they'd left Gabriel and Micah, not when they'd already lost Nadira and Jericho.

One person couldn't fend off the demon hordes of hell. Li Jun needed backup. If they couldn't stop the rats here, the beasts would hunt her friends down—Benjie and Finn and everyone else. She had to protect Benjie, no matter what. "Keep him safe."

"With my life." Finn met her eyes for an agonizing moment. She couldn't read his face in the flickering shadows. "Don't you dare die on me."

"Just go!" She watched Finn flee with Benjie safely tucked in his arms, then spun back to Li Jun. She kicked two screeching rats against the wall and lifted the flamethrower. "Show me how this bad boy works."

30

MICAH

"What's the plan?" Micah asked, so low his voice was a breath against his brother's ear. They huddled side by side, their backs pressed to the marble pillar. Their rifles lay beside them, empty and useless amid the spent shell casings littering the carpet.

"We need to get lower," Gabriel said.

Micah nodded, though he wasn't sure how that would help. But in matters of combat, he trusted his brother implicitly.

They crawled silently down the curving ramp as it gradually lowered from three stories to two, to one-and-a-half as they circled back around to approximately the same position, though lower and much closer to the action now.

He could hear every word of Sykes and Horne's conversation.

"I'm sure we can come to an understanding," Horne whined weakly. "I can still offer value."

Sykes laughed, an eerily pleasant sound that raised every hair on Micah's neck. "I seriously doubt that."

"You have a rat problem," Horne said.

Sykes made an irritated sound. "I'd say we all have a rat problem."

There was about two inches of space between the floor and the railing's brass panel. Micah pressed his face to the plush carpet and turned his head. He could barely make out the figures below.

Sykes was still turned away, his black trench coat sweeping his shins. He gripped that deadly, curled scythe in his left hand, his bandaged right hand limp at his side. Horne knelt before him, sniveling and pleading. Two Pyros flanked Sykes, their guns trained on Horne.

"I know who helped us escape," Horne said. "Let me go, and I'll tell you everything."

Acid burned the back of Micah's throat. He felt sick with anger. Horne never stopped. He'd betray his own grandmother if it kept his sorry butt alive.

Was this the right thing? Should he really risk his life for Horne? His brother's life? Was it worth it? Horne wasn't worth it. Horne had betrayed them. Jericho was dead because of Horne.

But to abandon him to the cruel torture of the Pyros? It felt wrong. This brutal world had already taken so much from Micah, from them all. Trying to force him again and again to be something he loathed.

Be good. Be brave. He repeated his mother's mantra in his head. He wasn't doing this because of who Horne was. Micah was doing it because of who *he* was. Everything was a choice. In the end, he had to make the choice he could live with.

Horne didn't deserve to be saved. Micah was going to save him anyway.

"I can help you," Horne whined to Sykes. He squirmed wretchedly. "I can tell you who the rat is."

Sykes only smiled in cruel amusement. "You don't think I already know? I know everything that happens in this place. You don't think I know what that girl's up to? Who she's affiliated with? Moruga is too enamored with her hideously burned face. He can't see clearly. But I can. I've just been waiting for her to make her move, to reveal herself as the rat she is." He spat on the floor. "Judging by the wreckage surrounding us, I'd say she has."

Horne deflated. He'd played his last card and lost. He shuffled forward on his knees, groveling. "Moruga should be the one who metes out my punishment. Let him decide—"

Sykes recoiled in disgust. "Don't touch me, you filthy beast. Moruga isn't here now, is he? We don't bother him with such small, unsightly matters. He trusts his people to take care of business, which we do. As for you, little piggie, it's time we had some fun. Right, boys?"

Beside him, Gabriel stiffened. Micah turned his head and met his brother's gaze. Gabriel pulled out the hunting knife Cleo had given him and gestured for Micah's. Micah handed it to him without a word.

Stay here, Gabriel mouthed. He crouched, every muscle tensed, his jaw bulging, his eyes cold and calculating. Getting ready.

"Wait!" Horne gasped, cringing. "Don't kill me! I know where the escaped prisoners are going and how they plan to get there. I'll tell you everything—"

Gabriel leapt onto the narrow lip of the railing. Micah inhaled a single sharp breath as his brother sprang from the railing and plunged over the edge of the balcony.

He dropped silent and deadly. He landed on Sykes's back, sending them both sprawling to the floor. As they fell, Gabriel sank one knife deep into the man's upper back. Sykes's scythe went spinning across the marble floor.

No sooner had he landed then he was on his feet again. He spun and hurled the second blade at the startled, gaping guard to his left.

The blade struck the guard in the throat. He clutched at his neck, gurgling, sputtering, eyes wide and astonished at his own death.

Protect him, God, he prayed desperately. *Keep my brother safe.* Micah watched from behind the safety of a pillar, his mouth moving in a flurry of silent prayers. But it didn't look like Gabriel needed them. He'd seen his brother fight, but he was usually waist-deep in the battle with him. He'd never seen Gabriel like this, a deadly, skilled killer.

Gabriel was raw, vigorous power. He moved with precision and control, his muscles bulging, sinews straining, his body a well-honed weapon.

He didn't waste time to grab a gun. He leapt over Sykes's writhing body and hurled himself at the second guard, a thickly muscled white man with a bulldog face.

Gabriel was a streak of lightning coming at him, impossible to stop. Bulldog shot but missed. A crackling blue ball of death smashing into the base of the fountain behind him, marble shards exploding everywhere.

Gabriel barreled into Bulldog with every ounce of his considerable force, his lowered head slamming into the guard's soft gut. Bulldog cursed as he stumbled.

Gabriel took him to the ground, wrestling for the pulse gun. The guard struck him in the face and neck with his free hand, but Gabriel was undaunted. He grunted, absorbing the blows like they were nothing.

Bulldog managed to lift the gun, aiming unsteadily at Gabriel's head. Gabriel spun on his hands and knees and lashed out with his leg, kicking the gun out of the man's hands. Bulldog landed a savage punch against Gabriel's jaw. He fell back.

Micah flinched as if he could feel the pain himself. His lungs constricted. He was too terrified to breathe. It didn't matter how strong Gabriel was. A tiny mistake, a second of misjudgment, or a single bullet could still take him down.

What was he thinking? How could he allow Gabriel to risk everything for Horne? Gabriel was worth a hundred of the likes of Tyler Horne. Jericho would never have allowed this, would never have sanctioned so great a risk for so little reward.

Abruptly he remembered the girl whose hand he'd held as she died in the middle of the highway, slaughtered by the Headhunters. Jericho had forced him back, refusing to allow him to intervene, for saving the girl meant certain death for the rest of the group. *All bravery and valor have a cost*, Jericho had said. *Be damn sure you weigh the cost before you act.*

Jericho was dead. Micah had to step up, to be a man now, not a boy. To be the leader Jericho said he could be. To weigh the risks and benefits of every choice, to make the difficult decisions, both for himself and for the people he was responsible for. To somehow balance mercy with justice, compassion with self-preservation. A good leader needed to do both. Micah needed to do both.

Right now, it was his brother who needed him. He forced himself to breathe, to act. He shoved his skewed glasses into place and pulled himself to his feet. Crouching, he scrambled down the curving walkway, not yet sure what he would do but knowing he had to do something.

In the lobby, Gabriel punched Bulldog's gun-hand hard just above the wrist, then forced his hand inward at an excruciatingly unnatural angle until the guard bit out an ugly scream and dropped the weapon.

Bulldog headbutted Gabriel, sending him reeling backward. The guard rolled out from beneath him and stretched for the gun.

Gabriel shook his head, momentarily stunned.

"Gabriel!" Micah hit the lobby floor at a dead run. "The gun!"

He glimpsed Sykes staggering to his feet out of the corner of his eye. Micah swerved left and went for the other guard, the one Gabriel had stabbed in the throat. A pulse gun lay a foot from the man's limp, open palm.

He bent, grasped it, and whirled, his finger already on the trigger. "Don't move!" he shouted.

Horne had tried to run, but he'd slipped in a puddle of Sykes' blood. He was flat on his back, moaning, clutching his knee.

Sykes picked up the scythe. He loomed over Horne, the wickedly curved blade pressed against Horne's heaving stomach.

Another pulse blast crackled through the air. He hoped with all his being that it was Gabriel who shot the guard and not the other way around, but he didn't dare risk a glance.

"Don't move!" he shouted again at Sykes. "Back away, now! Drop the knife!"

Blood filmed Sykes's lips and spattered his chin. His pale eyes gleamed. "Which is it, little piggie? Move or don't?"

Micah's hands were slick on the gun. His arms trembled. It was suddenly the heaviest object in the world. "Drop the scythe!"

"You and I both want this filthy pig dead," Sykes said, his lilting voice taking on a heavy rasp. The back and shoulder of his coat were slick, drenched with blood. "How about you let me do the dirty deed and we both walk away from this?"

"Just kill him!" Horne screamed, sputtering incoherently. "What are you waiting for?!"

"I can't let you do either of those things." Micah's finger twitched on the trigger. He was willing to fight. He had killed in the heat of battle. But this was different. He'd never killed someone face to face. He didn't want to do this.

He hesitated.

"Micah," Gabriel said from behind him.

He nearly sagged in relief. Gabriel was alive. He was okay.

He was only distracted for a moment, but a moment was all it took.

Sykes plunged the scythe deep into Horne's belly.

Micah pressed the trigger. A crackling blast split the air. A hole the size of a softball opened up in the side of Sykes's skull, the edges seared and smoking. His limp body tumbled sideways. He was dead before he hit the polished marble floor.

Micah dropped the gun and raced to Horne. He knelt over him, heedless of the puddle of blood pooling beneath Horne's crumpled body. Horne's eyes were glassy. They stared up at the ceiling high above them, seeing nothing.

Horne wasn't a good person. Maybe he never would have changed, no matter how many chances he was given. Now, no one would ever know. Death was an ugly, terrible thing, no matter how much the victim deserved it. "He's dead."

Gabriel came up behind him and gently wrestled the gun from his stiff fingers. "And we're not."

He nodded dully. "I killed Sykes."

"He was a murderer. He would've hunted us down. And the others. Whoever got in his way. You did what you had to do, Micah."

Micah stared at the bodies. Bile roiled in his stomach, acid stinging the back of his throat. "If I hadn't hesitated, Horne would be alive."

"They both made their choices."

"I know." He did know. He would never condone violence, never choose it if there were any other way, but men who lived by the sword died by it, too. That was Jack London's law of club and fang, wasn't it? It came true for Sykes. For Horne.

Would it be true for Gabriel? For Micah? That remained to be seen. All they could do was their best. That's what Jericho used to say. The rest was out of their hands.

"There will be other Pyros," Gabriel said. "The hunting parties are headed back. The drones sent out alerts. Moruga is still out there. If he finds us, he'll kill us. We have to go now."

Micah rose to his feet numbly. It felt like hours had passed since the first bullet had struck the elevator doors. In reality, it had been mere minutes. So much destruction and death in so little time.

Gabriel placed a heavy hand on Micah's shoulder. "Let's find our people."

31

WILLOW

Willow tucked the gun inside her waistband and grabbed the flamethrower from its strap around her shoulder. She opened the ignition valve with trembling fingers, struggling to remember the hurried instructions Li Jun had given earlier.

Yuan reached over and pressed the button that activated the spark plugs. "Point and shoot. It has wicked fire-power. Streams of napalm that shoot fifty—"

He cried out as a rat leapt onto his shin. He dislodged it by slamming his leg against the wall.

Another rat climbed up her shin. She seized it with her free hand and flung it to the ground. She pulled gently, half-depressing the trigger. A searing, twenty-foot flame whooshed out, blasting the rat. "Take that, you bastard!"

The rodent squealed and skittered back, but it was too late. A sizzle of fire engulfed its fat, bristling body. She spun in a circle, obliterating anything that moved. Fifty rats burned to a crisp in an instant.

Hundreds of rats squeaked and chittered, scrabbling away from her in a widening arc. Their shiny black eyes reflected the orange, flickering light. "They saw their comrades die. They know what it means."

"Of course they do," Li Jun said like he was personally affronted. "I told you they were intelligent."

"I'll have to take your word for it."

Together, they drove the horde back. The rats squeaked and squealed in fury but scurried back from the flames. Gradually, the river of hunched creatures ebbed away like a fading tide. They slipped into cracks and crevices and pipes and grates.

"It's working. They're leaving."

Yuan scratched his head, frowning.

"What?"

"That was too easy."

She switched off the flame and huffed her bangs out of her eyes. "Maybe you need to check your thesaurus app. That did not at all fit into my definition of 'easy.'"

"We only killed a handful of them. The rest fled."

She remembered what he'd said about rats communicating with each other and suppressed a shudder. "You said they're smart, didn't you? I'd run from fire, too."

The remaining rats kept rising on their haunches to glare at them, if rats could glare. Li Jun let off a short blast. A dozen rats met their fiery demise. The rest of them scuttled into the darkness.

More sounds echoed further down the tunnel. Willow dropped the flamethrower and drew her gun. Li Jun did the same. Was it Micah and Gabriel and Horne? Or were the Pyros coming for them?

She gritted her teeth. "Come on, come on."

Li Juan peered down the tunnel with his night vision goggles. "They're human, at least. Two of them."

Micah appeared out of the darkness. He sprinted toward her, his dark hair a mess, his glasses skewed. Gabriel followed close behind, several fresh bruises and cuts marring his jaw and forehead.

She could have kissed Micah. She was so relieved. She pulled him into a quick hug. "Have I told you recently how beautiful you are?"

Micah gave her a shaky grin. "Not recently, no. But there's no time like the present."

"Save your flirting for later," Li Jun said. "Where's the traitor?"

Micah shook his head, his face pale. "He didn't make it."

"Horne is dead. So is Sykes," Gabriel said. "Moruga will be coming for us."

Willow pointed ahead. "They went that way. We're holding off the rats for a few more minutes, just to make sure it's safe."

Micah hesitated. "I'll stay—"

She waved him off. "We'll be right behind you."

Micah nodded. He trusted her to handle this. He and Gabriel sprinted down the tunnel. Willow watched them go.

"I used to work at Rodell Industries, you know," Li Jun said quietly.

She turned to him. He was definitely the brainy type, though he clearly knew his way around a gun, too. The digital snake tattoo winding up his neck shimmered in the dim light. His angular face was sharp and hungry-looking, but his eyes weren't cruel. She should hate him, but she didn't. "Yeah?"

"I was studying bioengineering at Georgia Tech. I interned at Rodell between classes. I wanted to be a scientist, one of the few jobs not taken over by metalheads. My family was barely hanging on, you know? My folks worked three jobs each and stayed in the slums of Doraville so they could send me to school." His features hardened, his face grave. "Two years ago, the rotting tenement building we lived in collapsed. My parents were inside. The governor sent some drones and cop-bots to sift through the rubble, but only a handful of human rescue workers. They said they couldn't waste valuable resources, claiming the drone scanners had determined everyone inside was already dead. But they didn't know. How could they know? What they meant was, the slums could burn for all they cared.

"When they finally uncovered my father's body five days later, they found notes he'd written to us on the slab of concrete crushing his legs. He'd still be alive if…" He cleared his throat. "Anyway, I dropped out of Georgia Tech and joined the New Patriots a week later."

Willow's throat thickened. She swallowed. So much grief and sorrow everywhere. Too much. "Why are you telling me this?"

"Because I saw the way you looked at us. But the New Patriots aren't terrorists. We're freedom fighters."

"Whatever you say." She felt a prick of guilt at the words. She understood Li Jun's suffering better than most. And his anger. She didn't dislike him, though he was both a Pyro and a New Patriot. She glanced down the dark tunnel, straining for sounds. "Why are you risking all of this for us?"

"Because of the girl who survived the Hydra virus. If it's true, if she's really got the vaccine or the cure or whatever inside her, that changes everything. We can stop brutalizing each other, fighting for the scraps of a dying civilization. We can build something new."

He sounded just like Micah. "I hope you're right."

Li Jun pulled something out of his pocket. She eyed it warily. "What the hell is that?"

Shadows flickered over Li Jun's features. His mouth tightened, his expression scared but determined. He hefted a dark, egg-shaped object in his hand. "Plan D."

Willow's eyes widened. A pulse grenade.

"You should go now," Li Jun said firmly. "The rats will come back. I'll do this alone."

"And leave you to be the hero and get all the credit? I don't think so. I have a kick-ass reputation to uphold. We do this together."

"Halvsies on the credit?"

"Done. Now tell me how to kill these flea-infested mutants."

"When the rats show up again, because they will, I'll hurl it down the tunnel. I'll activate it here," he flicked his Smartflex, "and we'll take out as many as we can. The explosion will kill most of the main colony, hopefully. At any rate, it will create a wall of fire that will stun and confuse them, for a few minutes at least. It should be enough time to get us all out of here."

She smiled grimly. "Then we run like hell?"

He nodded. "Then we run like hell."

Something heavy plopped onto her shoulder.

Something else landed on her head. A hairless, scaly tail brushed the side of her face. Faint and tickling, like a feather.

Human speech failed her. Her scream died in her throat.

She flailed at the creature clawing at her scalp. She jerked her head and flung the thing away.

Dark, squirming shapes fell all around her. Rats dropped from a large grate in the ceiling, oozing out from the holes. More rats scurried along the pipes above their heads.

Abruptly the entire tunnel was alive, writhing and squirming with thousands of bristling bodies.

The rat clinging to her shoulder chittered angrily in her ear. She punched it off with the butt of her gun. But there were more. So many more.

Li Jun was right. These vermin were smart. They'd pretended to flee, only to regroup and return through the ceiling, attacking from above. The cunning bastards.

She cowered, attempting to cover her head and protect her face even as she thrashed wildly with the flamethrower, trying to knock the thing off. A wriggling rat tangled in her hair. She seized it and hurled it against the wall.

She stepped on another rat, lost her balance, and fell to her hands and knees.

A huge rat as large as a cat slammed onto Li Jun's head. He stumbled, arms flailing. The grenade slipped from his fingers and rolled across the floor.

Before he could regain his footing, rats swarmed him. A squirming knot tumbled from the ceiling and landed on his chest. They slithered over him in seconds, a mass of quivering bodies and gnashing yellow teeth. He beat at them, sending a pile skittering off his torso. But there were more, scrabbling at his feet, his ankles, digging their claws into his pant legs.

Horrified panic coursed through her veins. Half of her screamed to run, get out, to *survive*, by any means necessary. The other half wouldn't let her flee. She couldn't just leave him behind. He wasn't one of them. But he had still risked his life to save them all. Benjie would live because of him.

Micah was right. There was more to surviving than staying alive. She decided who she was going to be. What she was going to stand for. Whether she was a hero or a coward. And she sure as hell wasn't a coward.

She hadn't saved Zia. She hadn't saved her mother. But she'd be damned if she left anyone else behind. She couldn't abandon Li Jun to die.

She forced herself to move. She scrambled to her feet and shot a blast of fire at the rats, aiming to either side of Li Jun. She couldn't get too close or she'd burn him, too. She killed a hundred rats, two hundred, their death squeals echoing through the tunnel.

A handful skittered away. They shied away from the blast, but they'd scented blood now. They were voracious, the virus boiling their tiny brains, forcing them to bite, bite, bite, even at their own peril.

She backed away, searching desperately for any way that she could help Li Jun. A hot wave of fear and revulsion burned through her. There were too many of them. She couldn't get to him. She couldn't save him.

Li Jun screamed. A rat clawed at his face and bit deep into his cheek. He shrieked in anguish as dozens of razor-sharp teeth sank into his hands, face, and neck.

"Li Jun!" she cried. She stared, helpless, horrified, frozen in terror.

Li Jun lifted his arm high into the air, his SmartFlex glinting. He intended to activate the grenade with his SmartFlex. But it had fallen on the ground nearby. There was no way to find it somewhere beneath the bristling sea of vermin. She only knew it was close. Much too close.

Rats crawled over Li Jun, scratching, biting, gnawing. The entire squirming, writhing horde burst from the tunnel behind them. He moaned. "Run!"

Heaven help her, but she ran. Ten steps, twenty, her heart in her throat.

A flash of white-hot light blinded her.

The blast knocked her off her feet and slammed her body against the concrete. Her forehead and nose struck the ground. Pain erupted in her skull, splintering through her brain, screaming through every nerve and cell in her body.

The explosion shook the tunnel, raining gravel and chunks of concrete down on her head. Heat seared her exposed skin. Her ears rang. Blood filled her mouth.

The world throbbed red, like a wound.

She shook all over, gasping, struggling to breathe, to suck oxygen into her starving lungs. She scrambled to her hands and knees, waves of dizziness pulsing through her, nearly bowling her over.

She blinked away the stinging tears streaming from her eyes, rubbing her face furiously, desperate to clear the blackness wavering in the corners of her vision.

Her hand came back streaked with red.

Her thoughts were scattered and broken. What just happened? Why was she on the ground? Why couldn't she get up?

The rats. Li Jun, fighting them off. The explosion. The rats. *Oh, hell. Li Jun.*

She vomited sour, burning stomach acid. Her trembling legs wouldn't hold her weight. They were liquid, weak as water. She tried to stand and collapsed. Abrasions scraped her hands and elbows. The knees of her pant legs were ripped and bloody. More blood dripped into her eyes.

Her head was on fire. No, that was the pain. She touched her forehead gingerly, felt split skin. Was that bone? White and scarlet and black swirled across her vision. Her mind went dark, came back again.

Li Jun.

She managed to turn, craning her neck. Her head splintered with the pain of moving. Everything was hazy and disconnected.

Fire consumed the tunnel behind her, flames licking the walls and ceiling. Orange shadows writhed over stone and concrete. Hundreds—thousands—of small, bulging shapes littered the ground. Some of them burning. Most of them charred and blackened. None of them moving. A giant rodent lay a few feet behind her, its head missing.

The rats were dead.

She blinked through burning tears. She glimpsed an arm. A twisted leg.

A devastated moan vibrated deep in her throat. Li Jun had died for all of them. For her, too.

She didn't know how long she huddled there in shock, curled on the ground, her mind sinking into blackness, into red fire, into pain like an axe shattering glass, shattering her body, her brain, her everything.

Maybe it was two minutes. Maybe it was two hours.

A large hand seized her arm. The voice sounded far away, so very far. "Willow...you're safe now...I've got you."

Someone lifted her like a baby and pressed her against a broad, warm chest. She recognized the smell, dense and woodsy and sweet; recognized the heft of the person who carried her, both softness and strength somehow combined in one.

Her vision dimmed, the darkness coming for her at last, but she knew the face looming over her, knew it like her own: mischievous eyes, rich brown skin, that goofy, lopsided grin.

Finn had come back for her.

32

GABRIEL

G abriel slogged through the snow. The bitter cold stung his face and throat. He checked his rifle with fingers he could barely feel. But he was alive. Everyone was alive. That was all that mattered.

Cleo's plan had been dangerous but brilliant. Two hundred Pyros hunting them, but in all the wrong places. No sane person would double back and infiltrate the very headquarters they were attempting to flee. No sane person would intentionally descend into the death trap of the sewer system.

By the time the drones alerted the Pyros to their plan, it was too late. They were gone before the hunting parties returned. Even if the Pyros figured out the sewer ploy, there were so many tunnels and escape routes, they were impossible to track.

The plan had cost Li Jun his life, and almost Willow's. But it had worked.

The snow fell thick and heavy. The tracks they'd left would be covered again soon. But even if their footprints were discovered hours or days from now, they would be long gone.

They reached the AirRail station two hours before dawn. Elevator pods took riders from the ground to the slim, enclosed platform three stories above them, but without power, they wouldn't budge.

They climbed up the service ladder built into the steel support columns to get to the tracks. Up here, there were no rat hordes or dog packs, no aggressive infected whatever creatures to worry about. They could spot potential hostiles from this vantage point, but the height also exposed them. Luckily, the night would hide them through the most dangerous part of the journey.

They turned off their lights and walked in darkness, their way guided by the murky glimmer of moonlight. The snow blew into their faces, a cold wind nipping at their necks and cheeks. The city below them blurred into dark shadows and pale white shapes.

Gabriel trudged along the snow-covered magnetic steel tracks, taking point with Cleo, who wore the only pair of night vision goggles. Silas and Micah guarded their rear. Amelia helped Celeste hobble along and held Benjie's hand to keep him from the edge.

Finn strode resolutely behind Gabriel, blood seeping through his bandaged shoulder, his teeth gritted against the pain. He cradled Willow to his chest in his huge arms. She hadn't regained consciousness since the tunnels.

No one could dissuade Finn from carrying her, though both Micah and Gabriel tried. "You're only hurting yourself. Let me do it," Gabriel offered.

"You don't feel it now because of the stims," Cleo warned, "but you're causing further damage to your shoulder, tearing tissue, muscle, ligaments. Our doctor can only do so much without a real hospital. We don't even have cell regeneration therapy."

Finn's face was set in granite. "This is not up for debate. I'm doing this."

Their pleading was as futile as wind battering a mountain. He would not be moved.

Finn may have been a pacifist, but he was huge and strong as a bear. Attempting force against him was a bad idea for all involved. "Leave him be," Micah said finally.

Finn carried Willow for long, dreary hours in the cold and wind. He uttered no complaints. He did not falter.

They all trudged in silence, thinking their own thoughts, lost in their own private fear and grief and hope.

Dawn finally came, the world gradually lightening to shades of charcoal and ash. Gabriel kept twisting around to take in the Atlanta skyline growing slowly distant, the skyscrapers jutting proud and unbroken, billowing smoke staining the fire-scarred sky.

The further away they got, the safer they were.

Northwest, the track hugged Interstate 75, toward the city of Marietta. Gradually, the tangled network of roads, highways, and overpasses thinned. The city gave way to dense residential areas; to suburbs, towns, and neighborhoods, the buildings and vehicles and streets blanketed in a shroud of pristine white.

As the day passed, hunger burned in his belly. They hadn't had anything to eat in thirty-six hours. Cleo had brought several water bottles to share, but it wasn't enough.

He was exhausted from the tremendous exertion of fighting for survival. Every muscle in his body ached. His bones ached. But he'd done his duty. He'd saved them. Jericho was gone, but he'd kept everyone else that mattered alive.

It felt like they'd been walking for days. In the distance, a pack of feral dogs howled menacingly. He stiffened, then relaxed. They were safe from the dogs, at least. Humans, however, were another matter. He glimpsed a few dark shapes darting between buildings, but no one threatened them.

Cleo had spoken little all day. Her eyes had gone wide and hard when Finn emerged from the dark tunnel with Willow limp in his arms, but without Li Jun.

"He was a good Patriot," she had said simply, her fierce expression closed and unreadable, then turned and marched off into the black subway tunnels ahead of them.

"How many New Patriots are left?" Gabriel asked now.

"Enough."

"Seriously."

She slanted her eyes at him. "How do I know I can trust you?"

His jaw twitched. "What part of the last twenty-four hours wasn't up to your standards?"

She considered that for a moment. "What's the New Patriot creed?"

The words had the bitter, ashy taste of death on his tongue. He said them anyway. "For the honor of true patriots and the love of country."

She blew out a frozen breath.

"Now do you trust me?"

"Nope. Not even a little." She flung her purple braids over her shoulder. "But I guess there's no harm in telling you what you'll find out anyway. We've gathered a community of over six hundred people."

Gabriel whistled.

"But half of those are families—women and children, non-fighters. And most of them are survivors we've recruited over the last several months. Our rank of actual New Patriots is only ninety or so. Which is why we need you. "

A gust of freezing wind blasted them. He shivered. Heavy flurries of snow swirled down from the gunmetal sky. There was no visible sun behind the haze of thick clouds, but it had to be late afternoon by now. The shadows were deepening, the cold sharp and bracing.

"How much longer?"

Cleo wrapped her leather jacket tighter around herself. She pointed to a copse of barren trees around a raised platform in the distance. An American flag tied to a pole on the roof snapped in the wind. "Up there. Less than a quarter mile."

He cocked his brows. "That's it?"

She nodded.

"Doesn't look like much."

"That's the point. Don't worry. They received my message. They're coming."

"So who's in charge of this place?"

She looked at him askance, sizing him up. "General Reaver."

"Never heard of him."

She smiled dryly. "General Reaver is the founder and leader of the New Patriots. Only the captains of the city-wide chapters knew the regional lieutenants, who knew the state colonels, et cetera. To protect the leadership and sanctity of the cause. Who was your captain?"

Gabriel's blood pressure rose. Instinctively, he curled his free hand into a fist. He never thought he'd have to deal with the New Patriots again. They were a blot on his past, the stuff of his nightmares, his deepest shame. Yet here he was, about to speak the name of the man who'd mentored him, who'd loved him and treated him like he was worth something, then betrayed him and everything he thought they stood for.

And Gabriel had killed him for it. He swallowed. "Simeon Pagnini."

"The name sounds familiar. General Reaver would know it."

"Are you close with him?"

She flashed that enigmatic smile again. "You mean her. General Reaver is my mother."

Before he could react, a sound came from somewhere above

247

them. An electric engine whine and the heavy whirr of thumping rotors filled the air.

"Look!" Benjie cried, pointing.

Amelia and Celeste gasped.

A military-grade Vortex hoverjet appeared over the tree line, zooming toward them through the thickly falling snow.

He'd grown up seeing planes and drones and choppers and hovercrafts of all kinds in the sky every single day. But after months of wondering if the whole world had died, the oblong aircraft hovering above them was disconcerting and strangely alien, like it was too good to be true.

Buffeting wind hit him like a slap. He bent against it, shielding his eyes with his hand.

The Vortex hovered over them then lowered slowly to the ground, rotors blasting swirling air, blowing away the snow and spitting up clumps of dirt and rock beneath its churning blades.

The Vortex settled on the ground about twenty yards ahead of them.

"Let's go, Miss Amelia!" Benjie cried, yanking on Amelia's hand.

"No running!" she admonished, though he was already pulling himself free of her grasp.

Cleo turned to Gabriel, her arm outstretched, that sly smile twitching her lips. "Your chariot awaits you."

33

GABRIEL

Three hours later, Gabriel sat at one end of a large, battered-metal table facing the surviving leadership of the New Patriots. They sat at the far end of the table, well outside the ten-foot infection radius. Several armed guards were ranged around the room. A woman in a hazmat suit stood ready to decontaminate every inch of the place as soon as the meeting ended.

Gabriel and his people were segregated in the isolation block due to quarantine, assigned their own barracks at the far east end of the compound. Everyone who came in contact with them remained several feet away and wore gloves and masks at all times. But they weren't treated with fear, only caution.

Gabriel's eyes were bleary from lack of sleep. After this meeting, he would sleep for two days. But now, he remained alert as he faced the New Patriots.

He shifted uncomfortably in the metal folding chair. There were five men and four women at the opposite end of the table, ranging from their mid-twenties to their mid-sixties, all armed and staring at Gabriel in open suspicion. Most of them wore gloves, but their masks were pulled down around their necks.

They held tablets and wore SmartFlexes. Cleo had explained that a tower at the top of the mountain gave them a secure, enclosed network for communication and tech support within the compound.

Cleo leaned against the far wall, her arms crossed over her chest, her expression impassive. A thick cigar was clenched between her teeth, a tendril of white smoke drifting toward the low ceiling.

Micah sat tense and fidgeting on one side of him, Amelia equally tense but completely still on his other side. The New Patriots had wished to speak solely to Gabriel, but he'd insisted Micah and Amelia join him.

"How are your friends settling in?" General Reaver asked, her voice deep and throaty as a smoker's. She was a stern but attractive black woman in her late forties. She and Cleo shared few physical characteristics, but they had the same haughty jaunt to the chin and the same cold, cunning eyes. She was dressed in a tailored navy blue wool coat buttoned to the collar. Her gloved hands were folded neatly on the table.

"Very well, thank you," Amelia said politely.

Willow, Finn, and Celeste were being treated in the infirmary for their wounds. Willow had awakened shortly after their arrival. She had several lacerations, a deep cut on her forehead, and a possible concussion, but she was lucky. She'd sustained no serious injuries from the explosion. Celeste had received a blood transfusion and stitches. Finn was still being examined.

"I know you would probably like nothing more than a good meal and a full night's sleep," General Reaver continued. "And I assure you, you will soon enough. However, Cleodora and her partner, Chen Li Jun, made great sacrifices to bring you to us. Chen willingly gave up his life. I hope you will respect those sacrifices."

"Of course," Amelia said demurely. Her short, choppy hair was tucked behind her ears. She sat ramrod straight, with perfect posture though she had to be as weary as Gabriel. She was as elegant as ever. "We are incredibly grateful to them both for saving our lives."

"We appreciate your cooperation," said a man to Amelia's right. His skin was distinctly olive-toned, with thick black brows connecting in the center of his forehead like a caterpillar. He was in his fifties and heavy, his jaw blurring into his neck, his plump belly bulging against his sweater vest.

"This is Colonel Patel Reid," General Reaver said by way of introduction. "He oversaw the East Coast before the collapse."

"You were on the *Grand Voyager* mission," interrupted a second woman. Her dirty-blonde hair was cut into a harsh bob, and her skin was the pallor of mayonnaise. Deep lines around her mouth and eyes told of a hard life.

"This is Liza Willis," General Weaver said. "A long-time solder recently promoted to colonel."

"You served under Simeon Pagnini," Willis said.

"Yes, I did." He felt Amelia's eyes on him. What was she thinking? Was she judging him, hating him? Remembering all over again every terrible thing he'd done on the *Grand Voyager*? How he'd betrayed her?

His mouth went dry, shame flooding him. He tried not to flinch, to keep his expression even. Whatever he personally felt for Simeon Pagnini, he knew better than to show it here.

The people around the table were nodding in admiration. "He was a good man," the woman said gruffly. "Very committed."

"He was," Gabriel said, then hesitated. "He taught me everything I know."

"He taught you well," Cleo said from the corner, a hint of admiration in her voice. She tapped ash from her cigar and blew out a circle of smoke. "This one's a hell of a fighter."

The blonde woman grunted, her gaze lasering in on Gabriel, appraising him. "Surely we're not here just for him."

"You're here for me," Amelia said calmly. "I'm immune from the Hydra virus."

Willis shrugged. She didn't wear gloves or a mask. "Many of us still left are."

"I am immune because I already had the virus."

The room fell completely silent. Her words fell into the silence like stones. He could almost see the ripples vibrating the air around them.

"That's impossible," Willis scoffed.

"It's not," Micah said. "She got sick, and she almost died. I saw the blood coming out of her eyes. It was the Hydra virus. Then she woke up the next day and she was cured."

"Cured," Colonel Reid breathed, like the word itself was a miracle.

"And why should we believe you?" Willis's eyes narrowed, her tone distinctly chilly.

Amelia squared her shoulders. "Because I am the daughter of Declan Black, chairman of the Unity Coalition, founder and CEO of BioGen Technologies."

There was an audible gasp.

"I'm sure you've seen vlogs and newsfeeds of me standing beside my father at numerous galas and press announcements. You may take a retinal scan to verify my identity if you wish."

Colonel Willis's eyes lit with recognition. So did General Reaver, whose gaze narrowed. "An elite," she spat.

"There's no place for you here," Colonel Willis said with a scowl.

Colonel Reid, however, smiled broadly. He exchanged glances

with the man next to him. "The daughter of the most powerful man in the country. Maybe we can find some use for you."

Gabriel tensed, his hand going to his gun. "If you think—"

Amelia shot him a look, stilling the words in his throat. Her expression was calm and determined. She didn't hesitate. "My father was taken by terrorists on the *Grand Voyager*. Any of the elites who may have considered me an asset are now likely long dead. My only value to you or the Sanctuary is in the cure that may reside inside me."

Colonel Reid frowned, seemingly disappointed.

"Then we have no need for her," Colonel Willis said, her voice dripping with disdain. "She and her corrupt kind can find their own way down the mountain." She crossed her arms over her chest. "Or maybe we dispose of her in a more...permanent fashion."

The air crackled with tension. The hostility emanating off the New Patriots was palpable. Beneath the table, Gabriel's finger twitched for his gun.

General Reaver pursed her lips. "And what of the cure?"

"A ploy," one of the women at the far end of the table said in a mocking tone, "to save her precious skin."

This conversation wasn't going well. This was a bad idea. They needed to get out of here. Gabriel needed to pull his gun and get Amelia and Micah out of here before things got really ugly.

"I believe her." Cleo pushed herself off the wall. "And so did Moruga. She did not volunteer this little nugget to try and save herself. One of her own group turned traitor and divulged the information."

General Reaver raised her brows, still skeptical.

Cleo sauntered to the head of the table next to her mother. She pointed her cigar at Amelia. "Someone somewhere had to survive this damn virus. Why not her?"

"Even if it is true, what are we supposed to do about it?" Reid asked.

"Send her to the Sanctuary," Cleo said. "Their labs will find the cure. Then she smuggles it out to us."

"We have a lab here," Reid said.

"Not a good one," Cleo said. "And not a research facility."

General Reaver leaned back in her seat. She glanced at Cleo again before sharing a long look with Colonel Reid. She seemed to respect Cleo's opinion, even though she was young and hot-headed. Maybe they'd make it out of here in one piece after all.

"They're right," the General said finally. "If this information is true, then it is imperative to act on it. The reward is too great not to take this seriously. But we will need the Sanctuary resources."

"We'll help get her in," Cleo said, leaning forward, her voice rising. This was the most animated Gabriel had seen her. Except maybe when she was torturing Willow. "We have a man inside. He'll help her. Then once their scientists have used her blood to manufacture the cure or whatever, he'll help her steal it and bring it back to us."

Amelia frowned. "Why would you need to steal it?"

Every eye turned to her. Their gazes were still closed and suspicious, hostile. Gabriel's gut twinged uneasily. He could feel the hatred pulsing in the air, all of it directed at Amelia. Because of who she was and everything she represented. He'd felt the same way, once upon a time.

Cleo's voice turned sharp as a blade. "How else would we get it? Do you think they're gonna just hand it out like candy?"

"It's the cure," Amelia said. "It will save thousands of lives. The world can begin again. Of course, they will—"

"They won't," General Reaver broke in. Her voice had gone as cold as her daughter's. "The Sanctuary isn't a sanctuary for all. It is only for the *elites*. Only those they consider the brightest, the wealthiest, the *best*. The rest are left to rot."

Cleo's anger radiated off her in waves. *"We're* left to rot."

Gabriel's own pulse quickened. Of course, the Sanctuary was too good to be true. The government had created it, the same corrupt government that destroyed its own country for years, for decades, consolidating all its wealth, power, and resources for the elites, and the elites alone.

Even with the world falling to pieces around them, the elites were still only concerned with themselves. They didn't care if everything else burned. He no longer hated Amelia, but his hatred for the elites remained, burning inside him.

Gabriel's jaw clenched, every muscle in his body tense and on edge, his veins boiling. *Stay in control.* Beneath the table, he dug his fingernails into his thighs.

"I see." Amelia's face darkened. Her lips pressed into a thin line, but she didn't protest. She didn't defend the elites like she would have only a few months ago. "I am willing to steal the cure for you. On one condition."

The men and women in the room stared at her like she'd grown two heads. General Reaver smiled indulgently. "What are your demands?"

Amelia stood up, her chair scraping across the floor. Gabriel couldn't take his eyes off her. Even with her loose, ill-fitting clothes, she was strong and determined. There wasn't a hint of hesitation or uncertainty in the firm set of her jaw. She'd never looked so beautiful.

"Last month, my mother was kidnapped by a gang of biker thugs and human-traffickers known as the Headhunters," Amelia said.

"We are familiar with them," General Reaver said evenly. "We are sorry for your loss."

"They trade with the Sanctuary on a regular basis. We have

reason to believe they are bringing my mother to the Sanctuary now. I will do as you ask, but I need you to help us rescue her."

The New Patriots shifted uncomfortably. Someone coughed into their mask. Colonel Reid and Colonel Willis exchanged irritated, disbelieving glances.

General Reaver's posture stiffened, nostrils flaring almost imperceptibly. "I'm sorry about your mother, but our numbers are critically low as it is. We cannot use manpower and resources—and risk precious lives—to save just one person. Everyone here understands that the mission is the most important value we uphold.

"Chen Li Jun understood that. He sacrificed his own life because he believed your life could bring about a greater good. My daughter risked her life for the same reason."

"And we appreciate that," Micah added, always the diplomat. Gabriel half-expected him to argue against Amelia. She was using the threat of withholding the cure—which would cost the lives of actual people—innocent men, women, and children. But he didn't. "We have also risked a great deal."

"You must understand," General Reaver said, her tone patronizing. "We cannot—"

"I need you to understand," Amelia interrupted. Her voice was hard as iron. "I watched your daughter stand by and do nothing while the man next to her shot and killed one of our own, Ed Jericho."

General Reaver's sharp gaze flickered to Cleo, clearly displeased.

Cleo's scowl deepened. "I did what I had to do. You knew that when you sent me in."

"Do not tell me the meaning of sacrifice," Amelia continued. "I know it, and I know it well."

Colonel Willis frowned. "Disrespect will not be tolerated at this table."

Gabriel knew how these people worked. They wanted Amelia

and the rest of their group to risk everything for the cause, but the New Patriots wouldn't risk anything in return. He shoved back his chair and stood next to Amelia. Micah shot to his feet on Amelia's other side. "Then we'll leave."

Everyone at the table leapt up, hands hovering over weapons. "Stay back!" Colonel Reid hissed, fumbling for his mask. "Remain outside the ten-foot infection radius!"

There was a long, tense moment of silence as they all stared at each other, sizing each other up, bodies taut, faces grim and wary.

"Are you threatening us?" Colonel Willis asked, bristling.

"You owe me your lives." Cleo's cigar trembled in her hand. She was angry. She had a right to be. Gabriel didn't care. Neither did Amelia.

"I am grateful to you, Cleodora," Amelia said without missing a beat, "but I will not be manipulated by anyone else, ever again. We made no binding agreement when you chose to release us. I owe you nothing." She turned back to the table, meeting the general's gaze with eyes of ice. Her tone brooked no argument. "I have laid out my terms. You may accept them or not. The decision is yours."

Amelia swept from the room. Micah stumbled from the table, his mouth gaping, and hurried after her.

Gabriel hesitated at the door, fairly bursting with pride—and an urge to laugh. These people hadn't expected to be outplayed by a young, puny-looking girl, too beautiful and fragile to pose any kind of challenge. They were wrong.

He gazed at each stony face, his own expression just as hard. "I'm sure we can come to a mutually beneficial arrangement. Let us know when you've assembled the rescue team."

34

WILLOW

"How's your head?" Finn asked.

"How do you think?" Willow gingerly touched the squishy white bandage affixed to her forehead. Beneath it, a nasty, two-inch gash was stitched closed. The concussion had left her dizzy for a few days, but there was no lasting damage. "No modeling career for me, I guess."

She was lucky to be alive. No, not lucky. She thought of Li Jun with a pang. She was alive because of him. He was a New Patriot, the enemy. The people who'd killed her sister and her mother. But he'd helped her—all of them—escape. He'd sacrificed his life for it. For her.

She couldn't wrap her head around it. Not yet. Things were so much easier when everything was black and white, when she could categorize people as good and bad.

They sat on either side of one of the picnic tables rimming the compound's rec yard. A handful of kids played soccer with Benjie, kicking the ball into an old, torn net and shouting gleefully in the winter air.

The New Patriots' base was an old low-security, self-sufficient prison nestled at the foothills of the Blue Ridge Mountains. Thirty or so miles north of Dalton, the Fort Cohutta Detention and Rehabilitation Center was nestled halfway up Wildwood Mountain. Its twenty acres were bound by a twenty-five-foot electrified fence topped with razor wire. The sheet-metal plates hammered around the bottom six feet of the fence looked new, as did the deep, freshly dug trench circling the compound.

The only road was a single gravel lane winding up a steep, forested hill bristling with pine, maple, walnut, and soaring hemlock and oak trees. The windows and doors of all exterior buildings had been painted black with light-blocking paint and then boarded up to make the place look abandoned from a distance.

But the empty guard towers were armed with automatic machine guns controlled from a command center deep inside the compound. Anyone stupid enough to break in would receive a nasty surprise.

Willow had spent a bit of time exploring, but they'd only been released from quarantine that morning. Christmas was in three days. Someone had planted a pine tree between the cafeteria and the women's barracks, and several children were decorating it with paper snowflakes, strings of shiny crimson beads, and various ornaments.

Willow glanced back at Finn. "How are you feeling?"

Finn shifted on the bench and winced. His right shoulder was bandaged, his arm in a sling to minimize movement. "A little like I've been attacked by a rabid skunk."

When Willow had woken up in the infirmary three days ago, Amelia told her how Finn insisted on carrying her the whole way— at least eighteen miles on foot, if not more, before the New Patriots had picked them up.

"You giant idiot!" she'd yelled when she found him in his own curtained cubicle in the infirmary, so huge in his hospital bed that his feet dangled off the end of the mattress.

The doctor, a middle-aged woman with short red hair, was scanning his shoulder with some kind of white wand, a 3D reconstruction of Finn's bullet-damaged shoulder on the holoscreen beside her.

"Hello to you, too," Finn said amiably, offering her his most adorable lopsided grin.

"Don't give me that!" She whirled on the doctor, her stomach knotting. If he'd done permanent damage to his body by carrying her, she was going to kill him. "How's his arm?"

"We performed a minor surgery to remove the bullet," the doctor said. "But that doesn't mean he's out of the woods. I debrided the area, removed several bullet fragments, and doused him with antibiotics, which should stop the infection in its tracks."

The doctor pursed her lips, scanning the holoscreen. "You're lucky the bullet missed the subclavian and brachial arteries. However, there is significant damage to your brachial plexus, the large nerve bundle that controls arm function. Neurological deficits due to nerve injuries may heal after a few months."

Willow's stomach dropped. She sank onto the edge of the bed beside Finn, careful not to bump him. "Will he lose the use of his arm? Tell us the truth. We can handle it."

The doctor hesitated, then shook her head. "You may never regain full or even partial mobility, Finn. You need a nerve cell rejuvenation procedure and flesh grafts. Unfortunately, our facilities are a bit…rudimentary. The best we can do right now is keep an eye on it. Keep it immobilized for six to eight weeks, minimum."

"Lucky I'm left-handed, I guess," Finn said, trying to sound upbeat but looking sick instead.

"Why'd you do something so stupid?" Willow asked as soon as

the doctor left. She hated that Finn was hurting, that she was help-less to do a thing. It made her want to punch something.

Finn adjusted the IV dripping fluids into his arm. He pushed himself carefully into a sitting position, looking embarrassed. "You don't know how useless I feel sometimes. Everyone fighting and risking their lives to save us. Everyone but me."

She blew her bangs out of her eyes with a huff. "You're not useless. Usually."

"This was something I could do." He had shrugged like it was the most reasonable thing in the world. "You were hurt and you needed me. That was all there was to it."

She'd had no idea what to say to that. She'd mumbled something about Benjie and gotten the hell out of there as fast as she could.

Her cheeks flushed again at the memory of his words. She ducked her head so her hair—freshly washed and brushed—fell across her face.

"Earth to Willow," Finn said with a crooked grin. "I have some-thing to help you feel better."

With a flourish, he lifted two bowls with his left hand and set them on the picnic table in front of them. They were filled with an oozing dark brown substance, a single, lopsided candle at the center of each bowl. "You didn't think I'd forget to celebrate your birthday, did you?"

She had no idea what to say. Warmth filled her from her toes to the top of her head.

"So it's brownie batter, not a cake." Finn nudged the candle that was slowly sinking into the batter. "I tried to sneak into the kitchen to make an actual cake, but I'm about as sneaky as a bull in a china shop. The chef caught me. He wouldn't give me any oil, and they didn't have eggs. But he did let me steal the box of brownie mix I'd stuffed under my shirt. Turns out, if you mix in a tad of water, it's phenomenally good."

She took a bite, closing her eyes in pleasure as the sweet, gooey chocolate melted on her tongue. It was the most delicious thing she'd ever tasted.

Finn mounded the batter on his spoon and shoveled it in his mouth. "Scrumptious, right?"

She ate some more, every bite a luscious explosion of delectable sweetness. "Benjie will love this."

"Don't worry. I saved some for him."

Several crows flew low, black shapes carving through the cobalt sky. They pecked at the popcorn strings strung around the pine tree the kids were decorating, black wings flapping. A dozen children shrieked in alarm and waved their arms, looking like little birds themselves.

She thought of Benjie's wooden carving. She thought of Raven. They'd promised to meet her. Was she still there, skulking in the woods, Shadow by her side as she watched the highway, waiting for them? She put down her spoon. "I've been thinking about Raven."

Finn wiped a smear of chocolate from his mouth with the back of his left hand. "Me, too."

"She said she'd watch I-575 for us. The town of Ball Ground, exit 27, remember? But we aren't there. She'll think we didn't make it. Or that we abandoned her. Neither of which are true."

"I'm sure she can handle herself."

"I know. But still." The girl had seemed perfectly capable out there in the forested wilderness with her wolf. Raven was a survivor. Willow still felt crappy about it, like she was breaking her word. Besides, she'd be far more comfortable with Raven than these enigmatic New Patriots.

"Willow, I've been meaning to talk to you about something." Finn moved his bowl aside. His gaze dropped to the table, then lifted to meet hers, his expression suddenly uncomfortable, even embarrassed. "I've had time to do a lot of thinking, and—"

Everything fell completely silent. Abruptly, she was very aware of his large, masculine hand resting on the wood picnic table inches from her own.

Panic seized her. She shoved off the bench and brushed fiercely at the snow crusting her pant legs. "I forgot I'm supposed to meet Silas to go over choke-holds and neck-punches."

"Willow—"

"I'll see you at dinner!" She forced brightness into her voice, though she felt like biting her tongue in half. *Stupid, stupid, stupid.* Finn probably thought she was an idiot.

She strode across the yard, forcing her head up and her shoulders back. Her skin prickled, sure his eyes were on her, judging her. She'd just acted like a complete moron. And for what?

It was Finn. Big, goofy Finn. Her constant. Her rock.

What was she so scared that he would say? Or maybe it was what she wanted him to say. What she was afraid he never would.

In a world where you counted yourself lucky to even be breathing, wasn't it hubris to long for something more? She'd done her best to keep those thoughts locked out of her head.

She didn't think about the adorable gap in Finn's front teeth. She didn't think about how it made her chest expand to see him with Benjie. She didn't think about how warm and secure she felt curled up next to him every night. How, no matter where they slept, he would always be there. And she certainly didn't think about how it felt to be wrapped in his strong arms, pressed tight to his burly chest, his heart beating steady against her ear, reassuring her that it was all going to be okay.

She couldn't think those thoughts because it didn't matter. It wouldn't matter. The world was ending and even if it wasn't, she was still just a poor Filipina girl from the slums. Just plain, chubby Willow. Not beautiful and captivating like Amelia or Celeste.

Finn thought of her like a kid sister, or at best, a good friend. Just like everyone else.

All she was really good at was injuring people on purpose. Not exactly a romantic draw. In a fight, she wanted people to underestimate her, to ignore her, to not even see her.

In real life, it sucked.

35

MICAH

"We'll do it," Cleo said with a scowl. "But you haven't made any friends with these unreasonable demands of yours."

The New Patriots had made them wait three days before agreeing to mount the rescue mission, perhaps hoping they would back down. They didn't. Micah adjusted his glasses. "We don't need friends. We need allies."

"Those either." She rested her hand on the butt of her holstered pulse gun as they walked. Cleo was giving Micah and Gabriel a tour of the grounds. She'd wanted only Gabriel, but his brother had insisted he join them.

The day was crisp, the sky a rich cobalt blue. A breeze rustled the giant pines towering around them. Tree limbs drooped, fattened with heavy, wet snow. Several children Benjie's age played tag between the buildings, stomping through melting drifts.

Adults crisscrossed the grounds, some directing hover carts full of vegetables harvested from the hydroponics farm, others working on repairing the metal roof of one of the barracks. Some were families strolling in the fresh air; others hardened soldiers—or maybe criminals—grim, armed, and heavily muscled.

Behind them, Wildwood Mountain cast a long shadow. The north end of the compound was pressed up against a sheer rock face that towered a good sixty feet above the single-story buildings. Sugar Spring River snaked along the east flank. The compound was surrounded by thousands of acres of dense woods that made up the Chattahoochee-Oconee National Forest.

"We leave Christmas morning before dawn," Cleo said. "Two days from now."

Micah nodded. He'd forgotten all about Christmas. He'd been too busy trying to stay alive.

He followed Cleo and Gabriel along the concrete pathways that wound through the old prison. Most of the compound consisted of squat, concrete buildings painted in dull brown and puke-green to blend in with the natural surroundings. The buildings spiraled off a large, snow-trampled rec yard in the center. Because it was a low-security prison built on theories of rehabilitation and community, there were few fences on the inside.

Cleo showed them the east and south barracks, which were the same as their own west side accommodations. The New Patriots called them barracks, but they were really just long rows of prison cells. Each concrete square allowed a dresser or bookshelf and a cot padded with an actual mattress.

"How do we know you won't withhold the cure once you get it?" Cleo asked abruptly. She wheeled to face them, her expression cold and suspicious. "We've already rescued you people at great personal expense, housed and fed you, and treated your injured. Now, we're going to fight a battle for you, all before you do a thing for us."

"A fair point." Gabriel's jaw bunched, his shoulders rigid. "Instead of joining the mission to infiltrate the Sanctuary, I volunteer to remain behind."

A slow, sly smile contorted the burned side of her face. "As a hostage, you mean?"

Gabriel's expression was pained. "If Amelia does not return, you may do with me as you wish."

"Gabriel, no—" Micah started, but his brother held up a hand to silence him.

"Is that a promise?" she asked carelessly, but he could tell it was an act. There was nothing careless about Cleo Reaver.

Micah glanced back and forth between them. This was a power play, one his brother was losing. There was a tension battling just beneath the surface that he didn't completely understand.

"Yes," Gabriel said heavily.

Cleo's smile was triumphant.

A seed of doubt sprouted in his gut. Would Gabriel really sacrifice himself? Or did he have another agenda in mind? Why would he willingly choose to stay behind with the New Patriots? They'd managed to find their way past the distrust, the lies, and the betrayals, but suddenly Micah wasn't so sure.

No. He trusted his brother. He wouldn't doubt him now. It was Cleo who deserved his suspicion.

"And how are we supposed to trust you?" Micah asked before he could stop himself. "We watched you torture our own people. You burned Willow."

"It wasn't personal. It was a job." She paused, a wicked smile curving her lips. "Though there's a lot to be said for enjoying your work."

"You take pleasure in hurting people?"

Her smile froze on her face. "Sometimes a sheep has to wear the wolf's clothing."

Gabriel shot him a warning glance. *Be careful*, his look said.

"How long have you been here?" Micah asked to change the subject to less hostile territory.

Cleo pulled a cigar and a lighter out of her pants' pocket and lit the cigar. "General Reaver made Fort Cohutta her chapter head-quarters six years ago, two years after the state abandoned the place due to resource shortages—aka nationwide drought and famine—and budget cuts. It's served as an emergency base ever since. Every chapter captain knew of its existence, though only a hundred or so lived here permanently before the world ended.

"Those of us who could brought our own families. We've also attempted to rescue people rejected by the Sanctuary where it was feasible. Many were members of the gangs the Pyros wiped out in Atlanta. We took them in over a month ago. The Earth Liberation Army, Right Hand of God, Latin Brotherhood, the Cobras."

"Thugs and killers?" Micah's gut tightened. He recalled his conversation with Jericho before he died. *He who fights with monsters...*

"Survivors." Cleo's eyes flashed. "They're people willing to do what needs to be done."

The look in her eyes chilled Micah to the bone. He longed to flee with every ounce of his being. There was danger here. It was dangerous for Gabriel, for all of them. But if they left, they were risking Elise's life. They were risking their own.

Where would they go? It was winter. They were in the middle of the wilderness. Outside of this place, there was no power, no heat. And they'd made deadly enemies of both the Headhunters and the Pyros.

Their options were limited. And without Jericho, they were leaderless.

Later that night, he found Amelia outside their barracks. He'd been wanting to talk to her since they'd arrived. She understood him in a way no one else did, not even Gabriel.

The cold air was sharp in his lungs. The stars were glittering shards of ice sprinkled across the black bowl of the sky. The world was hushed with an almost reverent silence.

"Maybe we should leave," he said, speaking the misgivings he was hesitant to share with his brother. "I don't have a good feeling about this, about these people."

"We need them," she whispered back, her expression determined in the pale moonlight. "How can we take on the Headhunters by ourselves? Especially without Jericho. We don't know where they meet with the Sanctuary. We don't know what road they'll come in on. We don't know the territory or the possible traps. We need help."

Micah's stomach twisted uneasily. "We'll figure something out. We always have."

She rubbed her charm bracelet, which she wore outside her sweater now, but still bound to the leather cord he'd given her all those weeks ago. It suited her. She met his gaze, the set of her jaw firm and uncompromising. "Maybe not. But if the Sanctuary is what they say it is, then we need their help to get inside, too. We can't be stupid, Micah. We've lost too many people already."

Micah sighed in frustration. He hated it, but she was right.

"I know this isn't easy," She said gently. "You're always talking about being good, about choosing a better way."

"I killed Sykes," he blurted suddenly.

She cocked her head, studying him. "He would have killed you if you hadn't."

He tried to articulate the ugly tangle of emotions inside him. "I feel guilty because I killed him, even though I know I needed to. And I feel even more guilty because I didn't kill him fast enough. If I hadn't hesitated, Horne would be alive."

She clucked her tongue. "You feel that way because you're a good person. That's the burden of a leader."

"I don't feel like a leader," he said quietly. He felt weak, afraid, and full of doubts. "What if I'm wrong? What if I make a mistake? We trusted Horne. We almost died for it. Jericho did die for it."

"You offered mercy to Gabriel and Silas when neither of them deserved it. And they turned around and saved our lives. Horne made his own choice to betray us." Her expression softened. "Don't let people like him change who you are, Micah. You taught me that."

"You're right." He smiled at her, but it was stiff. Tension still twisted like a screw inside him.

"You're worried this is the *Grand Voyager* all over again."

For a moment, he didn't answer. Then, he nodded.

"It won't be." She reached out and squeezed his arm. Her touch was gentle and light, like the brush of a butterfly wing. She was so close, her eyes so bright. "Because this time, we aren't victims."

She looked like a warrior queen from some distant time and place, with her white-blonde hair a shimmering corona around her face, her delicate features carved in ivory, her eyes blazing with a fierce conviction. Moonlight spilled all around them, like diamonds reflecting off the snow.

"This time," she said, "we decide our fate."

She squeezed his arm, sending him both strength and comfort, reminding him who he was. He felt her touch like sparks shooting through his veins. He licked his lips, heat flushing his face. A tiny thing was loosed inside him, set free, like his heart had sprouted feathers and winged away.

He could have kissed her.

But he didn't. She wasn't his, and never would be. But he loved her all the same.

36

AMELIA

Christmas Eve dawned cold and gray.

Amelia and the others found a plot of unfrozen Georgia clay in a small clearing beneath a hundred-year-old oak tree, so tall its branches seemed to rake the sky. Half a mile beyond the compound, the dense and wild forest pressed in all around them.

Gabriel dug the grave. The ground was tough and hard, but he managed. The snow on the ground had mostly melted. The sky was a muffled gray, thick with charcoal clouds. Flurries of heavy, wet snowflakes dusted their heads and shoulders.

Micah found some scrap wood and cobbled together a small wooden cross.

Micah said a prayer for Jericho's soul and recited Dylan Thomas's famous poem from memory. *"Do not go gentle into that good night,"* he finished quietly, *"but rage, rage against the dying of the light."* Though they had no body and no coffin, they each wrote notes—memories, regrets, hopes—on old-fashioned scraps of paper and tossed them into the earth.

Silas stood stiffly beside her, his hands balled into fists at his sides, his face a rigid mask. Only his eyes betrayed a lost and wretched anguish. But he was here. He didn't run. He didn't scowl or sneer or scream or hit anything. He stayed present and a part of their grief.

She reached out and grabbed his hand. She pressed all her tenderness, love, and comfort through her fingers, offering solace in the only way he would take it. He tensed, but he did not pull away.

They stood around the grave in silence. All of them that were left, all of them that had been through hell together and come out the other side. They were family now. She, Silas, Micah, Benjie, Willow, Finn, Celeste. Gabriel.

After it was over, Amelia and Willow drifted back toward the compound, walking side by side along a snow-trampled path. Out beyond the fence, the ground was steep, the woods wild and untamed. They stepped over gnarled roots hidden beneath the snow as they trudged past brittle tangles of underbrush.

"We've lost too many people," Willow said quietly.

"I know," Amelia said.

"We can't lose any more."

Her stomach twisted. "We won't."

They walked in silence for awhile. The air here was clean and crisp, nothing like the fetid, smoke-choked air of Atlanta. The falling snow formed little drifts and ridges beneath the trees, covering the battle-scarred earth in a blanket of white.

Everything looked brand new. Like the world could start over if it really wanted to. Like they all could. She turned to Willow. "I wanted to thank you, for what you did."

Willow looked at her sharply. "For what?"

"Back in the mall, with the fire and the rats. When I—when I had the seizure. You could have kept going. You had every right to. But you didn't."

Willow kicked at a rock in the path. "Micah did all the heavy lifting. He's the one who carried you, who wouldn't leave your side. You should have seen him."

"What do you mean?"

"The way he held you, the look on his face, like he was watching you die right there, like it was the worst thing that ever happened to him."

Amelia's blush deepened. "What are you saying?"

Willow stopped and turned to look up at her. She fisted her hands on her hips. "He loves you."

She shook her head. "He feels pity for me. Because of my illness."

"No. I may not be all that experienced in the boyfriend department, but I sure as hell know love when I see it."

Amelia's hand strayed to the charm bracelet beneath her shirt. She tugged it out, but instead of rubbing the charms, she ran her fingers along the leather thong, remembering how Micah had given it to her, his expression so boyishly eager.

It was Micah who sat beside her hour after hour as the Hydra virus burned through her. Micah—who refused to leave her side, holding her hand through the awful seizure, never judging or shaming her for her weakness. Micah—who never pushed for more than she wanted to give. Who looked at her like a person; not a prize to be won, an asset to be manipulated, or a challenge to be conquered.

Was it true? Didn't some part of her already know it? "Love is a big word."

Willow shrugged. "Call it what you want. I just thought you should know. He's a good guy. He deserves to be happy. I don't know if he'll ever tell you himself."

"Because of Gabriel."

Willow rolled her eyes. "Gah, you people make everything so

difficult. I do not want to know about this weird love-triangle thing you've got going on."

"There's no love tri—" Amelia sputtered.

"Hey, I'm not judging. All's fair in love and the apocalypse."

"No, seriously. I just feel—"

"Please don't talk to me about your feelings. Finn says I'm not emotionally mature enough to handle it."

She needed a clever comeback to divert attention from her flushing cheeks. "What about you and Finn, then?"

Willow made a choking noise deep in her throat.

"Are you alright?"

She waved her hand dismissively. "Yeah, of course. I just—we're not anything. I mean, we're friends."

"If you're sure," she teased gently.

Willow jerked her chin, her hair falling like a curtain over her face. Hiding her own face. "Of course, I'm sure. I just said that, didn't I?"

They reached the fence line and walked alongside it toward the back gate, which was closest to the rec yard. On their right, the forest hugged the jagged hillside. Icicles dripped from the branches in frozen, glittering streaks. She blinked thick snowflakes out of her eyes.

As they got closer to the rec yard, the happy sounds of laughter and children playing filled the air, along with a delicious aroma that made her stomach cramp with hunger. The cook staff was busy roasting venison for Christmas dinner tonight.

Willow fingered the turquoise scarf wrapped around her neck. She turned to Amelia and cleared her throat. "Benjie really likes you, you know. You took care of him and kept him from feeling scared and alone during that whole quarantine thing…" She hesitated, as if struggling to find the right words. "I can't mess up. I have to do right by him."

"You will. And you are."

"Lo Lo!" Benjie called to Willow from across the fence. "Wanna play soccer? Mister Finn says we're gonna beat you so badly you won't know which way is down!"

Willow's lips twitched. The shadows cleared from her face. "I'd do anything for him."

Amelia thought of Silas. The damaged boy with the gaping wound beneath his hard, bristling shell. The brother she hadn't loved well enough. But she could change that now. She had another chance. As long as they were alive and breathing, they could change. "I know."

Willow watched her brother frolicking in the snow, laughing and shouting as he and Finn kicked around a half-deflated soccer ball. "We can't just fight against the bad. We have to fight *for* the good."

"That's profound, Willow."

Willow blew her bangs out of her eyes. "Yeah, well, don't expect more where that came from."

"Lo Lo!" Benjie shrieked, giggling as Finn stuffed a handful of snow down the back of his coat with his good arm.

"He's not supposed to be moving!" Willow muttered. "I'm gonna kill him." She glanced at Amelia, her jaw working. She licked her lips, pausing like she was trying to figure out the best— and fastest—way to get out what she needed to say. "You know we're here, all of us. Whatever we need to do. We're together in this."

Amelia nodded, a lump in her throat. That meant a lot coming from Willow. Before she could respond, Willow turned and dashed back through the gate to join her family.

Amelia blew an icy breath into her cupped hands. Her gaze shifted to the edge of the yard, where Gabriel and Micah sat side by side on one of the picnic tables. They had reconciled.

She was happy for them, but it also made her feel more alone. They could figure it out. Why couldn't she?

Micah hunched over an old paperback book, that wayward lock of hair falling across his forehead, his handsome, boyish features knit in concentration. Gabriel was polishing one of his guns, his every movement sure and steady and strong. Memories flashed through her mind—the passion and fire in his kiss, the fierce intensity in his gaze, undoing her piece by piece.

Her stomach gave a small flip, the hairs on her arms rising. Her skin tingled where his fingers had brushed her arm last night after dinner. A spark like an electrical current passed between them. His eyes had bored into hers, deep and searching. She'd strode away, unsure of her own treacherous feelings.

Now she found herself focusing on his face: his smooth bronze skin, the scruff of his goatee darkening his jaw, his full, sensuous lips. A memory of his mouth, hard and searching, and her own wanting in return, flushed through her. Her cheeks reddened in embarrassment, even standing out here behind the fence, alone.

It was disconcerting and infuriating how her body could still respond to him even after everything, the lies and the heartbreak and the anger. Like her heart was betraying her all over again. It was unfair.

Would she feel this way forever? She used to be able to control her emotions, to tamp down every dangerous, unruly feeling and bury it deep. But things were different now. She had changed.

Before the *Grand Voyager*, she lived in a gilded cage, numb and half-alive. Now she was fully alive. Now she felt everything. And it hurt like hell.

Micah glanced up suddenly, adjusting his glasses and smiling at her, so much warmth in his brown eyes. He was everything safe and good and kind.

Burning Skies

Gabriel felt like falling—intense, exhilarating, terrifying.

Micah felt like home.

But she couldn't think about all that now. Not yet. They weren't safe. Far from it. The Sanctuary waited. What would they find? Allies or enemies? Salvation or betrayal?

Tomorrow, they embarked on a dangerous mission to get her mother back. She still couldn't remember her mother's face. But it would all come back once they saved her. Amelia had to believe that. She clung to that hope, that she could still salvage some of what was lost.

It was all right there, just beyond her grasp. A new beginning. A new world. They just had to find it.

The End

I hope you enjoyed
Burning Skies: The Last Sanctuary Book Three!

If you liked *Burning Skies*, please consider leaving a quick Amazon review HERE. Reviews help readers find good stories and help authors reach new readers. I read every review.

Pre-order the final book in the series, *Breaking World*, HERE.

Want to be the first to know when *Breaking World* is available?

Join my exclusive VIP Mailing List
As a VIP member, you'll have first access to exclusive sales, freebies, and new releases.
Join my VIP list HERE.

I hate spam and cluttered inboxes as much as you do, so I won't send more than 1-2 emails a month.

Check out the rest of my books
Kyla's Author Central Page

Happy reading!

ALSO BY KYLA STONE

Beneath the Skin

Before You Break

Real Solutions for Adult Acne

Rising Storm

Falling Stars

Burning Skies

Breaking World

ACKNOWLEDGMENTS

I am eternally grateful to everyone who read the manuscript and provided feedback—a few of you read various versions multiple times.

Thank you to my awesome beta readers. Your thoughtful critiques and enthusiasm are invaluable, as always: Lauren Nikkel, Kimberley Trembley, Michelle Browne, Leslie Spurrier, Jazmin Cybulski, Jeremy Steinkraus, and Barry and Derise Marden.

To Michelle Browne for being an awesome person, beta reader, and line editor. And to Eliza Enriquez for catching those last little proofreading errors.

And especially to Becca Cross, for continuing to enthusiastically read all my books, even with a new baby. You rock, mama.

To my husband, who always helps with deadlines and plot holes and listens patiently to problems about imaginary people.

And to my kids, for being my everything.

ABOUT THE AUTHOR

Kyla Stone is an emerging author of contemporary young adult fiction and suspense/dystopian novels. She lives in Atlanta, Georgia with her husband, two children, and two spoiled cats. When she's not writing or spending time with her family, she loves to read, hike, draw, travel, and play games. Her favorite food is dark chocolate.

Kyla loves to hear from her readers. For news and new releases, visit her at:

www.FaceBook.com/KylaStoneBooks

www.Amazon.com/author/KylaStone

Email her at KylaStone@yahoo.com